I0660134

The Daddy Issue

by

Melissa Beck

This is a work of fiction. Names, characters, places, and incidents are either the product of the author's imagination or are used fictitiously, and any resemblance to actual persons living or dead, business establishments, events, or locales, is entirely coincidental.

The Daddy Issue

COPYRIGHT © 2008 by Melissa Beck

All rights reserved. No part of this book may be used or reproduced in any manner whatsoever without written permission of the author or The Wild Rose Press except in the case of brief quotations embodied in critical articles or reviews.
Contact Information: info@thewildrosepress.com

Cover Art by *Angela Anderson*

The Wild Rose Press
PO Box 708
Adams Basin, NY 14410-0708
Visit us at www.thewildrosepress.com

Publishing History
First Champagne Rose Edition, 2009
Print ISBN 1-60154-464-2

Published in the United States of America

"Would you like to see a picture of my goddaughter, Gretchen's little girl?"

"Uh. Sure." Kids weren't his forte. And to see the child Gretchen had with her next lover? *Weird.*

She rummaged in her purse, and pulled out a bi-fold wallet. Opening it, she held it out.

He reached for it, and gazed down at the child's image.

"Her name's Amy. She's four."

Daniel brought the wallet a few inches closer. Her eyes looked familiar. Damn the plastic sheath. He started to pull the photo out of it, then remembered himself, and with the edge of the picture between his thumb and forefinger, glanced at the woman. "Do you mind?"

"No."

He eased the photo out.

His breath caught in his throat. *Good God.*

"I—I better get going."

He gaped at the photo.

"There are photographers here, and I don't want to end up in the news as your latest date," he heard her say, around the pounding of his pulse in his ears. "My husband wouldn't find that funny."

He became aware of her tugging on it, and reluctantly released it.

"This probably won't happen," she said, as his gaze followed her every move in putting away the photo and wallet, "but if you happen to run into Gretchen, don't tell her I mentioned her. I promised I wouldn't." With one last look, she started backing away. "Oh! Congrats on your award."

Turning, she headed for the stairs.

Daniel stared after her, not seeing her. That photo, that image of the little girl, had burned itself into the front of his brain.

Advance praise for THE DADDY ISSUE...

"Beck's strong writing is definitely the high point of this enjoyable story. Both Gretchen and Daniel are well drawn and complex characters with their own troubled pasts, mannerisms, and goals."

~*BooksForABuck.com*

"This is a fun read that, while taking the oft-used premise of an unknown child suddenly being discovered, is still an interesting story. The small-town characters are quaint without being stereotypical..."

~*Romantic Times Bookclub*

"Melissa Beck's debut into the print publishing world comes with great promise. THE DADDY ISSUE...comes packed with emotional drama, humor, and a drop of truth that fills the reader to the brim. This reviewer has found a new author to follow, and knows readers who pick up Ms. Beck's novel will not be disappointed in any way. I highly recommend readers of traditional romance pick this novel off the shelves and bring it home into their hearts. This novel is one for the keeper shelf!"

~*Love, Romances & More*

"Melissa Beck's THE DADDY ISSUE offers readers more than just the typical 'secret baby' storyline..."

~*Romance Junkies* (Rated 4.5)

Dedication

To Mom and Dad and my sisters,
for your unwavering support.
And for Frank, Ben and Torie.
My greatest blessing is family.

Prologue

He hated crowds. No one would believe it, of course, and especially not tonight. But as Daniel Nicholson crossed the threshold of the Haley mansion with the beautiful Elena on his arm, he gritted his teeth in anticipation of all the moments of this awards dinner that would make him want to slip out the back door. Fortunately, he did it with his lips parted, so everyone would assume he was smiling.

In the well-lit foyer, he glanced around at clusters of men in tuxes and women in long gowns. They talked. They laughed. They drank. *He* could use a drink. Their head-spinning chatter made him want to stuff cotton in his ears.

Pressing his palm between Elena's birdlike shoulder blades, he guided her toward the grand ballroom. She drew murmurs of recognition. Her flawless face and body were, after all, plastered on a vodka billboard along I-90. But Daniel felt the love from spectators, too, in their expressions when he caught them glancing at him and in the way their gazes trailed him.

As he weaved his way toward his table, he paused to shake his peers' hands when they thrust them his way, and grinned at the banker who patted his back and assured him he was the shoo-in for tonight's award. Only *he* was aware that as he pumped each hand and acknowledged congratulations on his "Businessman of the Year" nomination, inside it was as if someone had poured concrete around his vital organs.

Finding his place in the front of the ballroom, he seated Elena and waited on the scotch he'd added to the banker's order from the cash bar. When his pal returned with it, plus champagne for Elena, he refused Daniel's money.

"On me this time, buddy. This is your night."

Left to himself again, Daniel lifted the highball glass. He turned it in his hand and watched the light from crystal chandeliers dance across its etched pattern. Gazing about the room, he thought, *This is what you wanted. It's where you belong.* But though he'd done lunch, been in meetings or taught seminars with many of the people around him, it'd never occurred to him until now that they didn't really *know* him, and he didn't know them.

He tipped the glass and swallowed a healthy amount of its amber contents. The pleasant warmth that trickled through his veins lent a hand to the buzz he'd gotten a head start on with champagne in the limo. It still wasn't enough to fully release him from the emptiness that had plagued him for months now. Futility gripped him with fierce determination, like the wind that whipped between Chicago's downtown skyscrapers, slamming into commuters and ripping scarves from their necks in an attempt to get at their cores. No, the booze proved no muffler against this gripping apathy.

Elena shifted in her chair and wriggled against him. "So how does it feel to be the main man tonight?"

He soaked in those exotic eyes of hers, incredible cat-like eyes that had already seduced a rock band's drummer, or so he'd heard.

She sucked in her full lower lip, and arched a brow.

The liveliness in her expression, the promise of fun, passion-filled nights, left him cold. Leaning in and catching a whiff of perfume that failed to register with his pheromones, he murmured, "Sorry to put you through this. It's got to be boring for you."

She tossed him a wicked smile. "I just want to be with you."

Why? They'd only met two nights ago, at a club. She'd come on to him big-time, dancing up and kissing him.

All that signaled was the start of yet another empty relationship.

What was wrong with him? Always before, "empty" was fine. Empty meant no real ties, so no loss and no pain. Why the problems with it now, of all times, when he was with one of the most beautiful women he'd ever seen?

After dinner, the Association president began the ceremony. "This year's nominees were all exceptional," he noted, glancing around the room and making brief eye contact with each of the four contestants for the coveted title. "But unfortunately we could only choose one." His gaze rested on Daniel as the last of the four, and lingered.

Pick someone else, Al. I'm a fraud.

What was he thinking? He loved honors. He loved the limelight.

"Our winner built his business from the ground up, and today his 'Little Advertising Agency That Could,' as the press once nicknamed it, is a force to be reckoned with. I remember the first day I met him. He came by my office with thumbnail sketches of print ads for one of my product lines. He wanted the job so badly, he offered to do the launch for free."

Appreciative chuckles rumbled through the audience.

"Instead I ended up paying him three times the going rate. You've all heard the story before. His ideas were so out-of-the-box, I had to have exclusive rights." More rumbles, this time accompanied by a few all-out laughs. "He was barely out of college, but he had *me* sold."

Daniel stared at his hand resting on the table as his friend elaborated on his accomplishments. Each sentence seemed designed to pound at him, to prod him back toward "them."

Whoa. When had he begun to think of it as "them" and "him?" His head throbbed, and he reached up and rubbed a temple.

"And of course, tonight's honoree is currently in talks with a very high profile corporation for an international TV-and-print ad campaign."

Daniel glanced around the room. Did any of these people, other than his big rival, The Chroma Agency, give a damn? Surely most were about to nod off.

They didn't love him. They probably loathed him.

"Before you go thinking all he does for a living is work," Al continued, "remember, just a few years ago, this man I'm proud to know and extremely lucky to be standing next to at certain times—" He paused for effect, and got the usual bawdy hoots from those who suspected what was coming—"This guy walked away with that other infamous title, *Chicago Bachelor of the Year.*"

Daniel groaned.

Elena squeezed his arm again. "You just hadn't met *me* yet. Maybe your bachelor days are over."

Considering his lack of interest tonight, he had his doubts.

He caught other women arching their brows at him as they clapped. Snatching up his drink, he knocked back the remainder of the whiskey. Wouldn't help the throb in his head, but at least it'd take the edge off before he had to proceed to the podium.

"So with that, ladies and gentlemen, I give you

our 'Businessman of the Year,' Daniel Nicholson."

He pushed his chair back and stood, dipping his chin to acknowledge the barrage of applause. As he weaved his way around tables, his associates offered more handshakes, and he performed in a grin-a-thon.

"This way, Mr. Nicholson," barked a photographer.

Pivoting in that direction, he barely blinked when the flash went off.

Stepping up to the dais, he took his spot behind the lectern. How many times had he carried off holding observers' attention as he pitched his agency? And yet, he wasn't "on" tonight. They couldn't tell, though. His voice came out smooth and flawless. His words flowed, from years of practice.

Thirty minutes later, he stood in the upper hallway and stared over the railing at the crowd below. His peers lingered in and around the tables, their conversations bouncing off the high ceiling and returning in a buzz of white noise. Off in the corner, a jazz band's fight for air space resulted in a pleasant melody trickling off the brew of voices.

He tracked Elena with his gaze, watching her move in her slinky red gown, straight platinum hair brushing her bare shoulders as she worked the men in the crowd. He'd grown used to the women he dated finessing their ways into the right circles. It wasn't a matter of not trusting them, but of understanding them. They were savvy about what they wanted. He wondered if dissatisfaction would set in once they got what or whom they pursued, the way it had his ex-wife.

Maybe that was what was eating at him tonight. Maybe he missed the rush he got from his job, back in the early days. You never really captured it again, did you? Just like with marriages, once it was gone, it was gone.

"Daniel?"

He turned, to find a thirty-ish dishwater blonde in a simple black dress standing at the top of the staircase.

"I'm Charlotte Singer." She didn't offer her hand. Hesitation seemed to flicker in her eyes. "My husband and I own Michigan Avenue Antiques?"

"Nice to see you again," he murmured, wondering what she was about to try and sell him.

She tilted her head. "You don't remember me, do you?"

"To be honest, no."

"I'm Gretchen Parks' college roommate. I met you when she brought you by the shop."

Gretchen. He frowned as a face with delicate features drifted to him through the scotchy mist in his mind—a face framed with medium-brown hair whose precise shade he couldn't recall. But her smile had been a sweet one, and even after five years, he remembered her girlish laugh. Still, she had that other distinction of being the woman who left him. His ribcage tightened. "I remember stopping in some shops with Gretchen. How is she?"

"She's fine. And doing a beautiful job as a mother, I might add."

The girl who'd been dumped at the altar and had been crying in her beer when he'd scooted his barstool over was a mother now? A twinge of some emotion he didn't recognize tickled his gut. So much for her solemn, if tipsy, pledge to never trust another man. He, on the other hand, had honored his drunken, divorce-papers-fueled vow never to trust another woman.

"She's married, then," he murmured. Probably went back to her runaway fiancé. "Good for her."

"No, no." Her forehead wrinkled. "Gretchen isn't married."

He stiffened. "She's divorced?" *Poor girl.*

Dumped again.

"No, she's never been married. She hasn't even dated much since she moved back home to Ohio."

"Huh." He frowned in confusion.

"Would you like to see a picture of my goddaughter, Gretchen's little girl?"

"Uh. Sure." Kids weren't his forte. And to see the child Gretchen had with her next lover? *Weird.*

She rummaged in her purse, and pulled out a bi-fold wallet. Opening it, she held it out.

He reached for it, and gazed down at the child's image.

"Her name's Amy. She's four."

Daniel brought the wallet a few inches closer. Her eyes looked familiar. Damn the plastic sheath. He started to pull the photo out of it, then remembered himself, and with the edge of the picture between his thumb and forefinger, glanced at the woman. "Do you mind?"

"No."

He eased the photo out.

His breath caught in his throat. *Good God.*

"I—I better get going."

He gaped at the photo.

"There are photographers here, and I don't want to end up in the news as your latest date," he heard her say, around the pounding of his pulse in his ears. "My husband wouldn't find that funny."

He became aware of her tugging on it, and reluctantly released it.

"This probably won't happen," she said, as his gaze followed her every move in putting away the photo and wallet, "but if you happen to run into Gretchen, don't tell her I mentioned her. I promised I wouldn't." With one last look, she started backing away. "Oh! Congrats on your award."

Turning, she headed for the stairs.

Daniel stared after her, not seeing her. That

photo, that image of the little girl, had burned itself into the front of his brain. She had his mother's eyes, with their tilted edges and earthy brown color. Prune eyes, he remembered his mother joking as she pointed from hers to his. Yeah, Gretchen's daughter looked a lot like the faded photos of his mother as a child, in the few albums he and Sam had been able to save.

What was he thinking?

No way. They'd used protection.

Sometimes protection fails. And she's the right age...

He turned and stalked blindly toward the hallway, nodding when some guy congratulated him. On what? Oh, yeah. The award.

He passed the men's restroom, and returned to shove the door open. No one was inside. Good. Heaving a frustrated breath, he went to the sink, turned on the faucet and splashed cold water on his face.

He stared into the mirror as water trickled down into his tux collar. *Me, a father?*

A surprise pregnancy might explain Gretchen's hasty departure from him, and from the city. He'd just figured by her vague "Dear John" letter that she wasn't that into him.

Had he gotten her pregnant? No. Come on. *You were together a few times, for a couple of weeks. That's some other brown-eyed guy's kid.*

He jerked the paper towel dispenser's arm up and down a few times, and wiped his face, neck and hands. *If she's mine, then damn you, Gretchen.* He didn't need this, not at this time, not when the biggest deal of his life was about to fall in his lap.

Yeah, it was some other guy's kid. Some guy who didn't mind the word "parent." For him, it refreshed the blurred picture in his mind of a mangled car and a rain-soaked double funeral.

Connect *parent* to *foster* and Ray's harsh features popped into his head.

He stared into the mirror, trying to recall how he'd looked as that lonely, scared kid. His passive adult reflection gazed back. But the glint in his eyes and the set of his jaw revealed to him what he kept from others—the frustration, the determination to survive.

The door creaked open. "Daniel?"

He turned and discovered one of his fellow nominees standing in the doorway. "Chris."

"You left this out there on the floor." His friend held up his plaque.

"Thanks, buddy." He reached for the award.

"Don't mention it." Chris grinned. "Especially since I'm taking your hot date home with me."

Daniel clenched his jaw. "If that's what she wants, that's fine."

"What she *wants* is your attention. But since you're so preoccupied, I thought you might not mind if—"

"I'm coming."

Holding the plaque with numb fingers, he followed Chris out of the restroom and walked downstairs with him.

But the image of the little girl so haunted him that he dropped Elena off early and spent the night in a state of restless sleep.

In his half-awake moments, he couldn't stop wondering what Gretchen was like, after all this time. Why had she left him? And what if the child was his?

Chapter One

"She's holed up on the potty."

Gretchen Parks' chest tightened. That explained why she hadn't seen Amy when she'd scanned the masses out front in the carpool line. Glancing past Mrs. Scarborough, she stared at the bathroom in the far corner of the pre-k classroom. "Is—is she sick?"

"No. It's that same issue that keeps upsetting her." Jessie Scarborough's grandmotherly gaze reflected concern. "She ran in there after I reminded the class we're hosting the annual 'Dad and Me' breakfast on Tuesday."

Gretchen stifled a groan. *Poor Amy.* "How long has she been in there?"

"Almost fifteen minutes."

Fifteen minutes. That was a lifetime for a four-year-old. She must be really hurt. And no wonder, since this breakfast was the second "dad" zinger she'd been hit with in her first weeks of school.

"When the final bell rang, I called her to be line leader." The teacher stepped out of the doorway to allow Gretchen into the room. "But she still wouldn't come out."

Gretchen headed for the closet-sized bathroom.

"After Miss Mary got everybody else in line, I went in and picked her up." The heavyset teacher's voice wobbled as she hurried along behind her. "But soon as I set her down, she ran back in there."

Gretchen stopped a few feet from where Amy had taken refuge. Stepping up to the pale yellow door, she remembered that it had been painted institutional pale green in her days at Marydale Elementary. Its bottom half was bolted shut, but its upper part had been unlatched and hung slightly open like a cabinet. After drawing a calming breath, she swung it wide. Leaning over the bottom, she saw Amy sitting on the closed toilet lid, her little shoulders hunched forward. Her lower lip quivered. Tears stained her pink top.

"Amy?" she breathed.

Amy lifted damp-spiked lashes, looking as if she'd lost her best friend.

"What's wrong, sweetie?"

Tears filled her earthy eyes. "I don't have a daddy to bring."

Gretchen's throat closed up. *Oh, sweetie, I'm sorry.* She unlatched the door and went inside. Dropping to her knees, she pulled Amy against her chest. As she kissed the crown of her baby's head, she caught a whiff of powder-scented shampoo that reminded her of Amy's splashing and laughing in the bathtub last night. Would that they could go back to that sweet, innocent time, and not deal with this heavy subject. The knot in her throat thickened.

Amy pressed her face into Gretchen's shoulder. "I wanna go home."

"Then home it is." Gretchen released her only long enough to stand, before scooping her back up into her arms. Then she stepped out of the musty, tight quarters of the bathroom and back into the tempera-scented room.

Mrs. Scarborough had hustled over to the coat hooks along the far wall, to stuff homework pages into Amy's Cinderella backpack. She carried her daughter over there, and the teacher slipped the pack's straps over Gretchen's wrist. Amy didn't look at her "very favorite teacher," but instead buried her head in Gretchen's neck.

"Sorry," Mrs. Scarborough mouthed, with a

sympathetic smile.

Gretchen nodded, appreciating her concern, despite the anger still knotting her stomach. Who the heck had thought up a "Dad and Me" day, anyway? She started to say as much, but decided Amy didn't need to hear that right now. Like her, all Gretchen wanted to do was go home.

"See you tomorrow," she murmured, stepping out into the hallway.

At the car, she buckled Amy in before looking hard into her big, dark eyes. "I'll come to the breakfast," she promised, brushing a tear off her sweet one's cheek. "It'll be fun. Okay?"

Amy shook her head, gold-tipped sienna curls shimmying against her shoulders.

"Joel can come, then." Gretchen and Joel had been buds since grade school, and he adored Amy. "I'm sure he'd love it if we asked him."

Again the adamant headshake.

Sighing, Gretchen climbed into the car and started for home. Her shoulders ached, and a headache hovered. She didn't know what to do, what to say to soothe Amy, which left her with the most helpless feeling ever.

Behind her, Amy began crying, a hiccupping sound that seared her heart. But then she rallied, certain that four was too young to be hurting the way *she* had when her own parents fought all the time. She'd been twice Amy's age, or so she remembered, and had blamed herself completely for her daddy's leaving. If she'd been a better student, a quieter little girl, more talented in ballet, if she'd made the spelling bee, surely he would have stayed.

She glared at the lines in the road. Stupid school. Would they ever stop talking about fathers, and having fathers come for show-and-tell, and feeding fathers pancakes?

She sighed. It wasn't the school's fault. It wasn't

Jessie Scarborough's fault, either. The teacher was only doing her job.

She was the one who hadn't provided a daddy for Amy.

But by the time he came onto the scene, you'd already shoveled aside a huge pile of garbage that men left behind in your life. Who'd want more?

Yes, she had vowed to end the Parks women's dirty laundry cycles when it came to men. She'd changed her ways so her daughter wouldn't suffer through twinges of abandonment, longing for the man who'd already left them, while she watched her mom get dressed and perfumed, eyes shining with excitement over the latest chance to meet Mr. Wonderful. And once the fighting grew fierce and doors began to slam yet again, Amy would never, ever have to curl up next to her, the way *she* had done, and murmur, "Please Mommy, don't cry."

When the car rounded the curve in the road and their property popped into view, she exhaled a long breath and released her vise grip on the steering wheel.

"Look, sweetie." She forced the lift in her voice. "Our scarecrow fell off his hay bales again."

No answer.

She stole a peek into the rearview. Had Amy cried herself to sleep? No. She was staring out the window, toward their house. Good. Maybe her mind was off that darned breakfast.

She glanced at their ranch-style duplex as they pulled into the driveway. Every time she saw that "For Rent" sign that Mr. Scott had hammered into the front yard last week, it dug at her, reminding her that she didn't own the real estate. Still, it was home. The swing set had sprouted rust and acquired a grinding squeak, but Amy didn't seem to mind. And the flag had fallen off the mailbox, but Max the postal carrier still managed to pick up and deliver their mail without complaint. So some things weren't perfect. They still said "home" to her. However, the sign reminded her that one thing wasn't even close to perfect anymore. Their former co-renter and adopted grandma, Beatrice Holtz, had moved away. And now she realized she'd been expecting to knock on Bea's door and ask her what she thought of today's situation. Bea would know, having raised three kids of her own. It'd been such a blessing to have her living right next door ever since Gretchen returned from Chicago, pregnant, scared and alone.

Now she'd have to figure it out on her own, and she was pretty certain she wouldn't find it in those stodgy how-to books. "Simply sit the child down and have a talk with her" was easier said than done. They never listed even half the answers to the "Why?" questions a child could come up with. They definitely never told you what to do when you could hardly look at your daughter because her pain seared straight through your heart.

She parked the car and got out to help Amy from her seat belt. Once freed, she hopped out and ran for the house, and Gretchen followed.

The instant she crossed the threshold, Amy waved the portable phone in her direction. "I wanna talk to Granny Bea."

"I was thinking of calling her myself." She read the number off a scrap of paper on the fridge and punched the Indiana exchange into the phone. When it started ringing, she handed it to Amy, and went to let Scooby in from the dog run.

Returning with the Great Dane scampering joyously at her heels, she heard Amy say, "Do you have a daddy, Granny Bea?"

Gretchen caught her breath.

"'Cause everybody has a daddy but me," Amy said, in a reedy tone. "BJ's daddy got divorced of his mommy, but he's coming. It's a daddy breakfast. You have to have a daddy."

Amy was quiet for a moment, then nodded.

Gretchen pressed her lips together. Just as quickly, she relaxed. There was nothing to worry about. Bea would have the perfect words of wisdom.

"When are you coming home, Granny? We live in Ohio, 'member?"

Hm. Gretchen wondered if Amy might be reacting to the lack of a father so intensely because she'd also just lost her "granny." Until now, she hadn't considered that.

"Okay." Amy stretched out her arm, still sweetly rounded with remnants of baby fat, and offered the phone to Gretchen.

Putting it to her ear, she watched Amy charge down the hallway toward her bedroom. When she was out of hearing range, she sighed into the mouthpiece, "Hi."

"Hi, yourself," came that familiar, grating voice. "What's this business that's got my little girlie-pie upset?"

She explained about Amy's situation at school. "Anyway, a dad breakfast is a good idea for most kids, and I shouldn't be upset," she said, finally. "I'm the one who caused Amy to be different. It's my fault she doesn't have a father."

"Don't sell yourself short. You give that little one twice the love some get, even with both parents around."

"That doesn't matter, though, if she doesn't think I'm enough." She sighed. "From the first second I held her in my arms, I thought she deserved a father. I wanted that for her. But look at the guys I pick! I'm cursed with my mother's bad taste in men, especially when it came to her father. And of course, right before I met him, David had run out on me."

"Well, I didn't know your mother, God bless her,

but I know you. You're strong. You can work this out. So quit blaming yourself. I can't grab you by the shoulders and stare it out of you, now Allison's moved me down here to her glass house."

Gretchen chuckled. "Is it that bad?"

"Huh! Don't get me started. For now, I'll simply say that my afternoon beer-and-peanuts break is a goner. *Beer is a man's drink*," Bea said in a singsong voice. "*Nuts are bad for your digestive system*." She groaned. "But that's a small annoyance compared with how they're ruining my grandkids with their paranoid coaching and tutoring and psychiatry." After a pause, she said, "Listen to me, going on about my silly concerns. What about you? What are you gonna do about Amy?"

Gretchen rubbed her forehead. "I wish I knew."

"Now that she's asking about him, are you still glad you never told the father about her?"

"Absolutely. There's a lot I don't know about Daniel Nicholson since we only went out a couple of weeks." *And slept together during a very fertile time...* "But I know how he feels about kids because we discussed it. He didn't want them. He was adamant on the subject." She remembered thinking it was odd that he'd even mentioned it.

"Did he say *why* he didn't want them?" Bea pressed.

"Who knows what his personal baggage is. He's a real man-about-town still, according to the newspapers. I'm guessing it would've seriously clipped his wings."

"Well. It's his loss. He's missing out on a wonderful child."

They talked on a while, about Marydale, the house and some mutual friends before saying their goodbyes. Afterward, Gretchen wandered to the high cabinets above the fridge, where she hid the box of newspaper clippings destined for Amy's scrapbook.

Pulling out the top photo, she tapped her finger over the figure of Daniel standing beside a slim blonde at some ritzy event.

Under his leadership, The Nicholson Agency had soared to great heights of advertising success in recent years. With that and his classic good looks, he now topped the list of the city's most eligible bachelors. But when she'd known him, he'd been a fed-up man going through a nasty divorce. A man who relished his freedom.

How well she'd learned that, when she returned to Chicago weeks later to tell him about the pregnancy. She'd squelched all concerns about telling him, on the chance that her child could have the father *she* never had. She steeled herself for whatever he had to say. But when she found him in a bar, laughing and flirting with another woman exactly the way he had with her, shame had frozen her in place.

From that moment, she knew she was on her own with the pregnancy. What he'd had with her was a rebound fling after his divorce. For her part, she'd had a no-strings-attached affair with him after having been ditched at the altar. How could she have ever expected more from that?

Now, if it wasn't for Amy, she wouldn't give Daniel Nicholson another thought, and truth be told, she resented it that she *had* thought of him today. She crammed the clipping back into the box, shutting the lid with a little extra force than was necessary.

Amy shuffled into the kitchen, carrying her ceramic piggy bank. The skin around her eyes was pink and puffy. "Mommy?" she said, sniffling, "Can we buy me a daddy?"

Pain radiated through Gretchen as she pulled her daughter into her arms. "It doesn't work that way," she said softly.

"Why?"

"I don't know, baby. It just doesn't."

Amy's tears soaked into Gretchen's T-shirt. Soaked straight into her heart, was more like it.

She closed her eyes, and swayed back and forth, making a vow while she rocked. She would show Amy every day just how much she cared about her, and that would be enough. It had to be enough. Amy would stop thinking about this daddy issue soon, and life would be sweet again.

Please God, let it be so.

Chapter Two

"I don't want another neighbor," Amy grumbled. She leaned in her chair to pass off her bacon to Scooby, who was in his usual sneaky begging position under the kitchen table. "I want Granny Bea back."

"I know. But her family needs her in Indiana now." Gretchen's gaze sharpened on the dog's smacking lips. Oh, to heck with mentioning table scraps were bad for dogs. This emotional seesaw Amy teetered on lately didn't need tipping in the wrong direction.

"I want Granny here." Tears slipped down Amy's cheeks.

Gretchen pressed her lips together, forcing control over her own glum feelings. "We'll visit her soon. I promise."

Beside them, Scooby whined for more bacon. But Amy's plate sat empty now. His angel-friend's little fingers delivered no more manna from heaven. After a moment, he flumped himself down on the floor with a heavy sigh.

Gretchen sank her chin in her hands. They should all be happy and having fun instead of this moping. After all, it was Saturday, and a day off from work. But the landlord's phone call just now, to tell them about a nibble from the "For Rent" sign, had set Amy off again. And just when they'd gotten beyond her upset over the "Dad and Me" breakfast.

She wished they could rewind their lives a few months, back to the lazy days of summer. To Bea and her, sitting in lawn chairs and watching Joel squirt the hose while Amy played in its spray. To laughing over her squealing, and falling on the wet grass, getting mud clear up to her ears.

The theme song to Amy's favorite show filtered through the air from a TV in the living room, but she didn't hop off her chair and hurry in there to watch like she usually did. She just sat there, fingering loops of cereal.

A car rattled across the gravel drive.

Gretchen twisted in her chair to glance out the front window. A burgundy SUV had pulled off the road. "Great," she muttered. "The guy's here to look at the other apartment and I haven't even had my shower." She shoved back her chair, at the same time grabbing her mug and swigging cold coffee for mouthwash. After tucking her hair behind her ears, she snatched up the key to the other end of the house.

Hurrying to the door, she told Amy, "You stay here while I show the renter around."

The minute she turned the bolt in the lock, the dog lurched out of hibernation from under the table, and then wagged and whined beside her.

"*Stay*," she commanded, noting with dismay his dilated pupils and lolling tongue.

She eased open the door.

Scooby leaped up. Before she could think, he'd slammed his full weight against her, buckling her knees. She struggled to keep her balance and snag his collar. But as she tried to grab him, he slipped through the doorway like a wily coyote, and galloped off to open ground.

"Scooby!" *Crazy mutt.* She hobbled after him in her slippers, across the wooden porch and down the steps.

He outran her, making straight for the man who'd climbed from the SUV.

"Oof!" the poor guy grunted as the hundred-pound beast pinned him to his vehicle.

"Sorry," Gretchen warbled, hurrying to haul her dog off the man. If she blew the duplex rental because of this, Mr. Scott would not be happy.

She gripped Scooby's collar as tightly as she could, but he lurched forward anyway for a slurpy lick across the guy's tightened mouth.

He groaned and craned his neck to escape the dog's reach.

"Amy!" Gretchen yelled toward the house. "Call the dog."

"Here, Scooby!" Amy's voice sounded tinny coming around the edge of the storm door. "Come get a treat."

The dog pricked his ears. Dropping to all fours, he did a one-eighty and galloped toward food.

Gretchen watched him as long as she could, afraid to turn and see the displeasure in the stranger's expression. But when she did look up at him again, she saw only her reflection in his sunglasses.

"Again, I'm sorry about the Welcome Wagon," she managed, hands on her hips and still breathing hard from the exertion. "I promise we usually keep our dog in his run or inside."

Brushing off his jacket, he didn't respond.

Oh, man. She'd probably blown the rental already. Watching his long, broad fingers work away the dog's dust marks, she lifted her gaze to the straight set of his shoulders, and upward again to his firm mouth. No. It wasn't—

He reached up and removed his shades.

Her eyes widened. *Daniel?*

"It's okay, Gretchen." The low tone of his voice vibrated up her spine. "I'm sure the dog wasn't expecting me, either."

Her mouth fell open. "Wh-what are you doing

here?"

"We need to talk."

"I, uh, I'm waiting on someone to come look at the house." *The house.* Panic gripped her. Amy was in there, only yards away. She could make a run for the door and lock the two of them inside—but could she trust her shaky knees not to sink her to the ground before she got there?

Across the street, Elmer Martin started his tractor. Her heart's pounding nearly drowned out its rumbling rhythm.

"Maybe you could make time for me since I'm here." Daniel's rich baritone somehow rose above the tractor's racket. His gaze penetrated hers, before drifting downward.

She dipped her chin to see what he was looking at. Her T-shirt had inched up, exposing bare skin above her hip-hugging yoga sweats. With trembling fingers, she yanked her shirttail down. When she looked up again, his concentration had shifted to a point beyond her.

She started to turn, but something about the way his gaze widened and his lips parted gave her pause. When his chest lifted and stilled, her heart leapt into her throat.

"Amy?" she called in a strained voice, eyes riveted to Daniel's.

A sticky hand slipped into hers, sending doom coursing through her. She slid her gaze away from Daniel, to catch Amy standing there, looking up at her.

"Mommy, is he a daddy?"

The innocent question rang in Gretchen's ears as she pivoted back to Daniel.

He stood frozen in place, his gaze glued on his daughter. Only his Adam's apple lifted and fell when he swallowed.

Amy dropped Gretchen's hand and hopped into

the space between them. Hands on hips at the waist of her pink corduroy skirt, she tilted her head way back to see six-foot-something Daniel. "Are you a daddy?"

He gaped at her a moment longer, before emitting a guttural, "No."

Her face fell. But in the next instant, she looked at Gretchen, shrugged and announced, "I'm gonna go swing."

"Okay," Gretchen scratched out.

Daniel's head swiveled as he watched Amy's retreat. Only after she'd climbed onto a swing and kicked herself into motion did he turn back to Gretchen. Fiddling with his sunglasses, he grated, "I wasn't prepared for that."

He wasn't!

His gaze roamed over her features now, as if he were seeing her for the first time.

Was he searching for a resemblance to Amy? Because now that he'd had a look at his daughter, he suspected the secret she'd been hiding all these years? She folded her arms across her belly, over the nausea churning there.

"We were going to talk." His voice seemed deeper, more definite now.

Forget it. Go away. On the other hand, he couldn't have come because of Amy. He didn't know anything, and ordering him off the property would seem strange and emotional.

She didn't have to tell him anything.

She turned and started trudging toward the house. Let him follow, or even better, stay put.

He chose to follow.

With each crunch of his heavier tread behind her, uneasiness rattled her bones. She had to concentrate on her steps because her feet seemed to have gained five pounds. One thought drove her on: *See what he's here for, and then he'll leave.*

As he walked behind Gretchen, Daniel glanced back at the small girl playing on the swings. Could she be his? He sucked in air, and then exhaled, attempting to clear the bunched-up feeling in his gut. Nope. No help at all. Whatever had tugged at him the instant he laid eyes on this child wasn't about to release him.

He lost his footing for a second, stepped on a rock, and it jolted him into paying closer attention.

Gretchen climbed the front steps.

He bolted ahead of her, to open the storm door and hold it for her.

When she brushed past, he glimpsed her taut body, medium-sized breasts and slim hips that he'd noticed earlier in her low-rise pants and clingy top. Hard to believe she'd ever been pregnant.

When she crossed the threshold, he came in behind her and they stopped in a narrow foyer with a worn slate floor.

He glanced around, easily taking in three rooms at once because someone had done some creative knocking out of walls. The diminutive galley kitchen to his left sported a small eating area with a table that he could reach out and touch from the foyer. The longer, wider room on his right—a living room with sofa and chairs—contained the square footage for formal dining on one end but instead provided storage space for a molded plastic playhouse and three piles of toys.

The entire place would fit into the kitchen of his new loft apartment.

Waving at the living room area, Gretchen indicated two chairs and a sofa corralled around a glass-and-chrome cocktail table salvaged from another decade. "Have a seat." She nodded toward the kitchen. "Coffee?"

"Black," he accepted as its aromatic scent registered around his nerves.

He moved onto worn carpeting with vacuum tracks at its outer edges. After tossing aside pillows lined up along its back cushions, he sank down on the sofa. Sitting felt good, considering he'd about been knocked off his feet at the sight of the little girl.

Tightness banded his chest. Swallowing around a dry throat, he kicked his feet out and then pulled them back. He tried to expand his lungs again, but the alien pressure remained, as if someone had tossed a heavy metal net over him.

Behind him, Gretchen banged cabinet doors, familiar sounds that seemed to come from another dimension.

He rubbed his neck. Why hadn't he asked his brother what one should expect, being a father, before he hopped on the plane and came here? How had Sam figured out how to be a good father to his three boys? But he was jumping ahead of things, as usual. She hadn't confirmed his suspicions yet.

Too keyed up to sit, he leaned forward, preparing to spring up and pace or something, just as Gretchen stepped from the kitchen into the living room.

He sat back again.

She bent to set the drinks on the table in front of him, and spilled coffee onto the carpet.

"Drat!" She frowned at the brown spot, before hurrying off, he assumed to find a towel.

Returning, she got down on one knee and began scrubbing away at the spill. Straight honey-brown hair slid over her shoulders. As she pushed it back behind her ears, he noticed how her black lashes fringed navy blue eyes. Eyes that belonged on a dark brunette. They seemed enticingly out of place on her, with her lighter hair and fair skin.

How could he have forgotten those eyes?

Because you were seeing her through a fresh-out-of-divorce-court haze, that's why.

She stowed the towel before coming to sit Indian-style in one of the matching armchairs. Picking up her steaming coffee, she sipped it. The mug teetered in her hand as she set it down on the table they shared. When she'd straightened again, she melded those pleasantly startling eyes to his. "Um, how'd you find me?"

The hesitancy in her tone was so unmatched with the directness of her gaze that it caught him off-guard. He frowned slightly, but then brushed it off. Of course she'd be anxious, if she'd really been keeping a kid secret from him.

"I ran into the college friend you'd been staying with when we met. She remembered me and kindly brought me up to date on you. Then she showed me a photo." A photo that looked very much like the ones of his mother that he'd saved in an old album. "From there it was easy to count back four years or so."

"I told Charlotte not to see you." There was no levity in the statement, and in her eyes he saw a storm brewing.

He answered by *not* answering, and watched her mouth tighten.

"Hey, it doesn't matter how I got here. The point is I'm here. We both know why."

He shifted in his seat. His knee jiggled up and down of its own volition. He stilled it, and stared hard at her. "Is she mine?"

Her lips parted, but she didn't say anything.

Emotion rose in his throat. "Well?"

She swallowed. She sat there, her breasts moving up and down as if she breathed thin air. Finally she closed her eyes and bobbed her chin.

So he'd been right. That was his child out there in the yard.

She was a blood tie. Related to Sam and to their parents.

He forced himself to grab air and fill his lungs, before slowly heaving it back out. "How?" The question that had threatened to burn a hole in his gut these few weeks since he'd bumped into Charlotte now grated out in a voice he barely recognized. "You told me you were safe."

"I thought I was, but it didn't work." She sat back a little then, her deep-water gaze suddenly colder. "It wasn't on purpose, if that's what you're asking."

He growled, and looked away. When he turned back to her, he said, "So I'm straight on this, we had sex and you got pregnant and decided not to tell me."

"Why would I?"

"Why *wouldn't* you?"

Her hand shook as she reached for her coffee. She picked it up, and quickly clamped both hands around the mug. Staring into its contents, she shook her head slightly. "It didn't make sense to rope us both into a relationship when the last thing we wanted was something permanent."

She looked up again, and Daniel noticed a fresh line of concern on her brow, and a shine to her eyes. Her breath shuddered as she inhaled. "My fiancé stood me up at the altar. You'd gotten divorced and were looking for fun. We went out for a whole two weeks, and then you quickly moved on. What kind of family starts out that way?"

"You opted to make all the decisions on your own, then?"

"Well, *you* weren't the pregnant one. You were free. Why saddle you with a child from our time together?"

"You didn't have to. All you had to do was tell me I had one."

"But you hated the thought. I remember you went off about it."

He shook his head, and clenched his jaw. This

whole thing revolved around one stupid comment he'd possibly blurted between beers? "I don't remember. But if I did, it's because I was pissed as hell at the time." He ran his palm down his weary face. "Let's just say I didn't realize until after I got served papers that my wife wanted my money and my sperm but not me."

She frowned. "What do you mean?"

I mean, the "promise to love" part of her wedding vows was a joke. "When Anne's biological clock started ticking, it started the meter running on our marriage."

She pursed her lips. "Because you didn't want kids."

Geez, she'd drive it out of him, anyway. "Because I discovered, during the course of our trying for a baby, that she didn't really want *me*." Humiliation burned inside him. "She blamed it on my being too involved with work. I'm sure that didn't help. But now I'm also sure our marriage was over from the start."

"Why didn't you tell me that?" she said, more quietly.

"I just told you more than I've ever told anyone."

She nodded, with a softer expression on her face. "I still say *my* forcing you to be a father would have been manipulative, too."

"And running away without allowing me a choice in the matter wasn't?" He regarded her with suspicion still, certain that she hadn't told him the real reason she left.

She shot up out of her seat. "Look, if we're finished here, I need to get going with my day."

He rose, too, and stood there a moment, drained of energy, before trudging after her on legs that now felt as if he'd run a marathon.

When she reached the front entry, she opened the storm door and called, "A—my!"

Daniel came up behind her in the doorway. He watched her look right and left for the little girl, leaning outside, her features softening when she'd located the object of her attention. The joy in her expression made something catch inside him.

Amy came skipping to the porch, and clambered through the doorway.

"Where's your jacket?" Gretchen scolded gently.

"On the slide."

Her mother sighed, but didn't look too perturbed. "Go wash your hands, then."

"O-kay!" Amy cut her eyes at Daniel before flitting through the kitchen to enter a hallway that he figured led to the bedrooms.

He didn't have to keep his gaze on her. He could have followed her trail by the little tune she hummed. And yet, he found himself staring at her bouncing curls until she turned the corner.

When he looked at Gretchen again, her gaze had sharpened.

"Well," she said. "Goodbye."

The finality in her tone was like being thrown against a concrete wall. It drew him up straight, made him realize he hadn't planned anything past coming here and getting at the truth. But something now made him reluctant to step back out into the day. Curiosity? Guilt? He raked his hand through his hair. Hell, how should he know?

Tilting her head, Gretchen fired off the same put-you-in-your-place look he'd seen high-ranked women executives employ, and just as effectively. No doubt about it, she wanted him gone.

He glanced toward the hallway, where he'd last seen the little girl. She was his. He still couldn't believe it, and shook his head.

"Do you need anything?" He made eye contact with Gretchen again. "Money, or—"

"No." Her mouth tightened.

He nodded, torn inside. Ripped, somehow, over this situation, so that he couldn't focus, couldn't solve it, the way he prided himself on solving things. He stepped through the doorway, and then he turned and blurted, "I want to see her again before I leave town."

"That's not a good idea." She darted a glance toward the hallway. "It'd be best if you never came back."

"I'm coming back."

Her gaze narrowed. "What is it you really want?"

"Gretchen, that's my daughter." The words sounded foreign to his ears, but he went on. "I want to make sure she's happy."

Pink spotted her cheeks. Her eyes flashed. "Of course she is. Why would you think otherwise?"

"People thought *I* was, when I was a kid."

The challenge in her gaze wavered, before she lifted her chin. "This isn't about you. It's about Amy. She deserves better parents than either of us, but she has me and I'm doing my best." She pressed her hands together in front of her. "You saw her. Now please, go back to Chicago."

He stared at her, feeling the rug being yanked out from under him.

Amy came back into the room, and they both turned at once and looked at her.

Moving to stand at her mother's side, she angled her alert gaze at Daniel. "Don't you want to live here?"

"Uh..." He backed up a step.

"It's a duplex," Gretchen explained, irritation barely banked in her tone. "The lady who rented the other side for a long time had to leave recently. We thought you were a renter when we heard your car pull up."

Right. The "For Rent" sign. "I'm just visiting

today," he told Amy. "Your mom and I are, friends."

She blinked, but kept looking at him.

"Well." He jiggled the keys he'd retrieved from his pants pocket. "I'll be on my way."

He started past Gretchen.

"Are you coming back?"

He froze, and pivoted back around to the little girl. In a softer tone, he said, "Would it be okay if I did?"

"Yep. 'Cause Scooby likes you."

"Scooby?"

She rolled her eyes. "Our dog, silly!"

"Oh." Disappointment lanced through him. It wasn't that *she* wanted to see him again. "I don't know about that. I like being alive, and I think Scooby thought I was his dinner."

"No he didn't. He liked you."

"Really?" He arched a brow. "I don't know about those things, since I've never had a dog."

Her eyes rounded. "*Never?*"

"Is that hard to believe?"

She bobbed her chin.

"Why?"

"I had to wait until I was three to get Scooby. But you're already old."

"Amy!"

"It's okay." Daniel flashed Gretchen a brief smile. "I remember when I thought thirty-four was old, too."

Amy turned and galloped into the living room, where she fell on the carpet in front of a TV tucked up on a shelf.

Kiddie music burst onto the airwaves.

"*Ahem.*"

Daniel dragged his gaze from the child to her mother. She looked ready to send him to that big dog of hers on a platter.

He'd shocked her, no doubt. Shocked himself,

too. He had no set road map for this meeting, for this day. The first map on parenting he'd been given had burned up in a fiery crash along with his mom and dad. The second had been torn and scarred by his foster parents until it was undecipherable.

Gretchen held the doorknob, and opened the door wider.

He moved toward her.

She drew back as he started past, but murmured, "Do me a favor. If you go in to town, don't tell anyone how you know me or how you're connected to Amy."

"I won't. I just need time to think."

Relief flashed in her cobalt eyes.

As he crossed the porch, he again promised over his shoulder, "I'll be back."

When he got to the SUV, he glanced back at the house.

Gretchen stood in the doorway, watching him.

Why had she moved away from him when he started past her? Was she afraid of him?

He frowned. That wasn't the emotion he wished to stir in anyone. Did she think he might grab Amy and run with her, like the fathers in the news? Definitely not his style, nor was he that confident about what he was doing. All he knew was, the child was partly his and that meant something.

He rested against the rental car a moment, palms spread and supporting his full weight. Trying to feel normal again, after days of this heaviness that had stolen his appetite and wreaked havoc on his gut.

After a moment, he climbed into his vehicle and started the engine. Drumming his fingers on the steering wheel, he mulled over the situation. He reached into the breast pocket of his suit, pulled out his cell phone and flipped it open with one hand. Swinging the SUV out onto the highway, he clicked on his brother's number.

It rang three times.

"Hullo?"

"Sam? I'm in Marydale."

"Did you find the woman? And the girl? Is she yours?"

"Yeah. I found them. And Gretchen says she's my child."

There was silence on the other end, and then Sam grated, "How much cash is she after?"

Daniel gritted his teeth. "Dammit, take off your attorney's hat for a minute. I just learned I'm a father. Anyway, why assume it's a setup? *I* sought Gretchen out. Not the other way around."

"I can set up a DNA test."

"Waste of time," he shot back. "Our genes for stubborn chins and Nicholson eyes seem a strong indication I was involved." He rubbed his forehead. "Look, I appreciate your concern. But give me time to adjust to the fact that I found them."

"Well, if she is your daughter, you need to decide if you'll seek custody. I'll put you in touch with Mack Adams. He wins tough cases for fathers."

"Good to know," Daniel said distractedly, as an image of Gretchen's worried face came to mind. "Sam, how does one go about being a good parent?"

There was silence on the other end of the line.

"Sam?"

Assuming he'd hit a dead zone, Daniel closed the cell phone and drove on.

To hell with Sam and his warnings. To hell with Gretchen wanting him to leave. For the time being, he'd plant himself somewhere in this ridiculously small town and figure out exactly what to do about the situation.

Chapter Three

As Daniel pulled onto the highway, the SUV's tires spit gravel. Gretchen watched his taillights until he rounded the bend toward town. Still staring out the doorway, but now at nothing in particular, she sighed.

Her arm tingled. Realizing she had the doorknob in a clench, she released it, shook the circulation back into her hand and pulled the door shut. Turning and leaning against its hard surface, she closed her eyes and focused on her breathing.

As if she could relax.

With a low groan, she opened her eyes. He'd come here and turned her into a noodlehead. Where was her brain? Down in her shoes? Obviously, since she'd sat passively in her own living room while he grilled her about leaving Chicago. On the other hand, maybe her brain had a right to go on vacation as soon as he showed up. *He'd shown up.* That fact alone was enough of a shock to her system, even before adding in his imposing gorgeousness, enhanced by the expensive suit that accentuated his height and the width of his shoulders. He still had that direct stare down pat, could still make her feel as if she were his only interest.

She should've told him to leave before Amy came out in the yard, even though he'd gotten her all flustered, and despite the fact she harbored some guilt over not telling him about Amy. But once they'd discussed the past, why had she *still* stood there and allowed him to talk her into coming back later?

"Because you're a noodlehead," she muttered low.

What'd he want, anyway? And what good could be gained by his returning?

The earlier tightness in her chest descended to her stomach. She pressed her hand against it, but the discomfort remained.

Daniel hadn't come all the way from Chicago to Marydale on a whim. Could it be that, now he knew he had a daughter, he wanted to play some sort of role in Amy's life? Fatherhood wasn't exactly in his realm of reality. He had no idea what parenting involved. You didn't pull out of anywhere slinging gravel if you had a child. You kept them safe. You taught them how to be safe.

She wandered into the living room, where Amy lay on her belly in front of the TV, absorbed in cartoons. Slipping up behind her daughter and sinking to her knees, she kissed the top of her head.

Amy flung her chin back and beamed up at her.

Soaking up the sight of those black-brown eyes, rounded cheeks and petal pink lips, Gretchen murmured, "I love you, Amy-Amy."

"I love *you*, Mommy."

A lump formed in her throat. "I can't hear that enough, you know."

Dipping her chin again as the TV commanded her attention, Amy recited, "Then I'll tell you a hundred million times."

Gretchen smiled. The phrase they swapped back and forth reminded her once again that the stretch marks, the laundry, three healthy meals a day and mind-numbing play dates were all tiny sacrifices, compared with the joy she got out of being Amy's mom.

She couldn't picture Daniel being corralled by parental duties. What would he be willing to give up for the sake of someone else? How much time off from his agency? How many nights of high living? Wouldn't he miss the champagne and caviar, the ladies, the publicity?

You're safe. Amy would be a rope around his neck.

So why this sense of doom hovering over her?

Because Daniel's features had softened when he first saw Amy. Just before he left, he'd smiled and tousled her hair.

What if he wanted Amy?

She lay on her back on the sofa, grabbed a pillow and hugged it to her chest, hoping for a moment's escape from her thoughts. Daniel's aftershave lingered in the fabric, releasing a faint clove-y, wood-shavings scent that drifted upward.

She pulled the pillow up to her nose and inhaled. Her scalp tingled.

She thrust the pillow away. So what if he smelled good? And who cared if he was so much more gorgeous in person than newsprint? He was the enemy if he had anything crazy in mind concerning Amy.

He'd only seen her for a few minutes. He couldn't understand the pure joy *she'd* experienced when a nurse first placed her baby, pink and squirming, in her arms. Okay, maybe it wasn't joy so much as fear mixed with excitement. Still, Daniel didn't have a clue.

But Amy was his child, too. Who else had those eyes, black-brown as the nuts from the buckeye trees out in the yard? Not to mention the wavy texture of his hair.

Reaching up to push some annoying wisps out of her eyes, she felt the bed tangles. Oh, geez! He'd seen her like *this*?

She shot up off the sofa. "Amy, I'm gonna go take my shower."

"'Kay."

On the way to her bedroom, she thought about what she'd say if Amy asked who this guy was, visiting them twice in one day. He'd called them friends. They were really just acquaintances. They hadn't had much of a relationship. They could forget it ever happened.

She would offer him that solution when he returned. Daniel didn't need to do anything with Amy. She had it all under control.

****

Daniel drove the mile back to town and pulled into a parking spot beside a diner. He sat in his car, fooling with his keys in the ignition and wondering why the gnawing in his gut refused to go away. He tried coughing and stretching. He concentrated on the things he usually fixated on, like how to keep the agency price-aggressive with reduced production costs. He even rehashed his biggest worry lately, the Toyco account and all the money that prospective deal could bring in if John Chroma's agency couldn't top their offer.

An image of his daughter floated over the figures in his head, and he grasped at it, tried to hold it and know it as well as he knew these other things. But Amy proved elusive, because he hadn't had enough time. You couldn't memorize your daughter that fast. This wasn't a two-minute memory game.

Climbing from the SUV and heading to the cafe, he tried to remember how the CEO of Toyco had looked the other day as they discussed plans for positioning the toy company in foreign markets. If he could focus on him and interpret his body language, he could determine how to proceed with their most important client to date. But all he conjured was Gretchen's worried gaze and tight lips.

"Damn," he muttered, and flung open the door to

the café.

Ring ring ring.

He frowned at the leather strap on the door with jingle bells attached. Why did little places like this feel the need to announce everyone's entrance? He preferred to slip in unnoticed and leave the same way.

Stepping up behind a customer at the cashier's station, he glanced around. Vinyl booths? A countertop with dessert under a glass dome? And was that Elvis swinging his hips to tick off time on that wall clock? "Huh!" he snorted, half to himself and half to the other diners. Surely they caught the humor here.

Ten sets of eyes blinked back at him.

He glanced quickly away again, pretending interest in the large "to go" order the cashier was ringing up for the guy in front of him.

"You the new minister?"

He swiveled around to find a rotund woman in black pants and leaf-patterned sweatshirt standing at his elbow. She toted a canvas bag stuffed so full of papers, it looked as if it'd explode any second.

"I'm Olive Barnes, your organist." Her gaze roamed over him.

"Did you say 'minister'?" Whew, she wore that perfume like a truck wore diesel fumes. He gritted his teeth to keep from wrinkling his nose. "No, I'm not. Sorry."

A waitress sauntered up and handed him a one-page laminated menu. "It's seat yourself."

"Thanks." He clung to the menu, grateful for the reprieve and wishing he could fan it under his nose.

He found a booth across from two teenagers who shot glances at him.

He averted his gaze.

"It's the suit."

Looking up from the menu, he discovered the

waitress hovering over him. "Excuse me?"

"Your suit." She pointed her pen at his lapel. "You wear something like that around here, we figure the bishop sent you. They keep telling us our new leader's coming any day now."

Daniel pretended disinterest, and ordered his coffee. But as she walked away, he wondered, who were "they?" Where was their old preacher? People didn't speak to each other this way in his coffee shop queue in the city. There was no time for small talk.

When the waitress—*Crystal*, her nametag read—returned with his drink, she set the mug in front of him and smiled. "A few people around here have one, but not like yours."

He glanced around. "Like my mug?"

"The mayor has a striped one. A few of the councilmen wear 'em sometimes. Then there's Wally. He has a black one, of course. But it doesn't fit nice like yours."

"Oh." The suit again. Shrugging out of his jacket, he flung it over the back of the booth. There. Now maybe everyone could just relax.

He gulped down the coffee, paid his bill and left. Once outside, he inhaled deeply of the crisp fall air. Now what to do? He'd sensed he should give Gretchen time to consider what he'd said, but how much time would she need?

He paced around the corner of the café and back, jacket in the crook of his arm and hands in his pockets. Oh, well. He supposed he could check out the sights.

He started down the sidewalk.

At the corner, he paused to study a colorful window display. A stuffed toy cat sat in a miniature rocker, reading to an assembly of mice. A cloth mallard and her fuzzy yellow brood waddled over through real leaves to hear the tale. He tilted his head to see the title on the book spine. *Amazing*

Animal Stories. With a wry grin, he silently gave the window dresser credit for the display. This was basic advertising at its best, something that tugged at the heartstrings of all ages.

Stepping backward, he read the name of the place on its shingle above his head. "Gretchen's Cards & Gifts."

Huh. *That* was surprising.

He opened the door, went inside and glanced around the shop. It wasn't one of the typical gimmicky places importing tourist items and cheap souvenirs. This was definitely classier stuff.

Gretchen was classy and intelligent. What was she doing here in this town? How could his daughter benefit from being raised here? Where would she go to school? He turned and saw a little boy in the next aisle begging his mother for a watercolor set. What about the arts? Was there a museum? A theater? A symphony?

He went back outside, and walked to the square across the street to stand in front of a bench where he had a good wide-angle view of the town. The whole place was one L-shaped stretch of shops.

What was he supposed to do now?

He checked his Tag Heuer. It hadn't even been an hour since he'd left Gretchen's.

Cramming his hands into his pants pockets, his fingers knocked against his cell phone. He pulled it out, figuring he could touch base with the marketing department and see what the news was on their end concerning Toyco. He sat on the bench to search for the number and saw that he had a message. Keying in the code to retrieve it, he heard:

"I haven't gotten my money yet. What's the deal?"

Ray. He closed his eyes.

"I know you got plenty cash to spare," his foster father went on. "I read the paper and I see your fancy company deals. Well, remember where you came from, pal. Remember who raised you. If it wasn't for me and Barbara, you'd be out selling dope on the streets. That's the way you were headed. You were a loner, an antisocial. We made you what you are and you owe us. Don't you forget that. And make it seven grand this time. Got a little gambling debt to cover."

I'll bet you do. Clenching his jaw, Daniel snapped the phone shut and just sat there. He'd talk with his office assistant later and have her send Ray a check. He rubbed the nape of his neck, wishing again that he'd gotten good foster parents like Sam's. Or better yet, if they could have fostered the both of them. Sam would kill him if he knew he was still sending the checks. He could hear it now, his "Why are you still letting that S.O.B. intimidate you?"

Because he was all I had, he and Barbara. He supposed he was still willing to do whatever, just for a jot of the affection they showered on their own kids.

He sighed. Sam was right. He had to stop sending the money. Next time he wouldn't.

"Hey. You."

Flinching, he nearly dropped the phone. Whipping around, he discovered a guy in a rumpled suit standing on the dulling lawn area behind him.

"You're in my spot." The guy waved a brown paper bag toward the bench.

Arching a brow, Daniel slid to the other end of the bench.

The guy came around from behind him then and plopped himself down where Daniel had been. He had those cheeks that seemed to hold a perpetual flush, like the Brits. Pale skin and red hair, cut short and looking thick as Astroturf, only accentuated it.

Daniel wondered if *he* was the new minister, and if he should warn him about the café. The ladies in there sure were eager for spiritual enlightenment or *something*, and this guy looked ripe for the picking.

"Visiting someone?" he said, opening his sack and digging out a wrapped sandwich.

"Yeah." Daniel eyed him. Was this some new opening for reeling in religious converts? He thought he'd heard them all on the streets of Chicago.

His bench partner raised the white-bread sandwich and took a bite, before squinting one eye against the sun and fixing the other on Daniel. "Who?"

"Gretchen Parks," he said, out of politeness. Not that it was any of his business.

"You a cousin of Gretchen's or something?"

"No. I knew her in Chicago."

Down came the man's red brows as he took another bite, chewed and swallowed. "Chicago," he mused. "Not a good time for her."

"Are *you* a relative?"

"Nah. Friend." Brushing crumbs off his hands, he held one out to Daniel. "Wally Williams."

He gripped the guy's hand. "Daniel Nicholson."

"Gretchen know you were coming?" Bottle green eyes blared into his.

"No. Why?"

"Surprised her, eh? She doesn't like surprises."

"I didn't stay long," he found himself saying in his defense.

Wally cocked his head. "You're brave, anyway."

"How so?"

"'Hell hath no fury like a woman scorned.'" He chuckled. "Know what I mean?"

"Yes, as a matter of fact." He'd scorned more than his share. "But I think you're getting the wrong idea. Gretchen and I are just acquaintances."

Williams' eyes narrowed. "What you say your name was?"

He repeated it as he rose from the bench.

Wally appeared to ruminate on that, before his expression mellowed again. Reaching into his breast pocket, he retrieved a business card that he thrust toward Daniel.

He took it and read "Marydale Casket Company," with "Wally Williams, Owner" printed under it.

"If I can be of any help, call me."

Daniel quirked a brow and said dryly, "I hope I won't need you anytime soon."

Wally grinned. "One never knows. Especially if one is dealing with Gretchen."

"What do you mean by that?"

"Stick around. You'll see."

Daniel studied him a moment longer, before turning and walking away. When he'd gone a block or two, he stopped and glanced back over his shoulder. The park bench was empty.

Strange. Strange guy, too. And yet, he'd seemed sharp-witted and funny. His advice about Gretchen had been meant to help him, as far as he could tell. And as for the little crack about needing the casket if he dealt with her, luckily there'd been some humor in Wally's eyes then. Daniel suspected the implication was that Gretchen was willing to step to the center of the ring when it came to her daughter.

He widened his stride. Time to get back to Gretchen and Amy.

Reaching his SUV, he hopped inside and drove with his windows down. The wind whipped at his hair, and the sun warmed his face. The air smelled like leaves or crops or whatever. Not smog. Huh. Nice.

He thought about Williams again. He seemed to know Gretchen pretty well. Had they dated? He'd said he was a friend, but maybe he'd been a very good friend. He couldn't see them together. Wally seemed too laid back. And yet, Daniel could see he might be endearing to women in a puppy-dog-to-take-home-and-nurture sort of way. Gretchen had returned here for some reason. Maybe it was Williams.

Frowning over that as he pulled into Gretchen's drive, he suddenly realized he'd given no thought to what he was going to say to her. And he prided himself on being a strategist. He didn't trust people who winged it in confrontations and seemed to go on intuition. And yet, here he was, without a plan because he couldn't wrap his mind around the situation. Parenthood? The idea popped in to tease him, to make him grit his teeth, only to vanish as soon as he tried to concentrate on solutions.

What the hell was he going to do?

Walking to the house, he looked around for Amy and saw the jacket she'd discarded on the slide. He went and picked it up. It hardly weighed anything. Wadding it into a loose ball, he carried it with him to the front door.

He knocked.

No answer.

Probably couldn't hear over the TV or something. Or maybe Gretchen would refuse to see him again.

He pounded with his fist a few times.

She yanked the door open. Her wet hair hung straight, making circle puddles on her pink T-shirt just above her breasts. A little more drip and—he jerked his gaze up, to catch the wrinkled brow and wary look in her eyes.

"I wasn't expecting you back so fast." Placing one bare foot atop the other, she jutted a hip closer to him. "I'm not ready."

"I have to get back to Chicago. I really can't give

you any more time."

She sighed, glanced at the jacket in his hand, and opened the door wide. "Come in, then."

He moved inside. After setting Amy's jacket on the kitchen table, he turned and checked out the living room. "Where is Amy?"

She picked up the jacket, shook it out and slipped it over the posts of a straight chair. "She's taking a nap. She woke up too early this morning."

Disappointment flashed through him. He raised his brows. "Can I see her?"

She looked doubtful. Finally, with a sigh, she said, "Follow me."

He shadowed her down the narrow back hallway to a darkened room.

Stopping in the doorway, she touched an index finger to her lips.

He caught the hint, nodded, and moved to her side. Amy lay in a frilly canopy bed, curled around a huge stuffed bear. Her lips were parted slightly, but she didn't make a sound.

Daniel's throat clamped shut. His heart thudded in his chest as he resisted the urge to step closer. She looked like the most innocent thing he'd ever seen, like an angel resting there.

Gretchen turned, and motioned him away from the door.

He gazed at Amy again, and swallowed around the lump in his throat, knowing it might be the last look he got of her today. Finally, turning, he followed Gretchen back toward the kitchen.

As she moved into the living room, he noticed the feminine sway of her body.

He sat on the sofa in the spot he'd occupied earlier.

She took the chair, straightening her back and placing her feet on the floor this time instead of tucked up beside her. She appeared ready to stand up fast, as if she might suddenly end their visit. "I thought we'd said all we needed to earlier. But if there's anything else before you go—?"

He had an idea of what he wanted to say to her now. A plan had developed as he stood in the doorway of Amy's small bedroom and watched her sleep. No, maybe it'd started when he listened to Ray's message earlier. Amy was his. His flesh and blood. He couldn't abandon her. He couldn't live with himself, knowing she might want her father the way he'd wanted his own parents.

He looked around the room, from the flowered curtains in the window to the cuckoo clock ticking rhythmically on the wall of the toy-filled dining area. He breathed in the scent of warm toast, something he'd failed to notice earlier. "You've given our daughter a nice home," he said. "Obviously you care a lot for her."

"I don't just care about her, I love her. She's all I have."

He nodded, the wheels turning in his mind now. "I live a comfortable life. I have my apartment, a staff, and money for the best private schools."

Her gaze narrowed. "Are you saying I'm not giving Amy what you think she deserves?"

"No." He wasn't sure how to go about this. His body thrummed with adrenaline, as if he'd just come in from a steep-incline run. "I'm just saying I have a good life, too, and there's room in it for my daughter."

Her mouth tightened. "Did you come here to tell me you want to take her?"

"No, I only wanted to find out if she was my daughter." He leaned forward, pressing his forearms hard against his thighs to keep from jiggling a heel up and down. "But now that I've seen her—" He bowed his head. When he looked up again, he said simply, "I don't have relatives. Just my brother and his boys."

So? her slight frown seemed to imply.

"I'm saying I have room in my life for this child."

"Huh!" Turning from his gaze, she shook her head. "You don't know what you're talking about. You don't even know her." She swung her attention back to him. "You say you can give her school, a penthouse and money. Servants, too?"

"Staff, yes." He raised his brows, and quickly added, "I can give her anything she wants."

"Four-year-olds have unique concepts of what they want. Right now she wants a purple tutu and a fairy wand."

He nodded soberly. "My administrative assistant could track those down."

"She also wants a pink motorized car."

"Then she'll have it."

"No she won't."

"If she wants it—"

"There's a difference between 'want' and 'need.' Amy wants it, but she doesn't need it. It's expensive and she's only four. If you give her a toy worth hundreds now, what will you give her when she's six?" Her eyes had widened slightly as she spoke, and her words had taken on more emphasis. "And even more important, what about broken bones? I don't know how fast those things go, but they have some speed. She could get hurt."

He frowned.

"Where would she ride it in Chicago? Up Michigan Avenue?"

"Okay." He held a hand up. "For now, no motorized car."

"And no living in Chicago."

"Why not?"

She heaved a sigh. "I have another solution."

"What's that?"

"Go home. Forget we ever knew each other."

Another door closing on him. In self-defense, he fired back, "I want to know my daughter. I want her to know me."

"She isn't something to own, Daniel. We're not fighting over a possession here."

"I'm just saying I can take care of her, same as you can."

"I don't doubt that your money can buy her things." She speared his gaze with those powerful navy eyes. "But can you give her love?"

His temples throbbed. His ex-wife claimed he was closed and coldhearted. Selfish. Maybe he'd forgotten how to care. "I can try," he said softly.

She shook her head. "Not good enough."

Finally, in frustration he blurted, "Why are you the one who should raise her?"

Her eyes darkened. "I told you. She's my life."

He sat there, thinking things over, until an idea formed. A ploy that wasn't in his best interest. But it could keep the door open, keep this link that he needed more time to come to terms with. He sent her a guarded smile. "I've been meaning to take a vacation. This might just be the time and place for it."

She thrust herself out of her chair. "You are *not* staying here."

He held her gaze as he stood up, dropping eye contact only long enough to pull his cell phone from his pants pocket and punch a number from his directory. While Gretchen shot him daggers, he said, "Valerie? I'm staying in Ohio a few days. Mind going over to my place and packing my things?" He chuckled. "Yes, you can leave my tux out. Forward all Toyco-related emails and calls for now. Oh, and send seven grand from my personal account to Ray Irwin ASAP. You have the address." Then he hung up.

"What, exactly, are you trying to prove?"

Gretchen demanded, hands on her hips.

"That you can trust me with my daughter. That I really do want to be in her life in whatever way you'll allow."

She chuckled and waved him off. "I've got a big picture of you, Daniel Nicholson, hanging around Marydale."

"I won't be hanging around *town* per se," he said, striding to the front door. "I'll need to be right here, so I can spend as much time as possible getting to know Amy."

"You're not staying here," she blurted, quickly catching up to him.

"Oh, I'm not planning on staying *here*." He stepped out onto the front porch and glanced back at her as she braked at his heels. He pointed to his right, toward the "For Rent" end of the house. "I'm staying there."

Chapter Four

Daniel forced his eyes open and squinted at his watch dial. Five-thirty, his usual wakeup time. Good. He'd get up in a minute. His lids drifted down again. He could afford a few more winks, a little more shuteye before—

Snapping his eyes open, he quickly surveyed the darkened room, the thrusts of his heartbeat thumping him back into the land of the awake. He wasn't in a hotel room on a business trip. He was in Gretchen's house. He'd found her.

Found his daughter.

He hadn't seen either of them since demanding to stay here, a fact Gretchen was none too happy about as she threw spare towels at him and threatened to have the landlord charge him double.

This bare-bones side of the duplex evoked memories of Gretchen's space, brimming with rugs and chairs, pink walls and crayon drawings, photos on the fridge, dishes on the table and kid toys on the floor beside dog toys. Here, you got the big fillers, the furniture, and that was it. Back home, he would have fallen asleep to the TV last night, and be catching up on world news right now. But no TV. Oh, well. He'd slept like a baby in the quiet room.

Even now, he could hear himself breathe, which made him aware of that same odd weight that had compressed the air in his lungs yesterday, like a cement mixer dumping its load smack on top of him. Why wouldn't it go away? Was this what being a father meant, this sense that something hidden deep inside had been laid open and exposed? He didn't even know the child. If just knowing for certain that he was a father meant he had to deal with feeling this way, then maybe he'd made a mistake with this mission.

He climbed from bed and stared at his naked reflection in the full-length mirror. He *looked* the same as always, even if he felt different.

Desire to know his child had brought him here. Seeing the little girl, something had made him want her, want to be her father.

What if she wanted him, too, and Mommy Gretchen wasn't saying so? What if she missed having a father? He could be a father. He could achieve it somehow, some way. He'd prove to Gretchen that he was willing to take this step. Screw the mixed feelings. Chalk them up as nerves and move forward.

He headed for a shower and a shave.

After checking his email, he went out the front door, strode to Gretchen's and knocked.

The door opened just wide enough for him to glimpse Amy's pink cheeks and bright eyes.

Scuffling noises sounded behind her.

"*No!*" she yelled over her shoulder.

Suddenly the door flew open and a pair of hyper-tuned dog eyes and gigantic, drooling jowls popped into view.

Uh oh. The damned dog.

Daniel backed up so fast he tripped over his own feet.

Scooby bounded at him, happily taking advantage of his wavering stance to plop plate-sized paws atop his chest.

The dog's weight bent him backwards toward a glass patio table. "Back off!" he bellowed, dodging wet swipes from a tongue the size of a cow's.

He wrestled the amorous beast off of him, and

when Scooby danced back for more attention, grabbed the big goober by his belt-sized collar and held on.

"Move out of the way, Amy," he commanded. After turning the dog around, and with an encouraging shove, he managed to get him safely back inside the house. Stepping in behind Scooby, he shut the door.

"What on earth is going on?"

Daniel looked up to find Gretchen standing in the hallway, glaring at him. Noting the terrycloth robe she gripped closed at her neck, he frowned in surprise. "Are you just getting up?"

She nodded toward the window. "It's still dark out. What time is it?"

"Six-thirty."

She scowled. "Go away."

"To where? You're the only person I know around here."

Her frown deepened. Seeing it, he bit back a rush of humor. Angry or no, she looked pretty cute standing there in that frumpy robe, her hair all tumbled, like yesterday. Her pretty eyes bleary. Sleepy-sexy.

A hand slipped into his.

He jerked his attention downward and found Amy standing there, face upturned, brown-eyed gaze hopeful.

"I got new cereal," she said, eyes twinkling in the same way as if she'd announced instead, "They crowned me Queen of The World."

His throat tightened. Her fingers fluttered against his, warm and light, reminding him of a baby bird he'd once held.

"Want some? It's got a rainbow in it."

"A rainbow, eh?" Her Winnie the Pooh nightgown, riotous honey-toned curls and small bare feet made him feel awkward, out of sync with her,

52

and at the same time, strangely comfortable. "I, uh, don't eat breakfast."

"That's silly!"

"You called me silly yesterday." He tried but failed to keep a note of humor from his tone. "Is that your favorite word, or what?"

She shook her curly head. "You're just silly."

"How can I avoid being silly, then?"

"Eat cereal!"

He glanced at Gretchen and caught her yawning.

"You could go back to bed," he suggested. "Amy and I can hang out and get to know each other."

"No, I'm fine," she insisted, straightening. "Let me change and I'll be right back."

He watched her hustle down the hall. Why the hurry? Did his presence bother her so much that she didn't want him spending any time around Amy without her?

When he looked back at Amy, she was in the act of pouring cereal into her bowl. Half of it landed on the kitchen table. Observing the pile of flakes and seeing her slight frown of concern, he said quickly, "This part can be mine."

"Okay!" she said, brightening again.

He grinned. Scooping up the spilled cereal, he put it in the other bowl she'd gotten out.

She went to the refrigerator and pulled out a jug of milk that she carried toward him, biting her tongue with the effort.

He gritted his teeth as he watched, but resisted the urge to rush over and relieve her of her burden. She was making such a valiant attempt at it on her own, and if she were anything like him, she'd prefer to be the one in charge. At any instant, though, she was bound to drop it and they'd catch hell when Gretchen returned to find them standing in a sea of white. He didn't want her to get into trouble. She was too happy-go-lucky. She wasn't sullen, the way he'd been. She didn't deserve the "heat."

When she scooted safely to within a few feet of him, he grabbed the jug, and with a sense of relief and pride in her ability, poured milk into their bowls.

They picked up their spoons and crunched away. Rainbow-colored cereal tasted pretty good. When was the last time he'd had cereal? Not in this decade.

While they ate, he struggled with something to say. What did adults say to kids, other than to scold them or tell them what to do? He wracked his brain, trying to recall some inspiring adult/child moment from his past. But all that came to mind were the tongue-lashings, or the growling belly he suffered after being excused from the table for one crazy reason or another. Pouring salt in someone's drink. Pinching someone under the table. Spilling milk. Any other infraction of the house rules that a foster sibling had committed and then blamed on him when they got caught.

He opened his mouth to say something, but nothing came to him. Finally, looking around for a subject, he saw two four-inch-long paws sticking out from under the table, and blurted, "Do you ever step on Scooby?"

"Nope." Amy didn't even look up. She was busy pushing cereal back onto her spoon before she stuck it in her mouth.

Silence.

Maybe she wasn't much of a conversationalist yet. He set his spoon down and just watched her happily chomping away.

"B-I-N-G-O, B-I-N-G-O." She looked at him, and giggled. "That's the doggie song."

"I don't know that one."

She rolled her eyes. "*You* know it. Everybody

knows it."

"Sorry." Who knew this song was a need-to-know thing? If his mother had sung it before her death, he couldn't remember.

Amy set her pudgy hands on her hips and sang more slowly so he, the obviously inadequate adult, could finally learn this important lesson.

He smiled and relaxed back in his chair. Inadequate or no, he wouldn't want to be anywhere else right now.

Gretchen breezed back into the kitchen, carrying a stack of folded towels that she put away in drawers.

Daniel followed her moves with his gaze. He couldn't help himself. She looked damned good. *Nice breasts*, the clingy sweater had him thinking. He dragged his attention away and it settled lower, on the jeans outlining her hips and showcasing the slender length of her legs. His body responded appreciatively. She was a beautiful woman, with soft curves, wide eyes and honey-brown waves of hair falling below her shoulders.

She came over to stand beside him, and as she lifted the cereal box to close it, he caught a whiff of her perfume. Vanilla? Some sort of flower? Whatever it was, it wasn't overwhelming like some women's.

"Who spilled?" she said a little sternly, pointing at the milk and bits of cereal on the table.

"I did," he quickly replied, to cover for Amy.

"Daniel didn't spill it," Amy piped up. "I did it."

Daniel tensed, awaiting the reprisal.

Gretchen cupped her daughter's chin, and patted it. "Thanks for being honest." She shot Daniel a condemning glance.

Amy peeked sideways at him.

Good. She hadn't had to suffer punishment due to a mere accident. He shrugged and winked.

With an impish look in her eyes, Amy hopped

out of her chair, came over and tickled his side, her little fingers barely pressing his shirt to his skin.

An enchanted warmth surged through him. He chuckled, and fibbed, "That tickles." He held his fingers out and wiggled them, as if to go after her next.

Letting out an ear-piercing squeal, she took off toward the living room.

"Thanks," Gretchen muttered, taking up their empty cereal bowls. "That's just what I needed to hear so early in the morning."

He watched her hair swing forward, and noticed the slim length of her fingers as she shifted crumbs off the table and into her palm. Her hands reminded him of when they'd met, when she'd been a jilted bride who'd returned her ring only days earlier. She'd told him about it in a defiant tone, as if she didn't care at all. But he had seen the pain in her eyes.

"Want me to go out and get us some coffee?" he offered, genuinely sorry for disrupting her morning two days in a row.

She eyed him. "I make it here." Then she went back to the counter area to start the pot.

He sat back, to await a cup. "I have a coffeemaker, but I've never used it. Never even taken it out of the box."

She cast him a knowing look. "Welcome to the real world." She came over to wipe the table. "And speaking of the real world, we don't usually get up around here for another hour."

"Sorry. I was eager to see you and start our day."

"*My* day starts with dropping Amy off at school. Then I'm going to the shop to supervise the unpacking of more Christmas stock." After a pause, she said, "What are you going to do around here all day?"

"I'll go with you to drop Amy off, if that's okay. Then I thought you and I could talk about the future. But if you're tied up, I guess I'll come back and work from here."

She stared at him a moment, before coming over to him and leaning in. Her scent wafted to him and wreaked pleasant havoc with his sense of smell.

Glancing toward the living room area, she murmured, "I let you stay last night because it was late and I was tired of fighting you. But now I want you to go back to Chicago." Turning her midnight blue gaze on his, she said, "I don't understand what you're trying to prove."

He moved an inch closer, saw her eyes widen as he invaded her space, and uttered a low, "It's simple. I don't want to be wiped out of Amy's life the way you wipe the crumbs off this table." His gaze locked on hers. "You've kept me away too long already."

He watched her swallow, before she tore her gaze away.

"Sorry if it makes you uncomfortable." He leaned back. "On the other hand, I don't think I'm asking anything unreasonable."

She glanced at him, her brow wrinkled, her eyes filled with—worry?

Not good. Making her skittish wouldn't help convince her that he could do this job of being Amy's father.

"How can you have any idea what you're asking? You're saying you want to try and do what I do with Amy?" She waved at the room. "Look around, Daniel. This is not you." She pointed the sponge at his chest. "People like you eat brunch. You don't eat frosted cereal."

"I just did." He eyed the sponge. "And don't point that thing unless you're gonna shoot it."

Her mouth tightened, and she set the sponge down. "You're trying to prove something now. But tomorrow you'll be bored, lonely and starved for the kind of fun that you won't find around here."

He shook his head. "If you're saying I'm on my best behavior around Amy to impress her, you're wrong. I don't know how to act around kids in the first place, much less finesse them."

"It's your business to sell things to people. Don't try to tell me you wouldn't know how to sell yourself." Her eyes held no humor. Turning away, she said, "Amy, turn the TV off now. Time to get dressed."

Daniel rose, reluctant to leave and yet pulled to the work that had followed him from Chicago. "I've got to check my email again. I'll be right back."

"If you're not ready when it's time to leave, we'll go without you."

"Oh, I'll be ready."

Following him to the door, Gretchen drew up close to him and said under her breath, "I'm not giving you custody."

He looked down at her flushed cheeks, full lips, thrust-back shoulders and pert breasts. He meant to brush her gaze with his, but such emotion flared in her eyes that he couldn't tear himself away. That look sucked him in, trapping him like a sailor swimming the ocean's surface one instant and in the next becoming lost in its depths. Energy surged between them, a sizzling hot push-pull that set pleasure throbbing through him.

Then she looked away.

The air chilled.

Frowning, he dragged his gaze from her, turned and shoved out the door.

Gretchen closed the door and rested her forehead against it. She turned and stared at the kitchen table, too numb to move. Daniel's mere presence intimidated her, with the way he carried himself, those blasted bore-through-you eyes and that quick mind of his producing irrefutable comebacks. All of it had her stomach tied in knots as if she were thirteen again, and "in crush" with her science teacher. On the other hand, there was a huge difference between puppy love and this situation. When Daniel moved in close, he reminded her with just a look and a change in his tone exactly what they'd had together. Without mentioning anything sexual, he zapped her back five years and into his arms.

Numb? Oh, no. She wasn't numb to Daniel Nicholson in any way. He just had this ability to sweep her mind of reason and permeate her body with feeling, separating the two in a way that made her bite her lip with concern.

"Why did I have to go and sleep with one of the most powerful, driven, spoiled men in Chicago?" she muttered under her breath. He could have just about anything and he'd come here for Amy. Well, he wouldn't get her.

I won't even allow you in close enough that you might hurt her with your leaving.

But he'd already held Amy's hand. Amy had warmed to him. She couldn't stop the sense of betrayal that flared over that.

She had to figure a way to get him to leave, and the sooner the better for Amy and for her. But right now, she had to get her daughter to school on time.

Heading down the bedroom hallway, she found Amy struggling to put on socks that didn't go with the outfit she'd laid out for her. As she helped her find another pair and get her sneakers on, she wondered what Daniel was planning. Was he going to follow them around all day?

"Owww!"

Glancing down, she realized she was trying to cram Amy's left foot into her right shoe. "Oh! Sorry, baby."

59

"I'm not a—"

"I know, I know." She kissed her head. "You're not a baby. You're my big girl."

Amy scooted around on her bottom to face her. "Is Daniel our new neighbor?"

"No, sweetie. I told you, he's just staying for a few days."

Amy's lower lip came out. "I want him to be our new neighbor."

Gretchen glanced at the Tinker Bell clock on the dresser. "Oops," she said, relieved that they had no more time for the touchy topic. "We need to get a move on."

After seeing to Scooby's needs for the day, she hurried Amy out the door and to the car.

Daniel wasn't around. Good. She wouldn't have to deal with the uncomfortable feelings he stirred up.

She'd hopped into the driver's seat and crammed the key in the ignition when the front passenger door opened and Daniel stuck his head in.

"You weren't planning on going without me, were you?" He sent her a knowing smile as he climbed into his seat.

"Daniel!" Amy clapped with delight. "Are you coming to my school?"

"Sure." He shifted in the seat to face her. "I want to see it."

He turned back around to Gretchen. "Well?" A facetious gleam lit his eyes. "What are we waiting for?"

She sent him a stony look and shifted into gear. Her fingers shook against the wheel as she started toward the highway. He'd stuck himself to them like glue—but only until she could get him back to Chicago. Until then, she'd have to grin and bear it or people might begin to suspect something.

Maybe her plan could be as simple as giving him

the runaround until he got bored and practically begged to leave Marydale.

Then she and Amy could be happy again. Happy and safe.

Chapter Five

Daniel wasn't sure what to do. Gretchen had dropped him off in the center of town, and with nothing but a "See you later" and "I have work to do," had left him standing there.

He supposed he'd eventually jog the three or four miles back to her house.

He walked over to the town square bench to call the office and check on things. While he waited for Valerie to transfer him to the creative department, he kept an eye out, expecting that character Wally Williams to show up any minute and demand his seat.

When he'd finished his call, he put his phone away. Reaching into his pants pocket, he pulled Wally's business card out of his wallet, flicked at it, and decided to kill time by checking into the casket business. Maybe Wally could fill in some blanks about Gretchen. The better Daniel knew her, the better he could deal with her. They needed to get along, for Amy.

The shops marching along Main across from the park formed the straight part of the "L," with Marydale Casket Company's stately brick façade completing its perpendicular end. He strode down the sidewalk and reached the old colonial-style building in five minutes, by his watch. He whistled, amazed by the efficiency of small towns. No having to elbow someone aside to get the taxi at the curb, no zipping across town on the raised rail or waiting in lobbies for the next elevator.

Once inside the casket company, he found himself standing on a hall floor constructed of old white marble that had him thinking, creepily, of grave markers. Now, where to find Williams? Spying a woman in an office to his right working at a desktop computer, he popped his head around the door. "Excuse me? I'm looking for Wally Williams."

"Nicholson, right?"

Daniel jerked around and saw Williams lounging in a doorway. Today he wore khakis, a wrinkled white shirt and a tie with color-splashed fish swimming across it. Good God. That fashion statement was more like "I rent beach property" than "I sell caskets." Oh, well. Maybe he had such a niche in the casket market, it didn't matter that he hardly dressed the part.

Daniel strode over and offered his hand. "How's it going?"

"Couldn't be worse." Williams grasped his hand, before turning and motioning him into his office.

Daniel looked around in surprise at the piles of papers, stacks of books and towers of miscellaneous junk. How could anyone work in such a mess? Maybe that was what Williams meant by "couldn't be worse."

"The truth is, business is really slow," the casket maker said, as if reading his thoughts. He hefted a pile of magazines out of a chair so Daniel could sit. When he had yanked his own desk chair out and flopped into it, his gaze landed speculatively on Daniel. "That why you're here? Decide you need a casket?"

He held up his hands. "Don't start sizing me up yet. I'm healthy."

"You never know. Best to 'be prepared,' to quote the Boy Scouts."

"Yeah, well, I'll get around to it one day. For now, I'm just here because Gretchen is tied up for a while."

Wally tilted his chin. "What was it you wanted with Gretchen? You say you're a friend. Then why haven't you been to visit her before?"

"How do you know I haven't?"

"Haven't seen you around."

Daniel frowned. "Do you see everyone who comes to Marydale?"

"Yup."

He figured that was an exaggeration. No place could be that small. "Well, I've been busy growing my business."

Wally was still eyeing him as if not completely buying his story. "What's your business?"

"I'm in advertising."

"Advertising," Wally groaned. "Finneyville Caskets is killing me with advertising right now. Horning in on my territory with telemarketing."

Daniel drew his brows together. "I've heard of them. They're out of Indiana."

Wally nodded.

"They're your biggest competitor?"

He nodded again. "They sent out a mail pack the other day. Laudermilk Funeral Home in Cincy told me about it when I called on them. They showed me Finneyville's rate sheet." When he shook his head, not a hair in the thick red hedge budged. "I can't match those rates. I've got bills to pay."

"This is interesting," Daniel murmured. "I've read that lately even the funeral industry has begun competitive marketing."

"My old man would turn over in his grave," Wally groused. "Word-of-mouth and handshake agreements, that's all it took in those days." With a low growl, he swiveled in his chair and stared at his bookcase.

Following his glance, Daniel noticed a car collection perfectly lined up on those surprisingly dust-free shelves. Corvettes, Porsches, Rolls, Bentleys, Lamborghinis, Ferraris, he had collected miniatures of the best makes from over the years, including a diminutive Spyder detailed precisely like Daniel's real deal. So he and the coffin-maker had discriminating taste in cars in common.

Wally turned back to Daniel. "Pop told me I needed to come out of my shell if I wanted to keep MCC in the black. He felt I wasn't personable enough." He paused. "Do you think I'm personable?"

"Sure." He couldn't be sure, though. He'd barely met the guy. All he knew for certain was that he needed professional marketing help. "You know, sales is all in the presentation. Maybe you're not going about selling yourself or your product the best way possible. I could help with that."

Wally tilted back in his chair and stretched his legs by putting his feet up on the corner of the desk. "I'll sell the caskets. But sell myself?" He shook his head. "I'm not Pop. I'm not glad-handing. I'm not running for office. What you see is what you get."

Daniel tried not to gape at the suede slip-ons he'd plopped on the desk. What the hell were they? House slippers? Moccasins? Slip-a-mocs?

Wally sighed. "Anyway, right before you and I met yesterday, I'd decided to throw in the towel."

"What? What are you talking about? People have to be buried in something."

"Yeah, a *Finneyville* casket." Wally's morose expression showed how much it stung to admit it.

Daniel pressed his lips together. *He'd* worked hard to build his agency. He wouldn't dump it just like that. Surely this company had some viability left in it.

He stared at Wally's car collection, trying to think of a way for the two of them to connect and be of help to each other. "You know, I have a Spyder like that one. A full-scale one."

"You do?" Wally's eyes lit. "Where is it?"

"In my parking garage in Chicago. It's this year's model."

Wally turned back to him, disappointment evident in his downcast expression. "I want one," he murmured, picking up the miniature version from the shelf and turning it in his hand, almost as if he could rub it and *poof* it would grow to full scale.

"But all your spare cash goes into MCC. Right?"

Wally nodded.

Daniel made a decision. "I'd like to help you get back on your feet and be able to afford your dreams."

"Yeah, sure." Wally scrutinized him. "Fancy guy like you wouldn't hang around here long enough to help anybody. Hell, I'll bet you wear those girlie tassel shoes because you don't even have time to tie shoelaces."

"And let me guess about *your* shoes," Daniel shot back. "You wear them because someone wouldn't let you bury their ninety-year-old grandpa in them."

They grinned at each other.

"You're right," Daniel allowed. "I won't be here long at all. But I can't stand quitters. I'm not quitting on something that Gretchen and I have going." *Meaning Amy.* "I want your commitment that if I'm not quitting on that, you won't close this place down."

"I don't see how you and Gretchen have anything to do with me. And I still don't see why you'd help me."

"I'm turning over a new leaf. I'm starting a new chapter in my life." Even as he said the clichés, Daniel realized how corny they sounded. "I like you, Wally. I don't want to see you fail."

Wally's face lit. Jumping up from his chair, he thrust out his hand. "Well, why didn't you say so?"

Because I thought you might be dating Gretchen

and I didn't like the idea. Now, though, he had a gut feeling that the coffin maker hadn't dated her. Wally meant it when he said they were just friends.

He smiled as they shook hands. It'd been a while since he'd had time for friendship.

Wally came around the desk and pointed at the door. "Want to go look at my coffins? I mean, you may like me, but if you don't like my products, you won't be able to help me sell 'em."

"Very true," Daniel concurred, and followed him out the door.

They left for the plant in Wally's cluttered truck. "So are you and Gretchen dating?" Wally asked as he drove. "Is that what you're working on?"

Daniel only raised a brow, a response that Wally didn't see.

"Better stay clear of Joel if ya are."

"Who's Joel?" Daniel asked, with an instant catch in his gut. Gretchen had a boyfriend?

"So you *are* going out with her?"

Daniel felt his collar getting tight. He needed some explanation for lurking around Gretchen. Caught between having to lie or reveal what Gretchen had forbidden him to say, he opted for, "You could say that."

"Guys usually run away from her fast," Wally said with a warning look. "So I won't expect to know you for long." He drummed on the steering wheel as he waited at a light. "You know about her fiancé leaving?"

"Right." Daniel eyed him, wondering where he was going with this line of conversation.

"Several of us tried to date her after David took off, and after she got back from Chicago. But she wouldn't have any part of it. Guys started calling her 'Ice Queen' behind her back."

"Maybe she had good reason to be cautious. Who knows what she went through in Chicago."

Wally leaned in a little. "Between you and me, I think she fell in love."

Daniel sat back. No way. They'd both hated the idea of love. Her fiancé hurt her. His ex-wife hurt him. So they were just toying with each other. "No. She didn't find love in Chicago."

"How would you know? Did she tell you?"

"Yeah, pretty much." No. She hadn't even told him goodbye, actually. "Anyway, she came back here alone. That says a lot."

Wally scratched his chin. "She never told us about her boyfriend there. We figure he left her for another and broke her heart. Then the jerk wouldn't even come and see his daughter."

I didn't know about her, Daniel wanted to say in defense. Instead, he bit his tongue.

Wally switched back to the subject of Spyders and filled the air space with his vast knowledge of the cars.

An hour later, riding back to MCC's offices, Daniel said, "That wood you're using is very impressive. And with the old-fashioned planing techniques, secret recipe polish and forged hinges, you've got a unique product. Without seeing your books, I'd say at least outwardly your company's solid. You just need to know how to compete in today's market. Finneyville jumped into the deep end. Now it's your turn. Only, you've got to jump off a higher board."

"I hear ya." Wally pounded his palm against the steering wheel. "I'm pumped all of a sudden." He glanced in Daniel's direction. "Thanks."

"No problem." Daniel hummed with energy too, from assessing a product and knowing he could help to promote it. Remembering his real reason for being in town, he hopped out of the truck. "Hey, thanks for the conversation and the tour. I need to run."

Wally grabbed the brown bag that had been

sitting between them and held it open. "Want lunch 'to go'? I've got an extra peanut butter sandwich."

When was the last time he'd had peanut butter? "Crunchy?" Daniel queried. "Or creamy?"

"Creamy. With grape jelly. I'm a purist."

Daniel reached out a hand.

Grinning, Wally plopped the sandwich into it.

"Thanks," he said, glancing up the street. "Now I've got to try and catch Gretchen on her lunch break. Think she eats in the café?"

"Chances are pretty good that she does. That or takes out food from there, since it's near her shop."

"Great. We'll meet tomorrow if I'm still here and Gretchen is tied up again."

Wally nodded.

He hurried out of there, eating the sandwich as he strode down the sidewalk. The peanut butter, his second departure from the usual, after the cereal he'd shared with Amy, tasted good. He sure was going all out on this break from his old way of living. But a familiar tension headache threatened near his temples as he considered what Wally had said about Gretchen. Scenes popped into his head, one of Gretchen standing in a white dress in church, waiting on a man who never showed up. That scene changed to one of her returning to town pregnant, and people staring at her and whispering speculations. And finally, he tried to picture her with this "Joel," but that proved more elusive, since he had no idea what the guy looked like. Still, he wondered. Maybe Joel was why she didn't really want him around.

He'd stopped in front of the cafe. He was early for Gretchen. Maybe she'd come early, too.

When the string of bells on the door jingled, Crystal the waitress looked up and smiled. "Hi, handsome!"

He looked around self-consciously at the

69

customers, who stared back. The geezer with the newspaper was there again, eating his toast and eggs. And there were the teenagers, allowing their gazes to slip away from each other only long enough to flick him curious looks.

He nodded at the room in general, sensing it was some strange ritual they awaited, and they bobbed and went back to their business.

He sat down in a booth.

Crystal, in black jeans and a turquoise tie-dyed top a size too small for her full breasts, sauntered over. "Coffee black?"

"Right."

"You should eat, you know." She squeezed his bicep. "Wouldn't want you going all weak on me." She arched a brow. "Then again..." When he didn't react to that, she said, "You're giving yourself wrinkles. Something that's troubling you stolen your appetite?"

He looked at her. The first thing he'd noticed yesterday—who wouldn't—was that wild hair of hers, a brownish-purple mass pulled back by a band that must be straining against all that thickness. Still, she had an open smile, and below the purple paint on her lids, her eyes seemed to reflect universal compassion. "Don't worry about me," he said, with a casual wink. "A guy just gave me a peanut butter sandwich."

Crystal's shiny lips formed an "O" before "You had lunch with Wally?" came out, each word more slowly than the last.

His brows lifted. "You knew that because...? Is he the only one around here who eats peanut butter?"

"No. But he may be the only grown man who does." Lingering beside his table, she fluttered a hand around on its Formica top, picking up the extra silverware and setting it right back in place atop a paper napkin. "I used to sit with him in school when he ate PBJs. And his secretary told me he still does sometimes."

"Well, I'm afraid I can't cure him of that. But he seems like a nice guy, and since marketing is my thing, I might be able to help him get out and get some exposure."

"Really?" Her face lit. "I'm glad you think he's nice. Wally doesn't see his good qualities. His father was a schmoozer, but he's quieter. I think he feels he has to live up to his dad's reputation. He's really funny, though."

"Sounds like you know Wally pretty well."

Someone rang the summons bell at the cash register then, and a blushing Crystal made a hasty retreat.

Smiling to himself, Daniel turned his gaze back to the table.

"I see you've discovered the local lunch hangout."

He swiveled around in his seat in time to appreciate Gretchen's approach in that red sweater and those hip-hugging jeans. "I was hoping to catch you here."

He noticed the flush to her cheeks. A result of the day's biting wind, most likely. Still, it made her blue eyes all the more striking.

"What have you been doing with yourself?" she asked, sliding into the seat across from him. "Have we bored you enough yet for you to leave?"

"Nope. I've been meeting with Wally Williams, actually."

Her brow wrinkled. "What for?"

"Offering my services. He's having tough times, and he needs marketing help."

She sat back. "Come on, Daniel. Your agency represents some big companies. What would you want with Wally?"

"Hell if I know." He clenched a muscle in his jaw. "I haven't worked with anyone on that small of a scale in years. But then, I never chased after a woman in my life, either. I've never been a father."

"I hope you didn't say anything to him about—"

He shook his head. "I promised you I wouldn't and I won't. But he did pin me down as to why I'm here. I implied that we're dating."

"What?!" Her eyes widened.

"Gretch!" hooted Crystal, breezing back with the coffee pot. "Get away from him. He's mine."

Gretchen sent her a wan smile. "We're just gonna talk for a few minutes. After that, you can have him." She ordered a grilled cheese and fries.

When Crystal left with the order, Daniel scowled. "You'd pass me off to another woman just like that?"

She arched a brow. "That's so you know for sure we aren't dating."

"Fine. I see what you think of me."

"Frankly I'm not sure what to think of you." She studied him with her head slightly tilted, her friendly expression replaced with a seriousness that made him shift in his seat.

"What are you still doing here, really?"

"I'm here to get to know my daughter and to understand what is best for her," he said, rather proud of his diplomatic wording. "Plus, I've committed myself to a small PR job for MCC."

"I don't believe you."

He took a swig of his coffee, and set his mug back down. "On which account?"

"Look. I agree we should be civil with each other and I'm glad that we've established that. I just don't want you coming here for something like, oh, I don't know—like wanting a relationship with Amy because you've decided you need it or something, and then leaving her." She pressed her lips tightly together, as if she'd just released something she hadn't meant to say, or at least hadn't meant to say it here. But then she added a quieter, "I won't let you do that."

Watching her, Daniel felt the full impact of what he'd stepped into by arriving in town yesterday. A past lover sat across from him, saying things he'd never planned on hearing. Things that had a lasting ring to them. And somehow he'd already committed to their dating. This wasn't his modus operandi. He walked out of relationships long before they turned the corner toward this arguing stage. But he couldn't make a scene because someone might connect him to Gretchen's past and she didn't want that. *He* didn't want that.

He felt Crystal watching them, leaning on the counter over there. He heard the old man on the stool in front of Crystal thrust his paper down with a crinkling sound.

He tried to relax, to stretch his legs out, kicked Gretchen and apologized. Then, in frustration, he thought of Amy. He thought of her big intelligent eyes and her teasing smile. He thought of her hand in his. "Let's talk about what I can expect from *you*, Gretchen," he said, very low. "You left town five years ago without telling me about my daughter."

Her eyes widened for an instant, and she glanced around before her expression grew passive again. Still, he saw her reach out and grip the leather backpack purse she'd set on the table. Was she considering running from this, too?

"How would it have been any different if I'd said goodbye?" she demanded.

"I can't say, since I wasn't given that option," he glanced away, before returning his gaze to hers. "But maybe I'd have been here a lot sooner."

Her lips parted at that, but she didn't say anything.

She glanced up as Crystal approached. The waitress set her food down, snatched ketchup off another table for them, and for once made a silent retreat.

Over at the counter, the old man rattled his crossword page.

Gretchen looked back at Daniel. "You men are all so honorable, anyway." She seemed to hold her emotions in check because of their surroundings. "I knew what your response would be. I knew you wouldn't come."

Picking up a fry, he waved it at her. "There's the real reason why you didn't tell me." He popped it into his mouth and chewed, but it tasted like cardboard.

"What?"

"You generalize when it comes to men. You don't trust any of us."

"I do not!" She rose from her seat. "I don't have to take this."

He stood, too, and reached into his pant pocket to retrieve his wallet. Plucking a ten from it, he tossed the bill onto the table. Taking her elbow, he said, "I think we both need some fresh air."

Something in her eyes stated plainly that she didn't want to go with him, the conversation was over and he should release her arm. But then she looked around at the other diners and the crew behind the counter. Clamping her lips together tightly, she walked with him to the door. Once it closed behind them and they stood on the curb, she whirled around. "I'm still angry with you because I had to deal with things on my own, okay? I thought I'd gotten over it. But now that I see you again, it all comes back to me."

With a quick nod, he indicated the group of ladies strolling along the sidewalk a few shops down from them. Crooking a finger for her to take the discussion walking, he had her follow him across the street to the empty park square. He waited for her to find a place on the wooden bench before he sat beside her.

Gretchen sat close enough to Daniel to feel the warmth of his body and hear his breathing. All day, she'd composed in her head what she wanted to say to him. But she hadn't considered how awkward it would be. She hadn't thought about how much his mere presence would make her forget her rehearsed lines and finally resort to the blunt accusation, "I didn't get pregnant on my own."

She wasn't looking at him, but she felt him turn and stare at her. Then he put his hand on her thigh. Why? She frowned down at his fingers resting there.

He moved his hand away.

Good. She didn't want him thinking he could just touch her that way. And yet, crazily, she instantly missed the warm strength of his hand.

"Not that it matters anymore," she said, "but I'd just like to know. What exactly does all this mean to you? I mean, was I the first? Were there others who could've had your baby?"

In the instant after she'd said it, she thought she saw hurt in his dark eyes. But in the next, he said in a flat tone, "This is my first and only child, Gretchen. And as for doing it on your own, you wrote that script and you didn't write a part into it for me."

She lowered her face. "Like I told you before, I was scared."

"It scared the crap out of me, too, when your friend mentioned Amy and I figured out I could have gotten you pregnant," he admitted in a lower tone.

She could tell by the lines on his forehead and the intensity in his gaze that he was telling the truth. For the first time, she realized he'd been scared. He seemed so determined now, she hadn't thought about his really fearing parenthood.

75

Consciously avoiding it and being narcissistic about it, yes. But fearing it? That surprised her.

He started raising his arm, as if he were about to put it around her, but lowered it again, probably remembering her earlier reaction to his touch. He moved a little in his seat. Something seemed to be bothering him.

Out of the corner of her eye, she saw him kick at the leaves. He stretched his legs out. His bones were so much longer than hers. Would Amy be taller, like him? She heard him sigh, and it sounded full of frustration.

She shifted. She wanted him to touch her again, and yet if he did, she would turn him off with a look. Why? Why did his presence confuse her this way?

"You should leave." If he stayed, she might do something stupid like let him get under her skin. "It'd be best for Amy."

He frowned. He sat there a moment, before fidgeting again. Finally he caught her gaze. "I want to have a relationship with Amy, whether it's in Chicago or here. So tell me now. Are you planning on denying me time with her if I stay these few days?"

She stared at him. Could she trust him? He looked sincere. But looks could deceive. He sounded like he meant it. But words were words.

She drew a long breath in and out. "I may be crazy, but I want you to know her. There's so much you don't know. But I don't trust you right now. I can't help it."

"I understand."

"So you have to do what I say."

He nodded.

"You can see Amy when I'm around and only when I'm around. And you can't tell her who you really are." It was deceptive, but what else could they do? "We really haven't discussed you, and I'm afraid of how she'd take it."

He nodded again.

They sat there in silence.

She pushed back some hair that had blown across her eyes. She felt him watching her. But she didn't want to look at him again. This was too intimate, this time with him. She couldn't afford intimate with Daniel.

"I have to go now." She stood. "I'll see you around."

He rose. "Can I come by when she's out of school? It's only a couple more hours. Right?"

Something about his eager tone softened her fear. "I should be there."

As she walked away, she felt his eyes on her. What was he thinking? He'd seemed as uncomfortable as she was over their topic of conversation. And yet he seemed earnest about staying, for Amy.

Well, she'd set the boundaries. She would stick to them, and see that he did, too.

As Daniel watched her go, he felt a new surge of respect for her. How could someone so small be so strong? When she talked about being pregnant and scared, she said it simply. Yet, he'd seen the truth in her eyes, and heard the hint of wavering in her voice. She had been alone. She'd managed, but it hadn't been easy.

He'd wanted to put his arm around her. But then he'd reminded himself that he wasn't going there with Gretchen. That'd be the last thing they all needed. He was here for Amy.

He would keep his vow to not tell Amy who he really was, and to only see her when Gretchen was around.

And he wouldn't touch Gretchen again.

He'd only been trying to show her a little empathy. If her leg had felt warm beneath his fingers and he'd enjoyed inching closer at that moment, it was just because she was sexy and he acted on impulse. Nothing else.

She'd given him the green light on being here. That was all he'd wanted to get out of their talk.

Chapter Six

"Where's the bread, Mommy?"

The bread. Gretchen glanced at Amy's reflection in the rearview mirror. "I forgot it."

Amy's face fell. "But the ducks are hungry."

"I'll call Crystal and see if she and BJ fed them." Even as she said it, Gretchen prayed she wouldn't forget, and disappoint Amy all over again. She had too much on her mind. Namely the big question of why Daniel was here.

"Can I hear my music?"

"Sure." She popped in the tape of favorite kids' songs.

Amy bobbed her head and sang along to the tunes, giving Gretchen free time to consider Daniel again.

He was probably in her house this very moment, seated at the secondhand desk in Granny Bea's old bedroom. He'd sure rolled up his shirtsleeves and settled down to business here. Was she making a huge mistake, allowing him to stay a few days?

She kept telling herself that deep down she wanted him to know his daughter. It was important to her, because of the tears she'd cried when her own father left. Seeing Daniel with Amy planted this weird hope in her, this wish that he could care enough. But enough to what?

To stay, maybe.

Of course he wouldn't stay. She knew that. She just couldn't stop herself from looking at him and wishing he were different.

She strained to see Daniel's car as she rounded the corner. There! There it sat, in the same place it'd been this morning when they left for town.

Uh oh. That white pickup pulled up behind him could mean only one thing—

"Joel's here!" Amy chirped.

"He sure is," Gretchen muttered. She'd forgotten all about him fixing the loose section of gutter in back of the house. She should've called and put him off a week. Now he'd surely met Daniel, without any prior warning or explanation on her part. She sighed. Just what she needed, those two male egos butting up against each other.

As she and Amy climbed from the car, she heard the telltale scraping and pounding created by her voluntary handyman. The racket grew louder as they rounded the side of the house.

She found Joel balanced high up on a ladder, sporting his usual ensemble of white T-shirt and carpenter's pants, and hammering away at the gutter. Only thing missing was his baker's apron, which she assumed he'd left hanging on the wooden peg in the shop. She inhaled deeply, certain her nose had picked up on the yeasty aroma of the shop that clung to him.

"Hi, Joel!" Amy greeted.

"What's up, Squirt?" He glanced down, his gaze resting warmly first on her, and then Gretchen.

"I'm not a squirt! I'm a girl."

"Oh. Excuse me." He pulled his brows together, all contrite, before grinning again.

"Come down, Joel," Amy implored. "I wanna show you my garden."

"In a minute, Little Bit."

"I'm not—"

"I know, I know." He slid Gretchen a bemused "Help me out of this" look.

She smiled.

He returned to aligning the gutter with the roof's edge and nailing it in place. The rough planes of his face held a fine sheen of sweat from his labor. His pecs shifted and his biceps flexed, reminding her of times when she'd visited him in the bakery's kitchen and he'd been kneading bread, rolling it out, carrying heavy-laden pans to the ovens.

She recalled standing by while two of his female customers blushed over his off-center grin, and murmured appraisals of his "cut" body. Little did they know that the first time he bestowed that teasing smile on *her*, he'd just beaten her in the seventh grade spelling bee with the word "flatulence." But his broad shoulders hadn't enticed her until high school. Even then, she'd only used him for comfort after Rick Floyd had asked Mitzi Chaplin to prom.

She left him hammering, and after a quick glance toward Daniel's windows at the other end of the house, went inside with Amy.

She scurried around, sorting the mail, filling the dog's water bowl and checking Amy's backpack for homework assignments. Maybe Daniel wasn't there after all. Maybe he was out walking, or running.

Ten minutes later, someone called to her from the doorway.

Daniel? Her heart pounded as she headed for the door.

Nope, it was just Joel.

"Wipe your feet," she directed, and he shuffled his Nikes back and forth a time or two on the mat.

He moved inside like the former football player he was, lumbering in an oddly agile way. In the kitchen, he opened the fridge and helped himself to a beer. Unscrewing the cap with his palm and flinging it onto the counter, he leaned against the counter and took a healthy drag from the bottle. Then he leveled his gaze on hers. "Whose SUV is that out

81

there?"

Heat tingled up her neck. "The new renter's."

"What new renter?"

"Just an acquaintance from Chicago."

He squinted at the bedroom hallway that abutted the other side of the house. "Is he here now?"

"I don't know," she snapped, and instantly regretted it. Joel wasn't prying. Of course he'd be curious. He sure was looking at her funny now. "Did you get the gutter fixed?" she asked, changing the subject.

Still frowning slightly, as if he hadn't quite made the switch of topics in his head, he nodded.

"Thanks." She sent him a brief smile. "I'm sure my landlord will be happy, too. He's got to be sick of hearing me complain, first about the gutter and now the leak in my bedroom."

He nodded in the direction of the hallway again. "Should I check it out?"

"Nah, I can handle a little primer and ceiling paint." She didn't want him getting any ideas about her bedroom. She'd been trying her best to keep such thoughts out of his head and out of their friendship. But things had changed since Debby signed his divorce papers. She could sense it in the way Joel looked at her.

He swallowed the last of his beer. Leaning around from the kitchen to the laundry room off the hall, he tossed the bottle into the recycling bin. Swinging back in her direction, he said, "You didn't come by for your bread today."

"True."

He held her gaze. Tenderness laced his expression. "I have two loaves for you in the truck."

She pointed out the window over the sink, at the shreds of plastic strewn across the driveway. "Sorry. I think they were a Scooby snack."

He moved to stand by her, brushing her hip with his as he leaned over the sink to see out the window. "What's that mutt good for? He can't hunt. And he's too goofy to be a guard dog."

"Yes, but he gives good kisses and we love him."

Straightening, he turned toward her. "I give good kisses, too."

"Be serious!" she scolded, knowing he wasn't joking.

His gaze drifted to her mouth.

She slid away, down the counter to where she'd been stirring brownie ingredients for the snack she'd promised Amy.

A door slammed. Shuffling noises, followed by a colorful curse, vibrated through the walls.

Peering out the window again, Joel groaned. "Look at that dog. Wagging his tail and making up to a stranger."

Stranger? Gretchen dropped the wooden spoon she'd been stirring with and shoved up against him. "Not again!"

She ran for the door, with Joel going, "What the hey?" behind her.

"Scoo-by!" she groaned, catching up to Daniel. He stood with feet planted in the gravel drive, hands at the dog's shoulders to push him off.

She grasped Scooby's wagging tail to get his attention, and through gritted teeth, said, *"Down."*

Ears flattened to his head in submission, the dog obeyed.

"Well, at least you don't have to worry about people sneaking up on you with him around," Daniel conceded, brushing at his chest.

"Your shirt," Gretchen moaned. Dirty paw prints marred its crisp whiteness. "I'll wash it for you."

"I might let you, since I can't seem to find the dry cleaners around here."

She arched a brow. "There's just the

Laundromat. But being a city boy, I doubt you'd know how to work the machines."

He glared.

She smiled.

For a few seconds, they stared at each other, until the little electric shocks of attraction running through her made her self-conscious. Breaking eye contact, she said, "So, what have you been up to since I last saw you?"

"I've been on a conference call. Right in the middle of it, some idiot started banging on the house."

"That's Joel," she explained. "He came by to fix the gutter."

His features seemed to register something, before he said, "Well, what he almost 'fixed' was an ad deal I've been working on. It was hard to concentrate with all that hammering."

"He's finished now," she assured him. "Come on in and let me wash your shirt."

As he followed her into the house, he began unbuttoning his shirt. But once he spied Joel standing there in the kitchen, his fingers stilled.

Joel nodded in greeting.

Daniel nodded back.

Gretchen cleared her throat. "Um, Daniel, this is Joel Osbourne. Joel, Daniel Nicholson."

Daniel stuck out his hand.

Joel gripped it. "Dog really nailed you."

"Yeah, he keeps mistaking me for a chew biscuit." He started buttoning up again.

"Oh, take it off," Gretchen prodded. "I'll wash it and throw it in the dryer with the load I've just started."

"Well..." His gaze drifted from her well-meaning look to Joel's narrow stare.

Joel's assessing reaction to Daniel surprised her. He was usually so happy-go-lucky. Maybe the disrobing had put him off. "See, Joel, in the city, people send their clothes out to be laundered," she quipped, hoping to spark some humor. "Daniel wouldn't be able to work the machines at Speedy Suds."

"Oh." There was no lightness in his tone or in the way he eyed Daniel.

Daniel returned to unbuttoning.

Gretchen stood by, waiting for his shirt and hating the uncomfortable silence.

Daniel's biceps muscles worked back and forth with little effort as he shrugged out of the garment.

Realizing she was staring, Gretchen glanced up at his face.

He lifted a brow. A twinkle of amusement glowed in his eyes.

Her face heated, and she looked away. What was she supposed to do now? This wasn't working, this plan to appear nonchalant about Daniel in front of Joel to maintain status quo. Daniel disrupted things. Maybe getting rid of one of them would ease her discomfort.

She turned back to Joel. "So...you were leaving?"

"Amy wanted me to see her garden." Before she could object, he turned toward the hallway and bellowed, "Amy? You coming?"

Amy skipped out from the back rooms, her pink stuffed bunny under her arm. When she saw Daniel, she stopped. "Mommy said you were working."

"I was, but I'm finished now."

"Yea! You can see my garden, too." Running to the door, she flung back, "Well? Come on!"

They followed her like army recruits. Daniel held the door for Joel, who tossed Gretchen a quizzical look. She urged him on with a wave of her hand. After they'd closed the door behind them, the worry set in. Joel's look had said it all. He wanted to know what was going on between Daniel and her. What would she tell him? And what would she tell Daniel about Joel?

She didn't owe Daniel any explanation, and yet she kept rehearsing one while she washed the brownie bowl and wiped the counter. Joel was a friend. They'd never been intimate. Thoughts of him hadn't kept her awake at night, the way thoughts of Daniel once had. Even after she left Daniel, knowing full well that she couldn't hold on to someone like him, she'd found herself dreaming of a life with him. But she knew it was a pipedream. Daniel Nicholson wasn't interested in settling down any more than he'd been interested in having a child, or so she'd thought.

But now, five years later, here he was, saying he was interested in his child. Could that mean she'd misread his vibes about settling down, too? More importantly, was she hoping that was the case? Was that hope the reason for this blasted confusion, these rolling emotions, the "You can stay," when it should be, "You go now."

She pressed the heels of both hands against her temples. *Ugh*. She couldn't take this much longer. He'd seen them. Time for the little reunion to come to an end, before it was too late.

As she returned to straightening up the kitchen, that "too late" nagged at her. Too late for what? No, she didn't even want to consider what that meant. Hurrying to the living room, she flipped on the TV and listened to the rattle of advertisements. Anything to clear her head and drive away this crazy anxiety.

Outside, Daniel stood across from Joel, eyeing him over Amy's dirt plot. What was the big guy to Gretchen? He frowned down at Amy as she poked her finger in the crusty earth, trying to find the seeds she'd planted yesterday. What did he care what their relationship was? He had no claim on Gretchen. And yet—

"You from Cincy?" Joel interjected into his thoughts. "Bengals fan?"

"Nah." Daniel met his discerning gaze. "Bears."

"Unh. Chicago." He flattened his lips together— a move that implied he liked the other team. The line on his brow deepened. "What's your business?"

"Advertising. Yours?"

"I've got a bakery."

Daniel nodded, somewhat deflated. He'd figured him for a day laborer. A painter, in his Mr. Clean clothes. He wouldn't have guessed he was an entrepreneur.

"Did Gretchen meet you in Chicago a few years ago? When she went to see her college roommate?"

Daniel looked down at Amy, squatting in the dirt like a little toad. She wasn't singing anymore. She'd tilted her chin up to them. Her earthy eyes captured his. She held her stick in mid-air, like a director's baton that'd paused and stopped her music. "Yeah," he said, keenly aware of the little girl's attention. "That's when we met."

Now the baker studied him with a new intensity. "That was a hard time for Gretch, after her fiancé left." Amy had gotten up, wandered over to some tired mums in the flowerbed and begun plucking them. "She went to find herself in the big city, but it ate her up and spit her out." He shook his head. "Made my gut ache, seeing her that way. But she's okay now. She look okay to you?"

"She looks great." No doubt about it, the country life had certainly put color in Gretchen's skin and a sexy glow in her eyes.

"You staying long?"

"I don't think so." Then, because Joel's not so subtle prying about Gretchen and him made him uncomfortable, he added, "I did promise Wally

Williams I'd help him with a bit of marketing."

The other man's gray eyes bore into his. "Don't work for him too long. He might start taking measurements."

Daniel grunted. Was there seriousness to the big lug's tone that didn't make the joke very funny?

Joel's gaze tracked their little tour guide, who'd moved on to the play area and started swinging. "I think she's bored with us."

"Come push me!" she called out.

Both of them moved, but Daniel moved faster, and got to the swing first. Grabbing its linked chains, he pulled back.

Amy wobbled in the seat, and slid sideways. Then, with a little "Uh!" of alarm, she suddenly fell forward and hit the ground knees first.

Still holding the swing back, Daniel stared in shock as tears welled in her eyes.

Joel reached her in two strides, and bent to gently wipe the dirt off her jeans. Pulling her into his arms and standing again, he said, "What a trouper." He patted her back as her lower lip wobbled. "Good thing you didn't cry. Mommy would've charged out here and given us a piece of her mind."

She nodded slowly, and cast Daniel a glance that wrenched his heart.

"Want me to swing you?" Joel asked.

She hesitated, but nodded again.

He sent Daniel a stern look, and he released the swing.

The baker set her down on it as if he'd done it a thousand times. "All situated?"

She didn't respond, but Daniel noticed how white her knuckles were this time as she gripped the chains.

Idiot, he berated himself, clenching his jaw.

Joel placed his big hands on her hips and pulled

her back. When he let go, she flew forward with a squeal of delight.

He pushed some more, and as Amy giggled, Daniel felt his heart lighten again. He caught himself grinning, and wondered when the fear for her had changed to this crazy sense of relief. Oh, well. She was in safe hands with Joel.

The admission brought a pang of emotion.

When Amy wanted to push off from the ground with her feet, he walked back over to Daniel. "Hey." He clapped Daniel's back. "Don't worry about it. When it happens, it's best to get her right back on. A 'hair of the dog that bit ya' kind of thing."

Daniel nodded. The guy could be Amy's father. He looked the part. Acted as if he wanted it, too. And by the way he'd ogled Gretchen, he seemed anxious to at least step into some sort of role here. Assuming, that was, he didn't already have one.

He watched Amy, who had stopped and was just sitting on her swing, digging a small trench in the dirt below with her sneaker.

She slid him a brown-eyed glance.

He lifted his brows.

Her rosy lips curved.

Good. She didn't seem to be holding a grudge over his dumping her like a sack of potatoes.

"Want me to show you how to whistle with some grass?" he offered.

"Okay." She hopped off her swing and came over.

Joel looked on with a skeptical expression as, with a satisfied grin, Daniel bent to pluck just the right blade of grass.

****

Gretchen had noticed Amy go flying past the living room window on her way to the swing set. Tiptoeing across the carpet, she'd holed up near the drapes and peered through the old sheers covering the window. The swing set was close to the house, in a spot where she could keep an eye on Amy whenever she played there. So she was able to see Daniel's eyes widen in shock and his jaw clench when Amy fell off the swing.

Gretchen's throat constricted, and she turned, ready to run out to them. But in the next instant, Joel appeared, wiping at Amy's knees and soothing her.

Thank goodness she'd had on her jeans.

As Joel settled Amy on the swing again and took up pushing her, Gretchen glared at Daniel. But he had eyes only for Amy. They made these little faces at each other, winking, grinning. Joel didn't seem to notice as he waited between pushes.

Then Daniel grew serious. He looked from Amy to Joel, and back.

What was he thinking? That Joel played the part of daddy well? Her heart dropped a few floors inside her. She didn't want him thinking that. Joel was not going to be Amy's father. Daniel was her father.

Not that she needed him to be. Just that it was a biological fact and she accepted that much of it.

After a few more pushes, Amy grew tired of the swing. She glanced at Daniel again, and then went over to him.

No one but Gretchen could see the look on his face as he bent to pick some grass—the most tender, sincere expression she'd ever seen on a man.

Her breathing stopped, and her heart seemed to, too.

In the next instant, he rose and turned away, and all three of them began picking grass, holding it to their mouths and attempting to whistle with it.

Gretchen pivoted around and stared blindly at the room. She realized she'd put her hand at her throat, and lowered it. Wow. Maybe Daniel was a little more complicated that she'd given him credit for. Or maybe she was being silly. Maybe she'd read more into that look than was there. What could he know about real feelings? He turned quick advertising sales and he switched relationships before they could head toward matrimony, which had already failed for him. She couldn't fault him on that, since *his* spouse-to-be had at least stayed through the vows.

Dreaming up feelings for him was crazy. She could be swallowed up by such nonsense and then unceremoniously spit back out, the way she'd been with David the Rat. Like her mother was with her father and the others that followed. No. She hadn't seen anything in that moment. Had to have been a dazzle of sunshine in her eyes, and not something dazzling about Daniel.

Daniel wandered back inside with Joel and Amy, and found Gretchen pulling a pan of brownies out of the oven. The house smelled like baking, like warm sweets. Gretchen looked warm and sweet, and deliciously cute, yelping and dancing when the heat began radiating through her baking mitt.

Joel snatched up a potholder and charged over to her. Whipping the hot pan out of her hand, he set it on top of the stove.

"Thanks," she said, pulling off the mitt.

"Burn yourself?" Daniel asked.

"No. But my attempt to look like a confident cook just went up in flames."

He snorted good-humoredly.

Hovering over the brownie pan as if he were a judge in a bake-off, Joel announced, "I should get back to the bakery."

"Okay." She nodded toward the back of the house. "Thanks again for fixing the gutter."

"No problem. See you tomorrow?"

"Sure."

Joel held her gaze until she seemed to grow uncomfortable, and glanced away.

Geez, couldn't the guy take a hint? She'd asked him earlier if he was leaving, and then had allowed him to stall with Amy.

Taking matters into his own hands, Daniel went to open the door for the baker.

Joel sent him a pointed look as he turned from Gretchen and headed his way, and after a less pointed, "See ya," he left.

Amy flitted to the door. "I'm going to my garden."

"Okay." Gretchen pointed at her feet. "Tie your shoe first."

Daniel moved back to stand awkwardly on the other side of the counter from Gretchen. Now that they were alone, he wasn't sure what to do. The gulf between them stretched pretty wide, it seemed, and he wasn't sure why. She didn't want him here. Couldn't she see he was harmless? She had Amy, and she had parenting knowledge. He had nothing but a little part of his heart to give the girl.

Gretchen glanced up from sealing the brownie pan with foil. "Better get that T-shirt off. There's dirt on it, too."

He looked down at his chest, swiped at a scrape of dirt, and then began pulling off his T-shirt.

Gretchen watched, appreciating the flexing of those muscles, amazed at the contrast of stark white undershirt against tanned skin and sparse black chest hair. Then suddenly he was standing there naked from the waist up and looking so good, her mouth went dry.

He handed her the shirt and their gazes met and held, before she turned away. "Uh, I'll be right back." Hoping he hadn't noticed how her hands shook when she took the shirt from him, she hurried to the laundry room. When she'd sprayed the mud with a soil remover, she popped it in with the load of lights still churning. Then she sped off to her bedroom to scrounge around in drawers until she found a T-shirt that might fit him. Returning to the kitchen, she offered it to him.

"It's pink." He held it out in one hand, angling a distrustful look in its direction.

"Is that a blow to your male ego?"

"No." He pulled it over his head and tugged it down over his solid-looking chest and taut abs. "I'm not so sure I like what it says, though."

"The Cincinnati Ballet?"

He shook his head, and pointed at the large scrolled letters below the company's name. "*The Nutcracker.*"

She laughed. "I didn't think about that."

"Sure you didn't."

They stared teasingly at each other a moment, and she basked in the warmth of his rich brown eyes, remembering how he'd looked with Amy, out there on the swing.

"I should start dinner," she murmured, and turned toward the refrigerator.

She'd thought he'd retreat to the living room while she worked. Instead he stayed at the counter, elbows propped, while she got out the chicken and spices and tied on her apron.

Daniel couldn't take his eyes off her. She'd looked good earlier in the blue wide-neck top that revealed her delicate collarbone, and black slacks that hugged her slim hips and rounded bottom. But once she popped that granny apron over her head, he knew he was in trouble. Its ruffles clung to the curves of her breasts, accentuating them. If that wasn't bad enough, she'd tied it snuggly at her small waist, which only made her seem that much more feminine and delicate. She didn't need to bother with dinner. She was edible enough herself. His body infused with heat. "What are you making?" he managed, in a gravelly tone.

"Nothing fancy. Roast chicken, mashed potatoes and green beans."

"Sounds great," he said, fishing for an invitation. He had to. She'd said earlier that she didn't trust him, and he had to have her trust before she'd let him get any closer to a relationship with Amy. Besides, when was the last time he'd had a home-cooked meal? In the next instant, he told himself to cut the excuses. Right now, he wanted to stay because of Gretchen. Her willfulness intrigued him. Her rare smiles enticed him. Her body reminded him of sex.

She looked up from the beans she was snapping into a bowl. A curve of chestnut hair loosened and fell forward. She tried to shove it in place with the back of her hand a few times, but it stubbornly refused to stay.

He leaned across the counter separating them and reached to tuck it behind the curve of her ear. When he did, he felt her skin beneath his fingers, warm and soft in that hidden place between ear and hairline. He should have pulled his hand away. Instead he lingered, rubbing the pads of his fingers lightly, rhythmically, against her skin. He gazed into her eyes to see if she was receptive. "You have nice hair," he murmured. "Soft. Like your skin."

She met his gaze. Her pupils dilated, and her lips parted.

Blood pulsed through him. He could kiss her and she wouldn't resist. Then something else flickered in her expression, something that should have doused the fire in him. Fear. She was scared again. What was that all about? He didn't want that. He meant to make things less awkward between them, not worse.

But he couldn't stop touching her, or drinking her in with his gaze. He wanted to feel her softness, pull her against him and see how she fit. He heard her breathe, lightly, and he swallowed and it seemed loud inside his head. Behind her, the stove's built-in clock ticked and ticked and seemed to signal that this must end. But his blood pumped fast again, its urgency overpowering the clock's warning.

He dropped his hand away then, but still held her gaze. Quickly, he rounded the edge of the counter, not wanting to make it a big noticeable thing so she wouldn't object. When his hip grazed her apron and he felt her body behind it, solid, he stopped. She'd turned toward him. That was a good sign.

He reached out, took her elbows in his hands, and started moving her into his arms. She didn't resist. She came to him. She looked a little pale, a little confused, maybe. But she went with the flow. Maybe she felt the same thing, that inevitable heat shooting through him. And if she did, they were about to—

Bang! went the door.

They both jumped.

Daniel turned to see Amy standing there, clutching her stick.

"Hi," he managed, in a gravelly voice as he dropped his hands back to his sides. "Finish digging your seeds back up?"

Gretchen had taken a step away from him the minute he released her. Now she said, "Oh, Amy! Did you really dig them all up?" She crossed her arms in a move that seemed to shut him out again. "You know they can't grow if you don't leave them alone."

"But I couldn't see if they were growing."

"Well, you have to give them time." She looked around, saw the brownie pan and pointed at it. "You wouldn't have brownies if you couldn't wait until they'd cooked and you ate the batter first."

Amy looked from Daniel to her mother to the pan of brownies. Her eyes shone. "I got 'em now!" She sprang into the kitchen, headed straight for the pan.

"Hold on! Let me cut you one." Gretchen hurried to her side.

Daniel stood back and watched. They both talked at the same time. They bent their heads close to each other, and Gretchen kissed Amy's muddy cheek. The little girl had pulled some very limp pansy heads out of her pocket, and Gretchen beamed over them and quickly got a bowl out to float them in water.

Watching them, he felt lucky to be there. He wasn't needed. He'd just somehow managed to worm his way into this little circle that was the two of them, this strange and different, warm and homey circle.

They all ate a brownie right before dinner. Gretchen had rules, she said, but sometimes she let them break the little ones. Amy had to promise to eat a healthy amount of her dinner, though. Then Gretchen sent her down the hall to wash up. Before she left, Daniel called out, "I'll come back and help you plant more seeds one day, Amy. We'll leave that batch in the ground and see how they grow."

When she'd gone, Gretchen said, "Please, don't go making promises you can't keep."

He held up his hands. "I was just making conversation."

She eyed him.

"Hey. It's clear you don't trust me," he said softly as he drew closer, "so why are you really letting me be here?" When he moved, he smelled the distinct odor of her fabric softener melded into the borrowed T-shirt. He liked that little intimacy for some reason, the way he'd liked the broken brownie rule, and the mashed pansies. "Are you sure it's just to see Amy?"

She didn't answer.

He wouldn't be scared away. She wasn't glaring at him now, being the Ice Queen that Wally had sworn she'd been to the local guys. "Talk to me."

"Okay!" Arms folded protectively in front of her again, she looked away. "I'm attracted to you. But I don't want to be. So stay away."

Like hell. He closed the gap between them. Reaching out, he set his hands on both sides of her waist and pulled her to within a few inches of him.

She gazed wide-eyed at him now, looking afraid and a little cross.

He didn't know how to right that, other than to kiss her. To show her he wouldn't hurt her again. Be gentle.

Her breath brushed his skin, and it made him want to taste her mouth. "There's something about us," he murmured against her hair.

"Yes," she said, after a quick intake of breath. "Something we should stop, now." She glanced around. "Amy'll be back any second."

"This'll only take a second. One split-second kiss for old time's sake, and these vibes will be behind us."

Her increased breathing made his scalp tingle. He could feel her hipbones beneath his fingers as he spread them low on her waist. His lips brushed her temple. "It's been a long time," he said, with a slow sigh. "I knew you were hot. But I didn't remember that you smelled this good, and felt this good."

When he drew back, he saw that a little pucker had formed on her forehead. He kissed her there. This time when he pulled back, she'd closed her eyes.

He brushed his lips over hers. He didn't mean to linger. He meant only a quick sampling. But Gretchen tasted sweet. And she leaned in to him.

She seemed vulnerable then, standing barefoot on the old linoleum.

He pressed his mouth against hers. She returned the pressure, and even made a small noise. Her lips moved as if she was opening to him, and he took the opportunity, plunging his tongue inside her mouth. She moved her hands to his neck, where she kneaded his muscles as her tongue played a rhythm with his.

Water's being turned off down the hall registered briefly, but then he was kissing Gretchen and she was kissing him and that was all there was in the world.

Until she broke the kiss and pulled out of his arms.

She stood there, staring at him, breathing hard.

He tugged on breaths, too, before reaching out and grabbing her hands. Moving sideways, he pulled her along behind him to the entrance to the hallway, where they could see what the source of her concern was up to. Watching Amy's head bobbing as she crossed the threshold at the other end of the corridor, he said, "She's going into her room."

Gretchen pulled away from him again. "It's not just that."

He held her gaze, frowning slightly. "What? What's wrong?"

"I can't do this. I have Amy to think about and I don't want her best interest clouded by, by this." She shook her head. "I made a decision to get away from you once, Daniel. I knew in my heart that it was the right choice and I'm not going to screw it up now."

Chapter Seven

Crystal swung around on the park bench so fast, she nearly spilled her takeaway cup of steaming cocoa in Gretchen's lap. "Did you say—?"

"Yes. He's staying at my house."

Crystal arched her brows. "You two sure have kept *that* a secret." Her violet eyes gleamed with speculation. "By the way he looked at you in the café the other day, like you were an ice cream sundae and he wanted dessert, I figured something was going on."

"Nothing's going on."

"You leaned toward each other and whispered, too, and then you cut out of there together."

Gretchen tried to appear calm as she stared off toward Amy and BJ, pulling day-old rolls from their bakery bags at the pond's edge. How could she keep Crystal in the dark? Whenever her best friend suspected anything, she'd pester and pester until she uncovered the truth. Scary thing about that in this case was, it could force Gretchen to face a few facts she'd rather avoid.

Joel had already quizzed her about Daniel when she'd stopped by the bakery. Darn it, why was everyone so curious about her private life?

Suddenly she noticed that every duck and goose within a mile radius had flown in for the kids' giveaway treats.

A big gray goose descended on Amy, flapping his wings. "HONK!" he squawked.

"AAAHH!" Amy squealed, eyes wide and frantic.

Gretchen leapt to her feet at the same instant BJ bellowed "Go!" at the bully goose and tossed a roll that bounced toward the pond.

The drake and his posse took flight in hot pursuit.

Glancing guiltily at Crystal, Gretchen sat back down. "Am I a nervous mother, or what?"

"Well, you don't want her to have waterfowl hang-ups."

"She's all I've got."

"Maybe that's about to change, with your new housemate."

Gretchen groaned inwardly. *Here she goes. And she won't let up until you tell her.*

Under Crystal's assessing gaze, she sighed. "Okay. The truth is, Daniel is Amy's father."

Crystal leaned back, staring. "No way. You would've told me."

"I haven't told anyone. Why should I?"

She laughed. "Because you live here and there are no secrets in Marydale."

"That's why this has to *stay* a secret, Crystal. Amy doesn't even know."

"She doesn't?"

She shook her head, and after admitting she'd given Crystal a sketchy explanation when she'd returned to Marydale, brought her up to date. "I never thought I'd see him again. But he's here now, and he's so good with Amy. Well, he isn't all that sure of himself, but he's trying really hard."

"Then quit wrinkling your forehead and enjoy!"

"I can't. I'm so scared he's going to hurt Amy."

"Why? Has he said anything to make you think he would?"

"No. And I've warned him there's no way he's taking her." She pressed her lips together and shook her head. "I don't know. It's just a feeling." Her cheeks flushed with heat. "God, how many times have I wished things hadn't happened so fast with Daniel? What was I thinking?"

"It's not like you hop into bed with a guy. But with *this* guy, who wouldn't?"

"It wasn't just that he was hot. I was in the city alone, and I'd never felt as worthless in my whole life as I did when David stood me up."

"I thought you were way over him. Dang! I can't believe I've been so blind."

"It's not about David. It's about how bad I felt after he left. Remember how Mom had come back, and when my wedding fell through, she left really fast with that bald guy, her fourth husband? I don't know...I just couldn't deal with stuff on my own then."

"*I* was still here. I never go anywhere."

"But you and Big Bobby were trying to work things out. You had too much on your plate for me to dump more on you."

"See, that's the thing with you, Gretch. You don't ask for help. I didn't know how bad you felt, or I'd have been over trying to cheer you up."

"I like to handle things—"

"Yourself. I know." She chuckled. "You're stubborn."

"So I've heard."

"And if Daniel was able to persuade you to let him move in with you, he must be hardheaded, too. He must really want to hang with Amy, or be around you, or both." She laughed. "You're perfect for each other."

Gretchen scowled.

Crystal stretched her tanned legs out in front of her. "I'll bet Joel isn't happy about this. Did you tell him?"

"Nope. As far as he knows, we're just acquaintances from Chicago. And I don't care if he isn't happy about it. I keep telling you, Joel and I are just friends."

Crystal chuckled. "That may be how *you* see it, but I'm telling you, he really—" She stopped in mid-sentence. "When you say Joel's just a friend, you mean, you guys haven't—?"

"No, we haven't had sex. It's been five years, since—since Daniel."

Crystal's mouth hung open. "Man. I just assumed you guys were beyond the middle school stage."

"Can we just drop this topic?"

"God, Gretchen! Sometimes you're *too* private. And here I was pitying me for my divorce and lack of action since then." She made a whistling noise. "But five years." She whistled. "That's forever."

"Yeah. It's five years of not agonizing over someone walking out my door. Five years of not constantly wondering what I did or didn't do that made him want me for a while and then want nothing to do with me ever again."

"And five years of lonely."

"I have Amy now. I'm happy."

"She'll have her own friends and her own life one day. So will BJ. Who'll be around for us to nurture once they grow up and we're empty nesters?"

"We'll have each other."

"No offense, but I'd like a man, too." Crystal reached out and gave Gretchen a quick hug. "You're great, and you deserve someone great. Just, promise me you'll be objective about Daniel."

"I can't afford to be objective about him or anyone else with the potential of using Amy's life like a revolving door."

"I understand. Just, don't run him off before you're sure."

Gretchen caught hold of her arm as they rose from the bench. "Don't tell *anyone* about this. And don't treat Daniel differently. Act like he's just a guy I know."

"Have no fear, the actress is here. Don't you remember my flawless performance in *Annie Get Your Gun?*"

"Our ninth grade play? All I remember is that hot kiss you planted on Bobby."

A bittersweet smile curved Crystal's red-tinted lips. "Ah, young love."

"And now you're just old and decrepit."

"*Hey*." Crystal swung BJ's backpack at Gretchen, who grabbed up Amy's and ran off, laughing.

When they reached their cars, Gretchen went, "Oh! I knew I had something else to tell you. On the way to school this morning, Amy told me she'd invited Daniel to the musical tomorrow night."

"So now he and Joel are both going with you?" Crystal's brows arched. "Sheesh! I can't even get *one*, and you've got two you don't want." She checked her orange bangle watch. "I wanna hear more, but Bobby's supposed to be at my house right now." Turning, she yelled, "Come on, Beej. Daddy's coming by the house to take you out for pizza."

BJ's freckled face lit. "Yea!" he whooped, racing over.

Watching him, Gretchen realized Amy was missing out on something her father could give her. Daniel cared. In this short time, she'd already seen it. She knew it, but Amy didn't know it was her father caring about her. And for the first time, instead of being frightened by the thought, she felt... oh, who knew what she felt?

Confused, that's what.

****

Daniel waited for Wally in the diner, in the same spot where he always sat. Crystal had deemed it his booth, since she now considered him a regular.

He flicked a few crumbs off the table and lined up the salt and pepper shakers, his mind on Gretchen's soft lips, and the restrained urgency he'd felt in yesterday's kiss. She was a passionate woman. Cautious, but passionate. The thought hardened his body as he considered how far that passion might have taken them.

He drummed his fingers on the wooden tabletop. What could be taking Wally so long to get here?

Minutes later, the bells on the door jangled, and Wally ambled inside.

When he'd settled in the booth, Daniel opened an email attachment on his notebook and turned the computer toward Wally. "Here's my marketing plan. First we print fliers with pictures of you standing in the town square." He pointed at the monitor, at the artwork file he'd had sent from his creative department. "The copy'll read like a travel brochure, beckoning your funeral director customers to the wholesome goodness of Marydale."

A "V"-shaped wrinkle formed between Wally's brows as he scrutinized the flier proof.

"In the direct mail video tie-in, you stand in front of the town square. The camera pans around, picking up on flowerbeds, storefronts, people strolling the sidewalk." Daniel waved his hands to demonstrate the flow of action. "Then your dialogue goes something like, 'Welcome to Marydale. I've lived and worked here my whole life. Now I'm offering your clients a touch of hometown comfort in the afterlife with my line of locally made caskets. While each casket is carefully sanded, stained and polished, the sun shines here in Marydale. The birds sing. Won't you feel comfortable knowing your clients take a little of that with them into the afterlife'?" He folded his arms and waited.

Wally's eyes glazed over. "How much did I agree to pay you for this?"

"You don't like it?"

"I hate it. How can *you* like it?" Wally scowled at the flier and copy.

Crystal breezed by then, with a soda for Wally and more coffee for Daniel. "Doin' okay, fellas?"

They nodded, but didn't look her way.

She stood there until Wally stopped in mid-sentence, and they both looked up. Then she blew them kisses and waltzed away.

They looked at each other. Daniel lifted a brow, and Wally turned red.

Daniel sat forward again. "Nothing is written in stone. Tell me your ideas."

"Hey, I'm not the ad man here. I just know you didn't put your heart in it." He stared at Daniel a moment. "Do you even *like* Marydale?"

"Sure. But I'm not sure I see the point in such an old-fashioned place."

The door's strap of bells jingled again.

Daniel looked up as Gretchen came toward them. His gaze traced her straight shoulders, followed the curve of her hips and stroked down her long legs. Remembering how well she'd fit against him when they kissed, he swallowed back a surge of desire.

Wally cocked his head at him, before glancing over his shoulder to see who'd distracted Daniel.

"Mind if I join you?" Gretchen asked, coming up to their table.

Daniel waved a hand toward Wally's side of the booth. "Please."

Wally scooted over. "You've arrived just in time to explain to this skeptic, here, what's so special about Marydale."

Her gaze flicked to Daniel's. "Hmm." She tapped her finger on her lower lip. "I think Marydale's special because of the people."

Daniel stared at her mouth. "There are special

people everywhere. What makes you people different?"

"The way we care. The way we protect each other. Our level of trust."

"So, you're willing to trust *them*."

She frowned slightly. "Wally knows what I mean. It's where you feel safe."

"Maybe because some people refuse to feel safe in other places." Daniel propped an elbow on the table, leaned his cheek against his knuckles and studied her expression.

Her mouth tightened.

Wally's cell phone rang, and he pulled it out of his jacket pocket. "Gotta take this," he said, motioning for Gretchen to let him out of the booth.

As he headed outside for privacy, Gretchen turned back to Daniel. "I should get back to the store," she said in a clipped tone.

"Something wrong?"

After a glance about the room, she slid back down in the booth. "What was with that undertone?"

He rubbed his forehead. "Hell, I don't know, Gretchen. Maybe it's about what you said yesterday, about not making the same mistake with me. I guess I've still got a chip on my shoulder from that 'mistake,' if you must call us that, five years ago."

The challenge in her eyes faltered. "I thought we'd moved beyond our issues for Amy's sake."

"I can't. The more time I spend with her, the more those four years I missed bug me." And the more moments he spent with Gretchen, the more he wished she hadn't cut their time together short. If she discovered his attraction to her now, she might "run away" again by shutting him out.

His own raw feelings that had surfaced after they kissed had him admitting, "I looked for you after you left, back then."

"You did?" Her gaze intensified on his, before

she seemed to come to a decision. "Because I didn't really leave right away. I decided I should tell you about the pregnancy for Amy's sake, so I went to find you at Cinna Bar."

"You couldn't have. I went there every night for weeks, and I never saw you." He'd spent hours watching that damned doorway. The memory stabbed at his chest.

"I was there one night. You didn't see me because you were busy."

"Doing what?"

"Kissing another woman."

He frowned. "What woman?

"It doesn't matter anymore."

He stared hard at her. "It was probably an old friend. I can't remember. What I *do* know is, you and I weren't over, as far as I was concerned. Yes, I did see other women after a while, when I had to accept that what you said in your letter was true and you were done with us. But I sure as hell didn't accept that overnight."

She glanced out the window. "I did what I felt was best."

"And walked out on me without telling me what was going on. Why would you do that, when you knew from firsthand experience how it felt?"

"That's just it." She looked down at her hands, folded on the table. When she looked up, her eyes shone with emotion. "I remembered being walked out on like I remembered my name. When I saw you with that woman, I figured you were already ninety percent of the way out my door. Maybe I made a snap judgment. And maybe it didn't help that we hardly knew each other."

He scowled. "That's a very roundabout apology, but I'll take it. Consider the subject dropped."

"No." She swallowed. "I'll admit it. I wasn't just protecting Amy. I was protecting myself, too. I

107

could've phoned you at some point. But as time passed, it seemed less, necessary."

He nodded, his mouth tight with regret.

Wally returned, and as soon as he reclaimed his seat, Daniel picked back up with his marketing plan. "As far as promoting the casket company goes, I'm thinking we need to have this place sell caskets the way Lynchburg sells Jack Daniels, or Louisville sells bats. In other words, we need a sales catch."

Wally and Gretchen looked at each other. Both turned at the same time and said, "What about the caves?"

Daniel cocked his head at Wally. "What caves?"

"Like Mammoth, in Kentucky. We've got 'em here, only smaller. There's rare fish in there that a scientist discovered a few years back. He was gonna publish a report on 'em in some journal. But he drowned in one of the cave pools." His mouth twisted at the memory, before he brightened. "I donated a coffin to his family. Felt bad about it happening here and all."

A macabre story, thought Daniel. Still, that sort of stuff sold. These caves were their special something, their Marydale pull. He could feel his adrenaline level spiking as he thought how he could use it.

Wally said, "We have a cave museum, you know."

"You have a museum, too? Where's that?"

"In a room in my building. The casket company sponsors it."

"Wally," Daniel growled, "why didn't you mention any of this?"

Wally looked at him as if he'd just said the dumbest thing in the world. "You didn't ask."

****

"I found out about these caves, Sam," Daniel blurted into his cell phone. "And you know my client, the casket maker you sent the flier proof for? His company runs the museum for them. I think we can use these caves! They have rare fish in their pools, and there's a bizarre tale about a scientist who drowned there when he was—"

"What the hell are you talking about?" his brother snapped. "First it was caskets, and now you're talking about selling the whole town. Are you okay?"

"I'm fine. I feel better than I have in a while. You wouldn't understand unless you were here." Daniel swept a palm across the top of the table. "I have my own booth now. It's prime real estate in the café, being by the window."

"Are you talking about a—a restaurant booth?"

"No. It's more like an old-fashioned diner."

"I'll have your doctor call you." Sam's voice took on a sense of urgency. "Maybe he can overnight you a mood stabilizer."

"I knew you wouldn't understand."

"Well, excuse me for under-reacting to your diner booth. It's probably because I was just at your ad agency, talking with your accountant about the discrepancies between your income and expenses."

Daniel rubbed his eyes. "How bad is it?"

"I'm recommending you lay off your most recent hires."

He swore. People could lose their livelihoods because of his mismanagement. "When?"

"I'll do it first thing tomorrow if you give me the go-ahead."

Neither of them spoke for a moment. The cell line crackled between them.

After sighing hard, Daniel said, "Do it."

"Toyco is back in talks with Chroma," Sam said then. "They've asked for other specs. Toyco's new top brass, Wickenham, heard you're out of town, chasing a woman." He waited, before adding, "You're losing the one deal that could save us. Only you can convince Wickenham you're serious. So get back here and do it."

Get back there? Daniel thought of how Gretchen had told him the other day that she was attracted to him. That'd been a good sign. She'd moved away from him after their kiss, though, and for some reason that bothered him. Joel had bothered him, too, with this little relationship he seemed to have going with Gretchen and Amy. He couldn't sort out his thoughts at all lately. Things seemed distorted. All of it cut into his gut, confusing and exhausting him. "I can't leave yet. I need more time."

"Wickenham is out of town, but he'll be back by Friday."

He nodded at the voice on the other end of the line. "I'll get there. And Sam? Thanks for all you're doing in my absence."

****

Gretchen stared into her closet. Why hadn't she thought of what she'd wear to the play before now? She groaned. Jeans, jeans, jeans. T-shirts and sweaters and casual jackets. Skirts too short or too long and all purchased over four years ago, after she'd lost her pregnancy weight gain. Well, there was the one short black one that might do, with the right pair of boots.

Suddenly she had an inspiration. Grabbing Amy by the hand, she hurried out the door. Twenty minutes later she was back, wearing Crystal's new high-heeled boots. They updated the skirt and made her feel sexier. Once she'd pulled a pearl gray sweater on and smoothed it out, she was satisfied that she looked okay. With her hair clipped back, she felt more sophisticated. More the way she'd been in Chicago, before Amy. Daniel saw beautiful women looking their best every day. She wanted him to see her at her best.

"Amy!" she called around applying tinted gloss to her lips. "Time to go."

As they climbed into the car, Amy said, "Are Joel and Daniel gonna meet us there, Mommy?"

"That was the plan. And afterwards we'll see if they want to come over for ice cream."

Crystal's, *He looks at you like you're an ice cream sundae*, popped back into her head. She nearly choked on the breath mint she'd been sucking as she drove along. Oh, well. Now she knew where the ice cream party idea had come from.

When they pulled into the school parking lot, she saw Joel standing by his truck. But it was when she looked around for Daniel's rented SUV and found it parked under the trees that her heart flip-flopped.

Amy scrambled from the car, ran to Joel and clutched his hand. "Where's Daniel?"

"Here I am." He strolled down the sidewalk, wearing a white shirt, open at the collar for once, and khakis. His eyes teased as he looked her up and down, before taking in Amy's transformation. "Wow. You two clean up well."

Her face grew warm. "Thanks."

Beside her, Joel murmured, "That's exactly what I was gonna say."

She laughed.

They all walked in together.

During the musical hour, Daniel fidgeted. Being around so many parents and kids made it hard for him to sit still. He could appreciate Gretchen's rapt attention to the music, but frankly, to his ears the group sounded a lot like the Chipmunks. Still, Gretchen's enthusiastic clapping and whistling had him grinning and enjoying himself.

Amy did look good up there on stage. Uncomfortable, but good. He recalled getting nervous in front of groups himself, before a few therapeutic bouts with speech coaches.

Breathe, Amy. He caught himself taking deep breaths for her and letting them out on counts of five.

At intermission, people climbed out of their seats and greeted each other. Gretchen leaned over Joel to say something to Crystal. When she stood to stretch, Daniel rose, too. "Think I'll go get us some sodas at the bake sale tables."

As he passed the drama room, he ran into children out in the hall talking and horsing around. It was all so surreal, these parents hugging their kids and patting them. His foster parents had never attended anything he was in at school.

Rounding the corner, he caught Amy talking with a sandy-haired boy. She looked over, noticed him and waved.

"Is that your dad?" the boy asked.

Daniel tensed.

Amy glanced his way. "Nope."

"*My* dad's talking to the teacher. My dad is Mark and he's a fireman." The boy took up rhythmic arm waving, as if he'd morphed into an airplane. "What's your daddy's job?"

"Don't have one," Amy mumbled, looking down at her shoes.

Daniel frowned.

"He don't have a job? That's stupid!"

"We're not supposed to say that word." Amy crossed her arms, covering the pompom eyes of a frog on her dress.

"Well, it *is* stupid. Stupid, stupid, stupid! Dads have jobs, that's all."

"I don't have a daddy!"

Daniel lurched backward. Wow. Well, at least she said it with confidence.

"My daddy is dead."

Hunh? Dead? *I'm standing right here.* What

112

lines had Gretchen been feeding her? Sure, she didn't know her father. But the poor kid should at least know one existed.

Then again, was it better to know you had parents who didn't care about you? His had died and he'd known he wasn't abandoned. They couldn't help the car accident. *He*, on the other hand, simply hadn't been here for his child. It didn't matter that he hadn't known about Amy until now. She would eventually hear of him and think he just didn't care, and blame him for not being here.

"Amy," he called.

She and the little wiseacre had begun kicking each other's shoes. She stopped, and walked over to stand in front of him.

He squatted on the industrial-grade carpeting. "Amy," he began, searching her innocent eyes, "I have to tell you something."

She tugged at the strap of her outfit that had slipped off her shoulder in her tussle. He reached out, lifted it and patted it back into place.

"Listen. I'm your—"

She turned to wave to another girl. Shiny curls bounced around her shoulders. The girl said something, and Amy's responding laughter tickled his ears, even as he realized he'd lost her attention.

She turned and skipped over to her playmate.

"Daddy," he murmured to her back as he stood.

He was aware of a thickness in his throat as he stared at his daughter. Oh, well. At least Gretchen wouldn't be ticked off that he told Amy the truth.

She swung back around, and left her friend to come and stand in front of Daniel again. She looked up at him with those luminous eyes and he thought, *She can tell. She knows.* A thrill rushed through him as he waited for her to say—

"I gotta go to the restroom."

His stomach dropped. "Are you sure?"

She nodded.

Grabbing her hand, he looked frantically around. "We better find Mommy," he said, and they started walking.

Rounding the corner toward the lobby, they almost walked smack into Gretchen.

"What's up?" she said. "Where's the snacks?"

"We were waylaid." Dipping his chin toward Amy, he explained her dilemma. Gretchen took her in hand and led her to the restroom, and after a deep breath of relief and a silent reminder that he was not cut out for parenting, he went to get the drinks.

Gretchen returned without Amy, explaining she'd left her with her teacher and classmates so she could catch the older grades' performances.

"Good, because I need to talk to you." Daniel told her about the boy asking Amy about her father. When concern lined her forehead, he quickly added, "She handled his questions like a pro, though. And once she explained her daddy was dead, that was the end of it." He set his hands on his hips. "Wanna explain that one to me?"

Her gaze froze on his. Grasping his arm, she tugged him around the corner and out of view. "I never said you were dead. She didn't ask for that much detail. She just wondered why she didn't have a daddy and I said because I couldn't find one good enough for us."

He flinched. "I suppose you felt that was fair."

"I know now it wasn't, and again, I'm sorry." Her forehead lined. "As for why she's saying you're dead...maybe she's decided it's an easier explanation."

"She needs to know the truth. I almost told her just now."

Panic filled her eyes. "Thank God you didn't. Give me time to think what it'll mean to her to find out and then to have you leave."

"Think on it fast, then." He stared hard into her compelling eyes. His gaze lowered to her lips, full and dark. What was it about her? Even when he should be angry with her, he just wanted to kiss her. No wonder Joel was on the prowl.

Where was her "shadow," anyway? "Did you leave Joel somewhere chatting about honey buns?"

She smiled. "He had to go to the bakery to finish decorating a wedding cake for tomorrow. He's going to try and stop by after. I bought some ice cream for us to celebrate Amy's first stage performance. Can you come? She'll be upset if you have to go now, too."

"Hey, I'm available." Good. He'd have time alone with them again. "My only plans were to flesh out my ideas for Wally for tomorrow's meeting. But I can do that later. I'm a night owl."

"I remember."

When they'd returned to the auditorium, he thought about those two words, *I remember*. The way she recalled that detail about him made something expand inside him. What was she implying, though, with that sexy lift of her brow? Sitting close to her in the theater seats, he stole a sideways look at her. He took in her jaw line, and her collarbone, exposed by the wide scoop neck of her sweater. *Nice angles.* His gaze lowered to the small mound of breast, so close to his elbow. So close that his body hardened as he tried to picture its whiteness, and imagine its soft, firm texture in his hand.

His gaze traveled back up to her mouth. Now, that he *did* know. He knew she tasted sweet and hot. She kissed with abandon, too, leaning closer to his body, pressing her tongue further, until...

His body throbbed, ached, even, and he gritted his teeth.

He should go back to Chicago tonight. All the ice cream in the world wouldn't cool him off now.

****

When the performance ended and they'd collected their little singer, Daniel followed Gretchen and Amy home. After Gretchen started the coffeemaker, she told Amy to put on her nightie and they'd have ice cream. Afterward, she helped her brush her teeth before tucking her in and listening to her prayers.

Flipping through the newspaper at the kitchen table, Daniel heard Amy bless her mother, her friends, and poor people. He smiled. She had a soft heart.

"Oh! And could I get a new daddy?"

His heart contracted.

"Amen."

He sat there, his breath echoing in his ears. She wanted a daddy? Elation shot through him, followed by fear. The father she prayed for was probably more like a fairytale, a guy who sat down to dinner with them each night, and ran with a kite and worked with his hands. A dad who stayed around.

Gretchen moved into the room. She'd climbed out of the tall boots and the short skirt that had hugged her slim hips, and slipped into relaxation mode in jeans, T-shirt and thick socks. She looked warm and soft.

He raised his gaze to her sexy eyes and met that look again, that reflective glance that made it seem as if she were hell-bent on reading his thoughts. Maybe she could discern his underlying fear. Maybe that was what made her want to protect Amy from him.

"Thanks for coming to the play," she said then. "It meant a lot to Amy."

"I liked it. I like her."

"She's doing all right, don't you think?"

"She seems fine. But I'm no expert on kids. I have nephews, but I—" He bowed his head. "—I think I bore them. Guess I'm a little too, preoccupied." The last word came out low. It sounded selfish. He couldn't explain that he avoided getting to know his nephews out of fear of rejection. That seemed immature. He looked up, expecting to see censure in her eyes. But there was none.

The burning ache in his chest reminded him of that cutting need he'd always had for a deeper connection with people. And over that need was the fear of causing some screw-up. He didn't do this. He took risks in business, not in relationships. But Gretchen sat watching him, her face unlined by judgment. Her full lips turned slightly up at the edges, welcoming, and over the fear spread warmth, pulling at him, making him linger in the moment.

She was a most attractive woman, with her soft features, her kind eyes. Five years ago, he'd put her in a predicament that should've been difficult and lonely, that should've made her sad and worn. And here she was. Happy. Vibrant. Forgiving.

He was the one who'd ended up lonely and tired.

Holding her gaze, he said, "Amy's lucky. Not everyone is cut out to be a parent, but you seem... exceptional." He thought of the little girl back in the bedroom, pictured her standing in the school hall in her dress and new shoes, gaping at him as if he were nuts to question whether or not she really had to go to the bathroom. "I didn't know four-year-olds could be so... I mean, the way she talks blows my mind, it's so straightforward. It's like, we adults quit being so open at some point. But she isn't there yet. And her face! Everything is right there in her frowns, her smiles." He remembered her kicking at the bully. "Or in her feet." He chuckled. "She's a whirlwind sometimes, right?"

"Oh, yeah." Gretchen's lips curved. Light flickered in her eyes.

He stared, entranced, thinking he could sit there all night and talk with her, and watch her, and it might be okay. Time really did stand still in Marydale, and now he was glad.

Bedsprings creaked. Footsteps sounded in the hall.

"Mommy?"

Gretchen turned. "What, honey?"

"I need a drink."

She hopped up and went to pour the child some water. After she'd walked her back to bed and tucked her in again, she returned to the living room. "I think maybe we should talk outside on the porch," she said, grabbing a granny-crocheted blanket off the back of a chair.

He rose and followed her out.

She settled on the porch swing. He considered taking one of the wicker chairs grouped around a glass-topped table a few feet away, but moved toward her on the swing. He eased down beside her, so as not to jar her. "I'm told my voice carries. I might keep Amy up if I'm over there by the door." It was the truth and not a ploy to get close to her. Still, he silently applauded himself for the thought.

She sat stiffly beside him.

"Relax." He started them swinging with a push of his foot against the painted wood floor. "I'm harmless."

She shot him a doubtful look.

"I'm harmless *tonight*."

She didn't insist that he move away. So he leaned back, content just to be there. For a while, they rocked back and forth, listening to the occasional whir of a car passing on the road. The night air carried a chill, and Gretchen threw the granny blanket over her shoulders.

Resting his arm across the swing's back, he moved himself a little closer.

He'd never just relaxed on a porch swing with a woman. He'd never sat anywhere with one for very long without the motive of becoming lovers soon.

His brushed his hand across Gretchen's shoulder, and squeezed it lightly. He felt great right then. Except, something nagged at him. "I heard Amy's prayer. I heard she'd like a new dad."

She sighed. "She's started that lately."

"What do you tell her?"

She stared down at the shawl's fringe, where she'd been slowly braiding little sections. "See, there's where I'm not the great mom you may think I am. I usually pretend I'm preoccupied and don't hear her when she brings it up. Or I just say, 'Maybe one day.'"

"Why?"

"Because like I told you, I'm afraid of how she'll react. How will I explain where you are?"

"You mean if you'd said I was in Chicago, she'd want to know why?"

She nodded. "'Why' is a kid's favorite word. And how would I answer her?"

"How about the truth for a change?"

She met his gaze. "How would *you* answer why you met her and then left her?"

He sighed. "I don't know."

"So we're right back at square one, with me not wanting to tell her that Mommy picks men who won't stay."

He reached out and touched her under her chin, and the feel of her warm skin beneath his fingers jolted him to sexual awareness. Gently, he turned her face toward him. When her lashes came up and she looked into his eyes, a glimmer of sadness touched her expression.

It got to him. It had him drawing an unsteady breath. "It's not you." He stroked her jaw. "You were right all along. It was me. I didn't know you five years ago. I didn't know you were the kind of woman who wasn't just out for fun. And frankly, I wouldn't have cared."

"Why?" Her gaze regained its spark as she searched his eyes. "Why are men allowed to be like that? They certainly don't pay for it the way we do."

He thought a moment, before admitting, "I've staked my business reputation on being able to analyze customers' needs. But in my private life, I guess I haven't worried enough about other people's feelings."

"Yes, but we've established that you're a guy."

He traced her profile, running his forefinger from her forehead down over her nose and lips. "Yeah. I'm a guy. I'll bet you think I can have my pick of women, too."

She eyed him, clearly not amused.

"I can. But then they ditch me."

"*They* ditch *you*?" Her eyes widened, then narrowed. "You're kidding."

"Nope. They leave. What do I have that they'd stay for? Money? Fame?"

"Well... yeah!"

His mouth curved up at an edge. "Gretchen. Tell the truth. Would that be enough for you? Would you sell yourself to be married to someone like me?"

She shook her head.

"See? I'm not so desirable after all."

"But you are!" Her gaze bore into his. "You just don't let them see the real you, Daniel. You're kind. You're honest. You're..." She bit her lower lip.

He reached out and touched his index finger to her mouth again, and the pressure of his finger tugged her lip from her teeth's grip.

Then he leaned in and pressed his mouth to hers.

Her lips were soft and warm, and she didn't pull away. She made a little sound, and he moved closer. Reaching under the shawl and accidentally under her sweater, too, he found her back and rubbed his palm slowly upward, feeling the fine bones and muscles there.

She tilted her head, adjusting to the angle of his kiss. The move made blood rush to parts of his body that reacted instantly, tightening, straining. He thrust his tongue into her moist mouth. She moaned, and he drew her closer, exploring with slow kisses as he kneaded her back, pressing her breasts closer to his pounding heart and feeling hers pounding in rhythm.

"This doesn't look like an ice cream social," came a deep voice.

Daniel opened his eyes.

Joel stood at the foot of the porch steps, hands in his pockets, his blunt features assessing.

Daniel swore under his breath as Gretchen pulled herself out of his arms.

Chapter Eight

Gretchen ducked, wrapping her arms over her head as pillar candles rained down on her.

When the stockroom was finally silent again, she straightened, lowered her arms and viewed the carnage. Wonderful. Now part of her freshly unpacked Christmas line would have to go on to the "scratch and dent" table. And all because she hadn't been careful when she moved a box of collectible ornaments beside them.

Bending to pick up the red and green wax cylinders marred by fresh white scars, she muttered, "One simple kiss and your brain goes out the door."

Only, it hadn't exactly been simple. And it hadn't been just one kiss. What Joel had interrupted last night was the second time in a matter of days that Daniel had taken her in his arms and mystified her with passion.

In her current state of confusion, one minute she'd love how they'd just grabbed those moments of pleasure together, and the next, she'd question whether he really was attracted to her, or if he was just trying to lower her resistance so he could worm his way into Amy's life.

She was probably just another pair of lips to him.

He'd probably found her inexperienced and fumbling, and the fact that she even cared how she kissed him was not a good sign.

She rubbed her shoulder where a candle had whacked it. The friction reminded her of the way

Daniel had touched her lightly there, gently urging her into his arms. Tucked against him, she'd breathed in his aftershave, caramel-spicy, mixed with his own scent and warmed by his body's heat. At the memory, she took a deep, automatic breath, but all she inhaled were the heavy scents of evergreen and bayberry candles.

"Oh, quit," she muttered. "You just happen to be the only woman in close proximity lately, and he's acting on male impulse."

"What'd you say, Gretchen?" Cile called from the other side of the closed door.

Gretchen jumped back in shock, hitting her head on a wreath hanging from a nail. Tugging her hair out of its leafy grip, she called back, "Nothing. Just, counting to myself. A little early inventory."

"Well, there's a guy out here asking for you."

"I'll be right there."

Daniel.

She picked up the bag of pencils and novelty toys she'd come in search of, for something the kids could buy at next weekend's festival. After brushing her hair back behind her ears and drawing a breath into nerve-tightened lungs, she opened the door.

Disappointment zipped through her. It wasn't Daniel. A skinny stranger with a cell phone pressed to his ear stared at her from across the room. As she moved toward him, he pocketed the phone, checked his watch and set his hands on his hips.

She stopped a few yards away. "I'm Gretchen."

"Miz Parks." He flashed a brief smile. "Friend of Daniel's. He here?"

"No." She scanned his wrinkled shirt, new jeans and pricey sneakers and considered his brusque tone and time's-a-wastin' aura. He could be a friend of Daniel's. She couldn't be sure, though. She hadn't been introduced to any of his friends or relatives. Their time together in Chicago had played out in bars and bedrooms, for the most part. "I don't know where he is."

"For real? I was under the impression he was with you."

She stood a little straighter. "Why is that?"

"People in the diner say you hang together."

"People in the diner have too much time on their hands." She set a hand on her hip. "Sorry, but I can't help you."

Out of the corner of her eye, she glimpsed Eula Miller scooting through the doorway, sporting that all too familiar knit shoulder bag that sagged down to her knees. But today she also clutched a knobby walking stick.

"Hullo, niece." She waved the cane toward Cile, who stood on the stepladder, dusting shelves.

Cile smiled and nodded before returning to work, bobbing to the tunes playing into her headset from her CD player.

Eula ambled over to Gretchen and the stranger. Lifting the cane, she tapped him on the shoulder.

His brows shot up, and he jolted back a step.

"Who're you?" demanded the town matriarch.

"Friend of Daniel Nicholson's." Keeping his eyes on Eula as if he feared she'd hurt him with her implement, he nodded toward Gretchen. "Miz Parks is a friend of his, too, right? A very *good* friend, from Chicago a few years back."

Why bring that up? Gretchen glanced quickly from Eula to Cile, who thankfully was still plugged into her music. She couldn't have her friends asking questions about Daniel and her. What if they figured out the truth?

"I guess we met, but I don't remember," she said, bristling at his speculative gaze. "Tell me your name and I'll tell Daniel you're looking for him."

"Don't bother." His smile didn't reach his eyes. "I'm sure I'll run into him." After a two-finger salute and a last wary glance at Eula, he headed for the door.

Eula followed his every move with her eagle eyes. As he screeched his car out of its parking spot, her fingers twitched on the crook of the cane. Once he'd zipped past the shop's window and they could no longer see him, she turned to Gretchen and muttered, "They're a strange lot, reporters."

Gretchen frowned. "He's a reporter?"

"Yup. Checked out his rental car on the way in. He had a stack of newspapers on the back seat, some legal pads with scribble all over them, five paper cups from coffee shops, and a black case, size of a computer."

"Maybe he's a paperboy."

"With a press badge hanging from his rearview mirror?"

She shook her head, smiling. "Wow, Eula. You're a regular Sherlock."

"Eh, I watch a lot of TV mysteries. What else is an old woman to do around here?"

Gretchen rolled her eyes. "You walk three miles to town every day and you read a stack of books a week. Don't try to tell *me* you're bored or old." Getting back to the matter at hand, she said, "So what do you think? What would a reporter want with Daniel?"

"To stir up trouble, most likely."

Gretchen pressed her lips together. What was the guy up to? Did Daniel have a part in it? She shrugged. A heavy feeling had settled in her shoulders.

"Don't frown so, child. You'll give yourself wrinkles. Anyway, time'll tell. It always does." Eula narrowed her faded blue gaze on Gretchen. "When you introduced me to your friend Daniel at the musical last night, he reminded me of someone. Does he remind you of someone?"

"No," Gretchen croaked.

Eula smiled. "Secrets are always safe with me." Turning away, she moved to another row to shop.

Gretchen's stomach lurched. Who else could she have meant but Amy?

She had to talk to Daniel and see why this guy was here. He knew about them. And now Eula knew. Their secret had protected them, but now she had this sinking feeling that someone might slip and say something.

Guilt permeated her for giving in to Daniel's kisses and letting her guard down, when she should've insisted, "You've seen Amy. Now go."

Even if their secret was still safe, the worst thing she could do was fall for Daniel, and because of *that* put Amy at risk. Memories of her mother standing in the doorway as her father left, and later, sobbing on the couch with a half-empty bottle of whiskey tucked under her arm after her latest lover walked out, made her even more determined. She'd never put Amy through the loss, fear, and sadness that she'd lived through. She never wanted her daughter to have to feel like the grown-up in their family, either. Amy was a happy, carefree child.

Making sure she stayed that way was more important than anything else in the world.

****

"I'm at Wally's plant, discussing marketing plans for the festival," Daniel told Gretchen over his cell phone around two that afternoon. "He set me up with Eula Miller for a tour of the caves since they're on her property. I'd like for you and Amy to come with me."

"To the farm?" She'd been distracted by his voice, rich as butter. *Butter is bad for you.* Coming back to her senses, she said, "I thought you were leaving today."

"I was. But Wally asked me to stick around and

126

help him at the festival. I gave him ideas for tie-ins to his sponsorship and I think he wants to show me he can pull them off."

"Tell me again why you're helping Wally?"

"Because I like him. I said I'd help him, and I'm enjoying myself."

Interference crackled over the cell.

"I liked last night, too, Gretchen."

Heat flashed through her, and she pressed the phone closer to her ear. Did he mean he'd enjoyed their kiss, or the musical?

"That's the main reason I want to stay a little longer. After last night, I'm convinced Amy needs me. She needs to know I'm her father."

He was right. But that didn't alleviate her worry.

"Come with me to the caves and we can discuss it."

She rubbed her forehead. "What time will you be here?"

"How about as soon as you get home from school?"

"Fine."

She set her phone down, though she wanted to beat herself upside the head with it. What was with her? The sound of his voice made her pulse dance. What had happened to her vow, only hours ago, to keep her head about this?

She leaned against the counter behind the cash register. And darn it, in the rush of their conversation, she'd forgotten to mention his reporter friend was looking for him.

****

Daniel pulled up in the driveway just as Gretchen unloaded Amy's schoolwork from her book bag onto the kitchen table.

Amy ran to let him in the front door.

Gretchen glanced his way. Their eyes met, and

his lips slid into a grin. He must have had his window down in the car, since his hair bent in more willful waves than usual. Plus, the sun had lightly tanned his skin these past few days. Sheesh, how much better could he look?

"What else have you been up to today?" She tried to sound casual around the nervous energy building inside her. "Other than hanging with Wally."

"I ran this morning. Then I had coffee. Then went to your newspaper office and placed an ad for the festival. After what you and Wally told me yesterday about the caves, with the scientist and the rare fish, I came up with this macabre sort of tour centered around the casket company and the caves." He raised his dark brows. "What do you think?"

"Sounds good." She moved about the kitchen, preparing Amy's snack. And thank goodness for the chore, which kept them from intimate conversation. Hiding how he affected her had become more and more difficult. "Could you get it in other papers, too? We need tourists, not locals."

"I put it in Cincinnati's and Lexington's." He frowned slightly as he leaned against the counter. "If I'd known about it sooner, I could've done more widespread advertising."

"How can you have time for this? Don't you have to get back to your own work?"

"You sound like my brother." He pulled out a chair at her breakfast table and sat. "He keeps calling and reminding me I'm losing money."

"That doesn't make you anxious to leave?"

"No, because I need to stay with Amy longer." His gaze lowered and settled on her mouth a moment before he lifted it again.

Uh oh. He's moving toward becoming a part of Amy's life.

She struggled around a dry throat and got out,

"What's the bottom line here, Daniel? What exactly do you want?"

He shook his head slowly. "I'm not sure. This is all new to me. I rarely take a vacation, much less visit a small town to see my daughter."

She crossed her arms—as if that'd stop the blast of fear assaulting her. His staying would only delay his inevitable leaving. While she fretted over that, she suddenly remembered his visiting friend. Maybe he'd come to take Daniel back to Chicago. "There was a guy in town today asking for you. He went by the café, and then he came to see if you were with me at the shop."

He frowned. "Who was it?"

"He wouldn't say. Eula thinks he's a reporter."

"What'd he look like?"

"About your height. Thin, with dark blond hair. And he seemed pretty hyper."

His frown deepened at first, and then she thought she saw a glint of recognition before he shrugged. "I don't know how anyone outside of my agency could've gotten wind of where I was. The only person I told was my brother, Sam."

"This guy knew we'd been together in Chicago."

"Like I said, I don't know how."

"So you don't have a friend who's a reporter? You didn't tell him about us?"

"Are you kidding? This is personal business. I don't discuss my personal life with anyone. I'm not a publicity hound."

"Really?" She went to the cabinets, pulled out her shoebox of clippings and handed it to him.

Lifting out a few of the carefully trimmed photos, he murmured, "Ugly mugshot." Tossing them back in the box, he looked at her with his brows raised. "Why do you have these?"

"They're for Amy." She took the box. As she returned it to its hiding place, she said, "It was for later, when she asked about you."

"Then I'm even happier about coming here, so she can know who I really am." Sincerity shone in his gaze. "The truth is it's easier for me to be around people I barely know than to be here, getting to know my daughter. Getting to know you."

She couldn't help herself. That insistent tone he used when talking about Amy made it hard for her to breathe and made her hands clammy. "Once you tell Amy, it can't be undone. Have you thought about what it would mean to your lifestyle? Do you really think it's fair to tear her away from the only parent she's ever known?"

He jerked his chin back. "What kind of guy do you think I am?"

"One with powerful lawyers who get you what you want."

He closed his eyes. When he opened them again, he said, "Gretchen, please at least attempt to trust me."

Off in the corner of the living room, Amy giggled over something on TV.

Daniel craned his neck in that direction. "Hey, Amy, guess what? I had breakfast today. Not just cereal, but a whole, big breakfast."

She turned and looked at him. Then she came and stood right at his knee. Her expression was as sober as a judge when she aimed the cookie she'd been nibbling on at him. "Me, too."

"Yeah, but I haven't eaten a real bacon-and-egg breakfast since I was a kid."

She pursed her lips. "That's not true."

"It is." He placed his hand over his heart. "I promise."

"Then it's silly."

"Silly to wait that long to enjoy breakfast, eh?" His eyes flashed with humor as he glanced at Gretchen, before turning his attention back to Amy.

"Guess I just need to keep smart girls like you around to warn me when I'm about to fall into the 'silly' trap."

Leaning on the counter behind them, Gretchen saw how the light in his eyes reflected in Amy's. When Amy giggled and he responded with a low chuckle, Gretchen's hesitant heart expanded. "C'mere, Amy. Let me tie those shoes again."

"I'll do it," Daniel offered, and bent to do the job. It took him twice as long as it would've taken Gretchen. She could have gone and taken over for him, but she didn't. She suppressed a smile, watching him struggle to form bows with his man-clumsy fingers. When he'd finished, one "rabbit's ear" was over an inch longer than the other. Gretchen swallowed back the emotion that filled her as father and daughter bent toward each other. Their similar mannerisms were so obvious to her. She couldn't believe nobody had noticed that, or at least remarked on their mirror image eyes.

"Let's go, then," she said. Maybe a little fresh air would clear her head.

Amy hurried out the door. Gretchen and Daniel followed, and before they reached the SUV and Amy, he said, "Mind if I ask you something personal?" His tone seemed lower, more tentative.

She glanced sideways at him. "What?"

"Are you in love with Joel?"

"No." A rush of nervous energy ran through her. "Why?"

"Just wondering." He never looked at her. He just dropped the subject and went to hold her door. But she thought she heard him whistling as he went around to the driver's side.

****

Eula was waiting for them when they arrived, cane in one hand and an old kerosene lantern in the other. She'd cuffed her jeans and donned a pale blue sweatshirt that matched her eyes and showcased her white puff-cloud hair. She'd also tied on her hiking boots. "Cile's looking for you in the kitchen, missy," she said to Amy in her gruff tone. But there was tenderness in her eyes when the child hugged her around the middle. "I think she brought home some of that ridiculous ice cream with gumdrop fishes in it."

As if on cue, Cile opened the front door.

Amy tore off toward her.

"Here, young man. Take this thing for me." Eula swung the lantern toward Daniel. "It's heavy."

Gretchen reached out to help her move forward then, only to receive a hard look and a curt, "I'm not ready for one of Wally's caskets just yet." She managed fine then, barely putting much weight at all on the cane.

Still, Gretchen thought Eula moved a tad slower today. Under the weather, perhaps. She stayed close by, and Daniel brought up the rear as they started out across the yard.

Gazing over the vast expanse of property, Daniel noted, "We *could* drive this in your pickup."

Eula eyed him. "Walking's good for you."

"True."

"By the way, some reporter man is looking for you."

"So I hear." He exchanged a look with Gretchen. "It seems he found everyone *but* me."

He listened as Gretchen explained how he had no idea who this guy might be. But sharp-eyed Eula glanced back at him long enough for him to see the speculation in her eyes and tightly closed mouth.

He was being paranoid, assuming suspicion this way. Still, by Gretchen's description, this mystery "reporter" stalking him could be his old nemesis, tabloid photographer Eddie Artis. Eddie had covered his divorce, lurking around corners and taking potshots that cast him as the guilty party. But why here? Why now?

Worst case scenario, whoever it was could somehow blow his chances with Gretchen and Amy. He clenched his jaw.

As they crested a small hill, Eula pointed with her cane. "There! See the cave there? That's Lion's Den. Then there's a string of little ones behind it that we call Ants' Hills."

Daniel nodded approvingly. Lion's Den looked the way he'd expected it to—a wide, dark opening in the stone-encrusted hill. Eula motioned for him to step forward and hold up the lantern. He did, casting light over craggy stone and exposing shadowy crevices. Upon closer look, one great shadow became an opening about five feet high and two feet wide where they could enter the hill.

With Eula up front now and in control of the lantern, Daniel motioned for Gretchen to precede him inside so he could watch their backs. They picked their way along, with the sides of the cave cool and hard and close to their bodies. "Have you been in here before?" he murmured in Gretchen's ear.

"A few times." She looked over her shoulder at him and smiled. "It was a favorite make-out spot when we were in school."

With his own make-out session with her last night fresh in his mind, he caught her arm and held her back a few steps. As Eula moved further into the cave, he said a low, "Why'd we have to bring her along?"

"That was *your* idea." With a grin and a lifted brow, Gretchen turned and hurried to catch up to Eula.

Daniel followed, touching the cold rock around him and hoping it'd cool him off. He wanted nothing more than to ditch their guide and spirit Gretchen away, deep into the cave, where he would make love to her. Hadn't he been thinking about that from the moment he stood in her yard and she came up in those ugly slippers to pull her dog off him?

Why hadn't he figured Gretchen might know her way around the caves?

They rounded a corner then, and the scene in front of him yanked even the lust from his mind for the moment. He'd never seen anything like it. The pool was black and liquid, stirred only where water dripped from stalactites overhead. It was cool, quiet, awe-inspiring.

What would it be like to make love to Gretchen here, on the banks of this beautiful water? Afterward, they could cool their bodies with a swim.

"Is the water just like a freshwater lake?" he asked.

"It's pure enough. But it's very cold." Eula's rough voice echoed off the dank walls. "And slippery. Watch your step."

He scanned the area one last time as they started away from the pool. It really was a pristine place, an oasis from the outside world.

"I can see why you'd want to preserve this place," he told Eula. "It's beautiful." Leaning forward, he murmured into Gretchen's hair, "I can see why people come here for lovemaking, too. It's very private." He couldn't gauge her response, because it was dark and she didn't look at him.

Moments later, they stepped out of the cave's mouth and into bright sunshine.

Eula headed straight for a crop of boulders, sat on a large one and fanned herself with her hand.

Gretchen went to stand beside her. "Are you okay?"

She nodded.

"I'll take Daniel to Ants' Hills while you rest. We won't be long."

Eula nodded again, and waved them off. "Gonna sit here and catch my breath."

"Sure she'll be all right?" Daniel asked as they started away.

"Huh! That woman's got more determination than most people our age."

He followed her over the next set of hills. Finally they came to a little range with three vertical openings into caves. "Do you want to find out what's behind Door Number One, Two, or Three?" she asked, humor lighting her eyes.

"Lady, I'm with you," he said in a voice gravelly from thinking about make-out caves, and lovemaking. "Lead the way."

"That's what I like. A compliant man."

"Hey, if it were up to me, I'd be beside the pool in the Lion's Den with you, behaving like the lion."

She laughed, a sound as light and gentle as the trickles of water down the walls of the cave. Taking up his hand, she said, "Come on, then." The thrill of the adventure sparked in her expressive eyes. "This might not be as impressive, but you need to see it, too."

I just need to see you. I just need to be with you.

He followed her into the cave, this one narrower at the beginning than the last, and darker. She held the lantern and moved adeptly over the smooth stone floor in front of him, since once again there was only room for single file. Minutes later, they stepped into an inner room ornate with icicle-like mineral deposits, cool and close. The entire space was nothing bigger than a walk-in closet, and a small one at that. There was room for both of them to stand or sit, but that was it. No cavorting. But he didn't wish to cavort. He just wanted to kiss Gretchen in this place where the pesky Joel couldn't pop in and break it up.

She set the lantern down and turned to face

him.

It was so dark, he missed seeing the marine blue of her irises. Still, he'd caught the teasing shine in her eyes when she swung the lantern toward her earlier. He wanted to bridge the gap between them, but something held him in place. What if she turned away from him? What if she made it clear that any advances on his part weren't welcome? He hadn't analyzed the kiss on the porch before he tried it. Why the hesitation now?

"I can't figure you out, Daniel." Her low tone bounced off the close walls and echoed sweetly in his ear. "What is it you want?"

I want you to come over here.

She stood there, still as the stone around them.

"Do you want Amy? Are you—are you being nice to me because of that? I need to know. I have to trust that you're being honest with me, because to be honest with you, I'm feeling vulnerable."

That wasn't what he wanted. All he wanted was to hold her, squeeze her and reassure her. But he couldn't guarantee her anything except that he'd have to leave Marydale soon. Everything about her, from her past to her present in this little town, in her cozy house, with these honest, good people surrounding her, screamed that she needed someone with staying power, and he didn't want to hang around long enough to hear "I don't want you anymore." Been there, done that.

He just wanted another kiss. One hot, deep kiss like the one interrupted one they'd shared last night that had left him hard and aching and, finally, alone. Maybe he wanted to avenge those feelings by making her at least crave him that way, too. Or maybe he just wanted more of the same because he was a glutton for punishment. A moment's worth of tasting her honeyed kiss and feeling her soft curves against him was worth the aftermath.

He raked a hand through his hair, dampened by the cave's humidity. "I don't want to hurt you."

"Not trusting you isn't personal. It's just how I feel."

"I'm taking it personally."

"I know. Why?"

"Because you're shutting me out."

She moved slowly across the wet, flat stone. Stopping inches from him, she set the lantern on a stone beside them. Tilting her face up, she caught his gaze. "But there's more to it, isn't there? I can see it in your face when you look at Amy. It's like, you want to be here, but you're scared of something. What?"

He swallowed. "Very few people I loved are still in my life."

She frowned. "Your parents?"

"Killed when I was a kid. Car crash."

"Who raised you?"

"Fosters."

"You're not close to them?"

"Let's just say they're close to me as long as I send money."

"But, you have your brother. He works for you, right?"

"Right. We were raised by different families. I found him two years ago, and hired him away from another attorney's firm after offering him a huge retainer."

"Are you saying you found your brother so you could *hire* him?"

He shook his head. "I found him because I wanted to find him. But we relate best on a business level. It's what I know."

He reached out and touched her jaw, and dragged his finger along it, to gently tap her chin. "I've kept my distance from his family. They're his. I don't want to poison their relationship with my coming around."

"How could you?"

"It just happens that way with me."

"You know," she murmured, after a moment, "I'm beginning to think we're not all that different."

"Why is that?"

"We keep our distance from people. We're our own persons."

He spread his fingers and cupped her chin. Then he leaned in and closed the gap, to brush his mouth across hers. He pulled back a little. "I could kiss you all day. Why is that?"

"It comes so easy to you. Like a handshake."

She kept her eyes closed while he kissed her nose, then touched his tongue to her earlobe. He'd made a promise to her about her safety. He'd keep it clean. Nuzzling her neck, he said, "There's something about 'shaking hands' with you, though, Gretchen, that's different."

Her lips curved at the edges, and she melted back against his hand resting on her back, keeping her close. It was a very vulnerable position, yet she seemed okay with it. She was a woman who knew her mind, but at the moment, she'd put that aside to go with what her body told her.

He'd do his damned best to keep her mind out of it.

He stroked up and down her back, nipped at her earlobe again, dragged his hand carefully around to where his palm pressed the side of her breast. "You feel good," he growled, before tasting her lips again.

"So do you," she murmured against his mouth, tucking her hips closer to his.

Damn. Did she know what she was doing? He pressed his erection closer, backing her against the wet cave walls in case she had any doubt that she was playing with fire. Then he leaned away, and sure enough, her eyes had opened in surprise.

They didn't need to play this game. He could go home and play it with anyone. Anyone but Gretchen, who he already knew couldn't be trusted to care. She'd left him once. She made it clear every single day that there was nothing for him here. Nothing but their daughter. So what was he doing?

In the lantern's light, he couldn't tell if her pupils were dilated, or if the pulse leapt in that telltale hollow of her neck. But her small ribcage moved in and out where his palms rested firmly at her sides, and her lips parted as she breathed.

She'd gripped his forearms for support while he leaned in to kiss her. Now that he'd steadied her against the wall, she drifted her hands up his arms to caress the nape of his neck. Fire shot to his nerve endings, sending his mind and body reeling.

She wanted something from him with those touches. Touches? She was stroking him!

With a groan, he bent and took her mouth, fast and hard. He pressed his lips to hers, and parted her teeth to plunge his tongue inside, to claim her sweetness with slower, more deliberate swirls and parries. She knew what they were playing with here. It wasn't unfamiliar territory. But if she must be shown that she was driving him to the edge, he would enjoy it. Then he'd stop.

But he didn't want to stop. Especially after she moved closer into his arms, pressing her breasts against his chest, her hips against his. She stroked his back with both hands. He followed her lead, kneading her muscles there gently, with the pads of his fingers, before tracing the delicate bones of her spine. He couldn't think. He deepened the kiss, moving his tongue, grinding his erection against her crotch, stroking her breast over her damned shirt one minute and in the next, sliding his fingers below the back waistband of her jeans to touch warm, firm flesh.

When his fingers found the crease of her bottom, he groaned. How fast could he get her out of these clothes? Hell, a minute longer and they'd burn themselves off.

He waited for her to realize his intentions and pull away. But she only kissed him harder and held him tighter, making him want her until he thought he would burst.

And then a face floated into his mind and fought to be seen. *Amy.* He could lose her if he couldn't control his lust and it scared Gretchen off again.

He broke the kiss and pulled away.

Gretchen came awake again more slowly, her half-closed eyes opening as she sucked in long, deep breaths. Finally, she murmured, "What is it? Did you hear something?"

"No." He stared at her mouth, swollen with passion. "It's just, what are we doing here?"

She blinked.

"I had to stop. I thought of Amy."

"She's fine."

"That's not what I meant." He looked away, and then back. "I thought of what happened the last time we acted like this." No way was he admitting his real fears. Best to just state the obvious. "I'm not packing protection."

Her lips parted in surprise.

"I didn't think we'd need it."

"Oh." Her expression closed.

"I didn't mean I wouldn't want to," he murmured. "I meant I didn't think you'd let me."

She turned away, to steady herself with the other hand against the cave wall. "I'm sorry. You're right. I didn't mean to—to lose control that way."

She looked beautiful and exposed in the lantern's light. What was she doing to him? He wanted to pick right up where they'd left off, to lay her down on the flat rock floor and penetrate her, and please her, until they were both satiated and panting. Instead he heard himself say, "If you want to pretend we weren't both worked up enough for sex just now, fine." Giving her a peck on the nose and grabbing her hand, he ground out, "Let's get out of here. Seems we needed a chaperone after all."

Chapter Nine

Gretchen scrambled from the cave's dank opening. She couldn't get out of there fast enough. Daniel had been truthful with her about his past, and she'd responded with a little too much compassion. Once she recovered from the erotic state of bliss his kisses left her in, uncertainty over what they were doing had quickly crept back in. Now, balancing on the rocky terrain, she blinked against stinging rays of afternoon sunlight as the field and the trees came into focus. She glanced toward the cluster of large boulders where Eula had said she'd catch her breath before trekking back to the house.

A pair of hiking boots jutted out from the far side of the largest stone.

"*Eula!*" She bolted for the boulder mass, acid fear pumping through her veins.

"*Damn.*" Daniel's low curse echoed against the rock walls as he emerged from the cave. Seconds later, his footsteps pounded the ground behind her.

She was fast, but he soon passed her. Reaching Eula, he knelt by her side.

Gretchen skidded to a stop on the opposite side of her friend. "Eula?" she forced out between gasping breaths.

Eula lay there, eyes closed and ghostly pale, her chest barely moving.

She's alive. Oh, thank God.

Daniel yanked the cell phone from his breast pocket and thrust it toward her. "Call 9-1-1."

His forceful glance eased her fears somewhat as

she took the phone, but her fingers still shook as she keyed in the number. When the dispatcher answered, she blurted details of the emergency. Once he'd promised the ambulance was on its way, she hung up.

Eula moaned and moved her head from side to side.

"Open your eyes, Eula," Daniel commanded, gently rubbing her upper arms.

She blinked, and squinted into the sun.

"Are you hurt anywhere?" Daniel's gaze, razor-sharp, searched hers. "Did you fall?"

She glanced from him to Gretchen, her face drawn and still drained of color. Her clear blue eyes seemed to reflect fear instead of recognition.

"Ssh. It's okay." Gretchen smoothed the wildness from Eula's cottony hair. Then she caught the hollow look in Daniel's eyes, and her heart ached with renewed fear.

She glanced at the house. Pushing herself to her feet, she said, "I'll show the EMT's up. Be right back."

She raced down the hill.

As she entered the house, she heard muffled voices coming from the kitchen, and bolted in that direction. Yanking the door open, she caused a clothesline of finger paintings attached to the knob to plummet to the ground.

"Mommy!" Amy scolded.

Glancing around, Gretchen saw Cile standing at the sink. As she turned, a jar of paintbrushes in her hand, she caught sight of Gretchen and her face brightened. Instantly, her smile evaporated and she rushed over. "What's going on?"

"It's Eula. She fainted or something."

"In a cave?"

"No. By the boulders."

Gretchen and Cile headed for the back door,

with Amy behind them, calling "I want to go, too!"

On the back porch, Cile touched Gretchen's forearm. "Did Aunt Eula get confused and fall?"

"We're not sure. We were in the cave, and—"

"She wasn't with you?"

"She had been, but not—not right then. She wanted to rest after Lion's Den. I took Daniel through Ants' Hills."

"Oh." Cile nodded, and turned and started up the hill, while Gretchen kept a protesting Amy back with her. She didn't want her to see Eula in that condition.

"Come on," she said, heading inside again. "We'll wait out front for the ambulance. They need someone to show them the way."

While they waited, Gretchen wondered if there was censure in Cile's "Oh" when she told her they'd left Eula alone. Or was it just her own guilt over feeling she'd let Eula down? How long had her friend lain there without any help? Her stomach clenched at the thought.

Amy sat on the porch and poked her stuffed bunny's head between its posts while Gretchen paced and watched the road on the horizon line. A few cars passed by. After a while, her attention drifted to the wide expanse of fading front lawn, peppered with oak and sycamore leaves. How many times had Eula crisscrossed the grounds in her worn hiking boots, scattering chicken feed, milking Jessie or riding the hay baler? Now she lay there, disoriented and weak.

She pressed her lips together in frustration as she glued her gaze to the road again. Why hadn't she realized her friend wasn't feeling well? She should have stayed with her. Instead, she'd focused all her attention on "exploring" with Daniel. Forget the excuse of his wanting to see the caves. There was no more denying it. She'd wanted to explore and maybe even lose herself in the sweet-salty taste of his mouth, the rough strength of his fingers holding her, and the heady scent of soap and man on his skin.

What was wrong with her? Her mother's blood pumping through her, always causing this lust for the wrong man?

No. She had long been responsible for her own actions. It'd be her fault if she couldn't stop wanting Daniel, and ended up hurting Amy and herself. Her own stupid heart's fault.

Finally a siren-blasting ambulance followed by a fire truck streaked down the road and braked in front of the property. Attendants tumbled from vehicles and followed Gretchen halfway up the hill while she filled them in on Eula's health history as best she could. Then she turned back reluctantly, to wait with Amy at the house while they saw to Eula's injuries.

Once they got Eula stabilized on the gurney and brought her down to the back porch, she adamantly refused to go any farther with them.

Daniel moved into their midst, and bent to stroke her forehead. "Everything's going to be fine. They're taking you to the hospital to make sure you're all right. You have to be back soon, because I plan on claiming the first dance with you at the festival. Okay?"

Her eyes opened, and she focused on him. Her lips trembled. "Okay," she said, in a reedy voice. Her eyes watered. "Okay, Isaiah."

She closed her eyes again, and as the rescue workers spirited her away to the hospital, with Cile riding along, Amy began to cry.

Daniel picked her up. Staring hard into her watery eyes, he said, "It's okay. She isn't hurt and they'll take care of her."

Her lips trembled. "Will they give her a shot?"

"If she needs it."

She wrinkled her nose.

He mimicked the action. "Me, too."

Gretchen smiled. He sure knew how to soothe both a worried old woman and a scared little girl. Catching his attention, she said, "Will you drive me to the hospital?"

"Sure." He looked down at Amy. "What about Little Bit?"

She took Amy's hand. "Wanna go play at Crystal and BJ's?"

"Yep."

So off they all went.

Once they'd seen Eula in her room and were convinced she was well cared for, Daniel drove Gretchen and Cile back to the farm. They stood on the porch and talked a while. Gretchen leaned heavily against the railing, drained of strength after the nerve-fraught day.

When Cile went inside to answer the phone, Daniel moved to Gretchen's side. Pressing his warm palm atop her fingers clamped to the railing, he murmured, "She's in safe hands now."

"No thanks to us," she muttered, blinking back the sudden dampness blurring her vision.

He shifted beside her. "Why do you say that? You called 9-1-1 and they came."

"We shouldn't have left her after Lions' Den."

"We didn't know she had a problem or we wouldn't have." He leaned forward, as if to catch her gaze, but she stared down at the boxwoods lining the front of the porch.

"Come on, Gretchen. Don't over-think this." He rubbed his palm across her knuckles. The gesture seemed so easy for him, but sent unbidden shivers of delight through her.

She pulled her hand out from under his. "Don't."

"Don't what? Don't concern myself with your feelings? Don't touch you?"

"Just, don't."

He snorted. "Whatever." When he shifted away from her, the air current chilled.

Her heart beat heavily in her chest. What was she doing? He probably had no idea what he'd done, and the truth was, he hadn't done anything. Nothing but be attractive and sexy, caring and strong. She was the one starting to feel comfortable with him. *She* was getting too close and too involved.

The screen door screeched open.

"That was Aunt Eula's friend, Martha," Cile said, rejoining them. "She said she's been after my aunt to go to the doctor for at least a month now, but she refused." Shaking her head, she sat down hard on the porch's top step. Her lower lip trembled, and she dipped her chin, as if to hide her true feelings. "Why does she have to be so hard-headed?"

Gretchen slipped down beside her, wrapped an arm across her shoulders and gave her a squeeze.

"She's been having these spells where she's confused." Cile rested her head against Gretchen's shoulder. "It happens one day, and the next, she seems fine. I begged her to go to the doctor, too."

"Why won't she go?" Daniel asked, leaning against the porch support.

Cile shrugged. She sent Gretchen a half-smile. "You remember when her stubborn streak first showed itself, don't you?"

She nodded, smiling. "Daniel might want to hear it, though, since she called him 'Isaiah.'" She wasn't sure why Eula had called him by her husband's name, but it probably had something to do with his staying at her side and murmuring words of assurance, his dark gaze filled with concern.

"Eula's dad was the preacher here," Cile began, her attention focused on Daniel. "He was really strict." She pulled her knees up under her chin. "Anyway, Aunt Eula fell in love with this guy,

Isaiah. But he wasn't good enough for the Miller family and their Quaker background."

Daniel shifted. "Why not?"

Cile's eyes danced with humor, reflecting Gretchen's own amusement. "He was the son of the woman who owned the strip club off the highway a few miles out of town."

He let out a low whistle.

"Eula met him at the lake on the Miller property one day. She secretly enjoyed an occasional skinny-dip down there. He'd happened by for the same purpose." Mirth lit her expression.

"It was Preacher Miller's worst nightmare. He'd never forgiven 'that heathen woman,' he called her, for making him baptize the boy 'Isaiah.' Everyone around here always thought she had something on him, to get him to do it."

Daniel chuckled. "She probably did."

"Well, anyway, Eula didn't believe anything they said about Isaiah. He'd grown up around what her parents called 'those' women, and people figured him for a slick womanizer. Eula didn't listen. What mattered was that he loved her, and he was good to her." She stretched her legs. "When her parents objected, though, Isaiah tried to break it off. He didn't want to cause trouble. But Eula made it clear that she believed in him and that was all that mattered. After that, it wasn't long before they eloped. And the rest is history."

Gretchen smiled. "It's such a great story. I'll tell it to Amy as soon as she's old enough."

Daniel studied her. "So you'd allow her to marry someone you didn't like?"

"I'd trust her judgment."

His gaze roamed over her. "I thought you didn't believe in fairy tales."

As Cile's attention flitted back and forth between them, Gretchen said, "Just because it hasn't happened that way for me, doesn't mean I don't think it's great when it happens to other people."

The lines around Daniel's mouth softened, and his gaze grew less intense.

"How about you?" Gretchen watched him. "Do you believe in happy endings?"

"No. But sometimes I think I'd like to."

She breathed in then, and a tingling sensation started in her scalp and settled in her lungs.

After another glance at Daniel, Cile grinned at Gretchen and wiggled her brows. When Gretchen flashed a warning look at her, she sobered. "Well, Daniel, Isaiah wasn't really convinced that things would work out for Eula and him, either," she said, continuing the story. "But he worked hard to make them a home after they married, and he worked to gain everyone's confidence in him. Eventually, he became head of the bank. Eula threw huge parties and invited the whole town. They proved their critics wrong. Everybody was always here on the farm, watching them dance, listening to their jokes and sometimes their fights. They raised four daughters."

Daniel's gaze bore into Gretchen's. But the setting sun suddenly cast him in shadow, making it hard to see his expression. She was wondering how he liked the ending of the story when he said, "It's funny, but Eula didn't strike me as a softie at all. Hearing about Isaiah puts a whole new light on her."

"She's a proud woman," Cile acknowledged. "But she has a big heart."

"Sounds like someone else I know." He tilted his head toward Gretchen.

She fidgeted, and checked her watch. "We've got to get going," she blurted, thankful for the reprieve from that fresh matchmaking gleam in Cile's eyes. "Mr. Scott's supposed to come by to check Joel's roof repair. And there's the leak in the tub. He'll want to see that."

She hugged Cile goodbye, telling her to come to work whenever she wanted tomorrow and allowing her leeway to go by the hospital. Then they walked to the car.

On the way to pick up Amy, Gretchen accidentally flipped the stereo from radio to a CD in the middle of one of Amy's songs. She hummed along to the tune.

"What is that?" Daniel asked.

"You're kidding, right?" She laughed. "It's 'Frere Jacques.'"

"Oh."

She glanced at him. "You don't know it?"

"No."

"Didn't your mother teach you—"

"I doubt it. She died when I was seven, in that car accident I told you about, along with my father." Stopping at a traffic light, he glanced her way. "My foster mother, Ellen, wasn't the type to sing. She was too busy keeping Chuck happy. Plus they had five kids of their own."

"But, didn't you hear other kids sing it, in school, maybe?"

"Nope. I stuck to myself. Tried to fly under the radar." She saw the muscle move in his jaw. "My foster siblings made sure everyone knew I wasn't a true Koontz."

"Wow."

"Wow what?"

"That's not what I expected."

He glanced her way again. "What *did* you expect?"

"I guess I pictured your mom driving you to Little League, cutting the crusts off your sandwiches. And for your dad, I thought he'd be a company man by day, but would watch TV with you at night."

He sent her a skeptical look. "Were your parents

like that?"

"No. My dad left when I was pretty young. My mom spent the rest of the time out a lot, looking for a replacement."

"Why? Didn't he give her any financial support after the marriage ended?"

"He did. But she couldn't cope on her own, I guess. I hated that."

He reached over and patted her leg in a quick gesture, before withdrawing his hand again. "Probably what made you independent."

She looked down at her thigh where her skin still tingled from his touch. The gesture made her think he understood her feelings, because in a way, he'd been in her shoes.

"So your mom was always going out and leaving you?"

She nodded.

"Is that why you don't go out? Because you're worried Amy might think she isn't enough to make you happy?"

"I—I hadn't thought about it."

"Well, we need to consider that Amy isn't me and she isn't you. She's a mixture of both of us. And thanks to your parenting skills, she seems very well-adjusted." He glanced at her. "She seems fine about having me around. I think you're underestimating her and I *know* you underestimate yourself."

"What do you mean?"

"I'm saying, I don't think Amy's holding you back from finding someone. I think you're just scared."

"No I'm not. I like being on my own."

The way his mouth quirked up at the edge implied that she hadn't exactly convinced him. But he didn't say anything else.

They stopped and picked up Amy from Crystal's, and then headed for home.

When they reached the house and turned down the drive, they saw Mr. Scott's truck parked up front.

As they climbed from the SUV, the elderly landlord ambled away from the far side of the duplex, with that wiry reporter friend of Daniel's on his heels.

Gretchen noticed how Daniel's shoulders stiffened when he spotted him.

The two men ambled over to them. After Mr. Scott had commented to Gretchen on the fine job Joel had done on the repairs, he said, "Mr. Artis, here, just paid me a month's rent on the other side of the house."

Disappointment washed over her. This could mean the end of Daniel's visit. "I thought we were looking for a full-time renter," she said quickly.

"We are." Mr. Scott removed his Bass Pro Shop baseball cap and scratched his bald scalp. "But a month is more than I've gotten lately."

"Mr. Scott?" Daniel shot a hand out toward the landlord. "Daniel Nicholson. Pleasure to meet you." Mr. Scott hesitated for half a second, eyeing Daniel, before accepting his hand. As they shook, Daniel said, "I believe Miss Parks mentioned that I've been living in the rental unit while you were out of town? I came to see her—she's a friend—and she let it out to me on a day-to-day basis. She told me about your having just lost a long-time renter, so I'm guessing our setup worked out well for all involved." Reaching into his jacket's breast pocket, he pulled out a leather checkbook. "How much is a month's rent? One, two thousand?"

Mister Scott's hound-like face wrinkled in a bewildered-looking frown. "Shoot, no! Eight hundred's what I get, and Mr. Artis here just paid it."

"Mm. Well, I feel bad for taking up the place

while you were gone and not giving you time to fix it up between renters." Daniel rustled around in the wallet and extracted several hundred-dollar bills. His lips moved as he counted them, before squaring them off and handing them to Mr. Scott. "There. That's all yours. Two thousand, for my rent and for a clean-up after I leave."

"You've only been here a week. That's too much, unless you've done some damage." His gaze narrowed a little.

"Nope. No damage. And I'll be here until the end of this week. I'm really enjoying the place. Consider the rest a donation toward—flowers, maybe. Some, uh, pansies for Gretchen and Amy. Some fertilizer, some soil."

Gretchen's gaze shot to his, and he met it with a lightning-quick wink. She slid glances at the other men to see if they'd noticed. Eddie stared straight at her, a knowing gleam in his eyes. But he only said to Daniel, "Ain't this one for the books! Thinking money talks in the boonies, just like in the city. Trouble is, you're late. I've already rented."

The landlord shifted his palm, crossed with all that cash, back toward Daniel. "He's right." Regret tinged his voice.

Daniel plucked the cash from his hand, counted out eight bills, and handed the rest back. "How about if Mr. Artis and I work this out between us? And in the meantime, you can consider the place rented to me."

"Oh, yeah?" the reporter snapped.

"Yeah." Daniel's jaw clenched as he thrust the eight hundred at Eddie Artis, who hesitated and then took it.

Mr. Scott looked from Daniel to Eddie to Gretchen, and shrugged. Rolling the remaining bills into a tube, he fisted them in his left hand. With a quick nod and "Gretchen's got my number, so call if you need me." He skedaddled to his truck.

"Money talks and he listens," Eddie muttered, watching him back out of the drive. Pivoting back to them, he appraised Gretchen with a leering grin before coming around to Daniel. "What the hell you doing here, anyway, City Boy?"

"Me? What about you?" Daniel's jaw clenched as he swept his gaze over him. "You're not on vacation. You never quit snooping."

"Maybe I *am* vacationing, on your ticket." Eddie looked down at the cash he still held. He counted it out, folded it, and finally pulled a silver money clip out of his pants pocket and clipped it. Looking up at Daniel again, he said, "Maybe you're gonna earn me more than eight hundred by the time I'm tanned and rested."

Daniel's mouth tightened. "Go home."

Eddie pulled a pack of Marlboros from of his breast pocket, pounded it on his palm and extracted a cigarette that he stuffed between his lips. "Sooner you tell me what you're up to," he said around it, "sooner I go back." He cocked his head, lit the cigarette with a lighter and inhaled deeply. Exhaling, he said, "Weren't you in the midst of some big scandal when you left? Something to do with a councilman's daughter?"

Gretchen went cold inside.

Daniel tensed.

"Maybe that has something to do with your flight from the Windy City." He puffed on the cigarette again. "But why here, in the middle of nowhere?"

"I'm helping a friend of Gretchen's keep his business afloat."

He sneered. "You expect me to believe you'd walk away from Toyco, that international account you're working on, to come here and help some mom 'n' pop shop?"

"And I'm visiting Gretchen."

The reporter glanced at her, narrowed his gaze a second, and then shifted his attention back to Daniel. "Why?"

"That's between us."

Gretchen folded her arms. "Yes. And I think you'd better go now."

Eddie's eyes glinted as he held up a key to the duplex. "I'm home."

Daniel took a step toward him, and Gretchen moved back when she saw the hard look in her ex-lover's eyes. "Gretchen suggested you leave," he said, his voice low and strong. "I gave you back your money, now give her back the key."

Eddie's brows shot up, but he said, "Aye aye, Cap'n. Miz Parks is a little old for you, though, isn't she? I mean, the councilman's daughter was, what? Twenty-two?"

Gretchen knew the instant Daniel's muscles tightened. He leaned threateningly closer to the other man.

Chuckling, Eddie stepped backward toward the road. He'd parked his car under one of the buckeyes lining the edge of the property. Turning and strolling toward it, he looked over his shoulder at Amy on the swing set. "When I do get the scoop on you, Danny boy, it'll go down the way it always does, to the highest bidder. So keep that checkbook handy."

He hopped into the car and drove off.

Gretchen turned to Daniel. "He knows."

"Let him. Let everyone know, for all I care." He squeezed her fingers. "Seriously, don't let a has-been photographer make you nervous."

"He's a photographer, then, and not a reporter?"

"Yep, he's a mid-level *paparazzo* who likes to talk big. He can't hurt us unless we let him get to us."

She took in his chocolate-rich eyes, his square

jaw line, his wind-rumpled hair. It wasn't just what Eddie'd implied about Amy that scared her. "What happened with the councilman's daughter?"

"Nothing. Someone set me up. I was in a bar and a woman came on to me. She was hungry, and I offered to whip her up some spaghetti in my apartment."

His gaze seemed earnest. But then, it always seemed earnest. It was part of his attraction, that deep, soul-engaging way he had of looking at people.

"I went into the kitchen to fix the pasta. Next thing I know, someone's beating down my door. I open it and there's a photographer there snapping shots of me and this girl, who'd stepped up from behind me and draped herself on me."

Disappointment enveloped Gretchen. "Let me guess. She was naked."

His gaze dimmed, and he nodded. "She'd said she was going to the bathroom. But she went into the back room and took off all her clothes."

She shoved out a breath, and looked away.

He stepped to her, and placed his hands gently but firmly on her upper arms. "Look at me, Gretchen."

With effort, she turned to meet his gaze.

"We didn't do anything. It was a setup."

"A setup. Right. Who would do that?"

"I don't know. Someone at Chroma Agency, maybe. They're competing with us for the Toyco deal."

She couldn't listen to his excuses. As she swallowed past the sickness bubbling up, the heaviness inside, an inner voice tormented her. *Here you go again. Here's proof that he's a player. You pushed it to the back of your mind today, because you want him.*

"Hey." His voice softened. He moved closer, so close that her breasts pressed against him and her hips brushed just below his. "I know I have a bad track record." He released one of her arms, to smooth back some tendrils that had fallen forward on her cheek. "It started after you left. I didn't want to work at relationships anymore. I went a little wild. But I stopped." His gaze hardened. "Unfortunately, my reputation was in place and the media kept building it even after I'd burned out."

She willed herself to be inured to the sales pitch. Not to be thrilled by the touch of his flesh against hers, or the way he looked at her as if she were the only one in the world who mattered. "I have to take Amy in now."

Shifting out of his arms, she stepped back.

He stood there, his hands at his sides, his gaze unreadable now. "You don't believe me."

She didn't say anything.

He nodded, and murmured, "So this is the Gretchen who walked away from me back then."

"Maybe I saw you more clearly then. Maybe I knew what you were going to do and my gut told me to go before you started it."

"Maybe it wasn't *my* issues that made you go. And maybe if you'd stayed, things would've worked out."

He watched her. But she wouldn't give him anything. Nothing in her expression. No words. Finally, in frustration, he ground out, "Don't listen to me, then. That's fine, as long as I have my daughter. If she believes me, that's all I need."

"And if she doesn't?"

His chest stilled. He drew his brows down slightly and stared at her.

She glared right back.

His shoulders suddenly sagged, as if a weight had dropped on them. He drew out a long breath. "I was hoping," he said, turning toward Amy on the slide, "I had it in my head that she would accept me." When he looked back at Gretchen, her heart contracted at the sadness in his gaze. Then he turned, and without another glance in her direction, strode off toward his end of the house.

She stared after him until his front door banged shut. Her bones ached. Her voice barely came out enough when she called to Amy. She heard her, anyway, and they went inside together.

As she went through the motions of making pizza, Gretchen longed to go to Daniel. She'd seen the hurt in his eyes. She'd heard the disappointment in his tone when she threw back at him that his daughter whom he'd come here to meet might not accept him.

She wanted to believe in him. So what if he'd messed around with a councilman's daughter? So what if it'd hurt Amy and her?

She wanted him, and it was becoming harder and harder not to throw caution, integrity and her future to the wind, just to be able to spend another moment in his arms.

Chapter Ten

On busy days at the gift shop when customers stood in line glaring and muttering under their breath for Eula to make up her mind about a purchase, Gretchen had wished the town's matriarch wasn't so obstinate. When Eddie Artis disclosed that Daniel and she had known each other in Chicago and Eula had figured out their connection, she'd wished Eula wasn't so smart. Now, sitting next to a hospital bed with sides locked like a fence around her friend, she longed for those days. Where was the fire that usually ignited Eula's blue eyes? Where was the resonance that so distinguished her voice from every other Midwestern twang?

Eula wasn't the type to allow something like a stroke to render her feeble. She'd never agree to this confinement. Yet here she lay, drifting in and out of sleep, scarcely aware of people she'd known their whole lives.

If it could happen to Eula, it could happen to anyone. One day, Gretchen could go to bed strong and wake up weak. Maybe it'd already happened, but in her case it wasn't so obvious as a stroke. Maybe it was just that she'd felt strong before Daniel showed up and now she felt vulnerable, unsure of her future. Yesterday, she'd pretty much admitted to herself that she was falling in love with him.

"Hey! Miz Parks!"

She glanced around. Eddie Artis stood in the hallway, grinning at her. What nerve, coming into the hospital at a time like this.

Tiptoeing to the doorway so as not to awaken Eula, she stepped out of the room. She pulled the door shut behind her, crossed her arms and stared hard at him. "What are you doing here?"

His fox-bright gaze swept over her. "Got a minute?"

"Not really. I'm visiting my friend."

"Come on, now. How about showing me a little small-town courtesy? Got something I'd like to show you. Something you'll be interested in."

She rubbed at a strained muscle in her shoulder. "I doubt that."

He whipped out a rolled newspaper he'd had clamped up under his arm. As he unfurled it, she recognized the widely-circulated Chicago tabloid.

He thumbed through the pages before spreading a section wide in front of her. "Well?"

She'd often searched for photos of Daniel, photos for Amy's memory shoebox. But now that Eddie obviously wanted her to look, she hesitated, the hair at her nape prickling in warning.

He shook the paper at her. "Middle photo, bottom of page three."

She found the photo and squinted. *Daniel*. In slacks and a white shirt, with his tie undone. A bare-shouldered woman stood glued to him from behind. No, it looked as if he'd intentionally stepped in front of her. A foot of her pale thigh was outlined along Daniel's pants leg. From all angles, it appeared she was naked.

The councilman's daughter.

Her stomach tightened, and she drew back. Then, recalling what Daniel had told her yesterday about a setup, she looked at the photo again. He was fully dressed and the blonde wasn't. She scrutinized Daniel's expression. He seemed about to blink, and his lips had parted as if he were about to say something. As if the photographer had surprised them. The woman's eyes were barely open. She held a champagne flute in her hand that was flung out toward the photographer. In stark contrast to Daniel's look of surprise, she smiled and posed for the camera.

"Well?" Eddie's angular face glowed. "How's it feel, seeing your lover with someone else?"

She shrugged a shoulder in a fake gesture of bravery. "Why are you showing me this?"

His smile wavered. "Just wanted to show you what kind o' guy you're dealing with."

"Daniel told me he was set up." She glared at him. "You wouldn't happen to know who did it, would you?"

"I never rat out my friends," he said, leaning closer.

She wrinkled her nose. His cologne smelled as strong as a plug-in deodorizer. Didn't he know people could still detect evil under it?

"Tell me why Daniel's here in Marydale, Sweet Cheeks. Give me that and I'll tell you who took this shot."

"I thought you never ratted out a friend."

Lounging back against the wall, paper folded and tucked back under his arm, he tapped his foot. "I'm waiting."

"What could I possibly tell you?" she shot out, cornered by that discerning gleam in his eye. "Daniel and I dated in Chicago a while back. It didn't work out in the romance department, but we're great friends."

"Nope. Not buying it." His eyes raked over her again. "I make a living watching people and waiting 'til I can get the most telling shots. No, there's something besides past history going on with you two."

"I have to go." She started around him.

"What's this hold you have over our boy Daniel

161

that you can pull him out of Chicago?" he called after her.

She stopped, turned and stared at him, and then glanced at an orderly pushing a cart down the hall, who'd craned his neck in their direction.

"I get the feeling you've got a connection that goes deeper than just the two of you." The photographer's voice echoed in the corridor. "If you get my drift."

A chill ran through her. She just stood there, afraid to move for fear he'd broadcast something else down the hall. They'd already drawn glances from the nurse's station.

He stepped quickly to her side, leaned in close and hissed, "That's his kid, isn't it?"

"No!" she hissed.

"Now, now, Gretchen. It's not nice to lie."

She glared at him, and stalked away. Once outside in the bright light of day, she stopped and caught her breath. She must remain calm and consider what all this meant. Was Eddie only threatening her, or was he planning on spreading what he'd discovered?

They had to tell Amy. But every time she considered it, she saw her own father walking out the door. She saw her mother running off with another husband. She saw Amy eventually blaming her for running Daniel off, and then...she saw herself alone again.

Still, they had to tell her. Where was Daniel? She had to warn him that Eddie knew their secret.

****

Crouching on hands and knees, Daniel peered under the crawl space beneath the bathroom on his side of the duplex. He needed a flashlight.

Forget the flashlight. He needed a plumber.

"What're you doing?"

Recognizing the voice, he squinted up into the

sun. "Joel." He shoved himself back on his haunches. "My shower sprang a leak."

Joel nodded. "Shower pan. I changed the one on Gretchen's side last year when it went."

"I bow to your superior knowledge on the subject." Daniel stood. Brushing dirt off the knees of his jeans, he admitted, "In the city, I just call maintenance and they fix it while I'm away for the day."

Joel didn't seem to find that funny. In fact, his normally friendly expression looked downright sour. "Where's Gretch?"

"Not sure, but I think she went to the hospital to see Eula."

Joel set his hands on his hips. He had on his white T-shirt and jeans. He looked big but not fat like the normal tendency for a baker. He wished Joel had that tendency.

"When will you be leaving town?" the bread man asked.

"I don't know. Why?"

"What's keeping you here? Crystal mentioned you're doing some work for Wally. Is that it?"

Hardly. That'd just been a way to fill his free time between seeing Gretchen and Amy. But what *was* keeping him here now? He'd already accomplished his goal of spending time getting to know Gretchen and Amy. "Yeah," he said, frowning slightly. "I'm working with Wally."

"That'll be over after this weekend, then. After the festival?"

He nodded. "It's a festival blitz. Though I told Wally I'd like to see him do like his competitors and go nationwide. But I'm not sure he's ready for that. At least, not yet."

"Or maybe never." Joel's hands remained on his hips, and his biceps bulged. "Some of us don't need the limelight. We're happy just being behind the counter." His eyes narrowed on Daniel.

There was something more to their conversation, Daniel thought. Something he wasn't saying, though he sure broadcast it with those body signals.

"Damn, I hate suspense," Daniel blurted. "You got something else you want to say to me?"

Joel's mouth tightened. "Are you in love with Gretchen?"

The old weight that accompanied the "L" word settled on Daniel's chest again. Love was death and disillusionment, disgust and divorce. It should be the "D" word. Then he remembered the sweet expression on Gretchen's face as she listened to Eula's love story yesterday. He saw again, in his mind, that little smile that had played on her lips in the car when they'd talked and he'd squeezed her knee. Some of the heaviness lifted. Still, he said, "In love? No, man. Are you?"

Joel's shoulders slumped, and he dropped his hands from his hips to hang loosely at his sides. Even his gray-eyed gaze seemed to sag. "I've loved her since she was eight and I was ten. But she tells me she doesn't feel the same way." He couldn't have looked less intimidating right then. It was as if with his admission, all the strength had drained out of him.

Daniel felt for the poor guy. He'd be better off lusting after his baked goods. Gretchen said she wasn't in love with him. Once again, love had been one-sided.

Joel lifted his doleful gaze to Daniel's. They stared each other down for a moment before the baker slowly stuck a hand out to him.

Daniel looked down at it, then back up at Joel. Cautiously, he reached out and grasped it.

As they shook, Joel's mouth set in a hard line. His gaze narrowed on Daniel's and his grip tightened. "If you hurt her," he muttered, "I swear I'll rip this arm off you." Just as quickly, he dropped Daniel's hand and turned away.

As he lurched around the side of the house, Daniel wanted to yell, "I thought you were a baker, not a butcher." But he knew when to keep his mouth shut.

He stood there until he heard Joel pulling his truck out of the driveway. Then he went around to the front of the house and sat on the porch to wait for Gretchen.

They had some talking to do.

****

Gretchen had kept an eye out for Daniel's SUV all over town, but hadn't had any luck finding him. When she turned the last curve before home and saw his vehicle parked in her drive, her heart rate picked up.

She scooted out of the car and headed for the house, where she found Daniel lounging on the swing, his long legs stretched out, feet propped up on its arm. As she approached, he opened his eyes and focused on her.

"I was looking for you," she said.

He pushed up to a sitting position, swinging his legs down. "I was looking for you, too."

"Behind closed lids?"

His lips quirked, and he held out a hand. "Come here."

She dropped her purse and went over to him. The instant their fingers touched, heat shot through her.

Placing his hands on her hips, he pulled her in between his knees and stared up into her eyes.

Her breasts tingled, and the place between her thighs throbbed. "What's wrong?" she murmured, suddenly aware of the dullness in his brown eyes.

A muscled played in his jaw. "I had a visitor."

Melissa Beck

"Eddie? Because he came by the hospital and flat out said what we suspected. He knows you're Amy's father, and he'll use it to his advantage somehow. I'm scared you could lose that big business deal."

"Maybe, maybe not. I don't care about that right now." He reached up then and stroked her chin. The intimacy of the touch, and the thrill of it, shocked her. But she didn't squirm away. The trouble in his gaze held her. "So who visited you?"

"Joel."

She frowned. "Joel came by? What for?"

"The usual. You."

He dropped his hands away—a move that left her with a torturous sense of loss—and clasped them in his lap. As he stared down at them, she suppressed the urge to touch the boyish waves crowning his head.

"Was he upset about something?"

He snorted. "You might say that." Hands on his thighs now, he regarded her again. "He told me how he feels about you. And he says you don't feel the same."

She nodded. "I told him earlier this morning." She shifted. "Crystal made me realize I might be stringing him along. I hadn't meant to, but I guess that's what I was doing."

He scowled. "Why do I feel bad about you shooting him down?"

"I don't know." She faked a gasp, and then smiled. "Could it possibly be that you're starting to believe in the transforming power of love?"

"Hardly."

"I didn't think so." The trickle of hope that had started inside her now ebbed. "Well, anyway, if you feel bad for him, you should feel bad for me, too."

"Why?"

"Because we're in the same boat." Oh, man. Was

166

she really going to do this?

He frowned. "You are?"

"Yep. We both care for someone and the feelings aren't mutual." Yeah, she was doing it.

His expression closed. "Who is it *you* care for?"

She lifted a brow. "A new friend of Wally's, Crystal's and Eula's. He has a little girl, and he's really into her. I can tell by the way he looks at her." She smiled. "Mr. Scott even called this morning and said he could stay as long as he liked, as far as he was concerned. What was it he called his new renter? Oh, yeah. 'That crazy city boy with the ready cash.'"

Laugh lines formed at the edges of Daniel's eyes. His chest rose and fell, before he reached out and touched the pulse point in the middle of her collarbone. It was a simple touch of his forefinger, but the smoldering heat in his gaze made the blood race through her, made her feel light on her feet.

"Why are you telling me this?"

"I don't know. Maybe because Eddie was trying to figure out our relationship and it forced me to think about it. He showed me a photo of you and the councilman's daughter, and I realized I believed you. I believed it was a setup." She reached up and pressed her hand over his, where he'd begun to massage her skin there at the base of her throat. "Anyway, why not tell you my true feelings? I'm really an honest person, even though I kept our daughter a secret from you."

"That secret was a biggie."

He looked up into her face, and the hunger she read in his eyes made her sway slightly in place. "Since you told me a secret, I'll share one with you." His voice, low and rich, stroked her ears. "It's the middle of the day and I want to take you to bed." His gaze drilled into hers. "But I'm not Joel. I'm not offering to bake you a wedding cake afterward and put little copies of us on top."

She laughed, a nervous sound that somehow made it past her suddenly dry throat. "No, I—I would never expect that."

He stared hard into her eyes. "The baker should have you. He loved you the first time he laid eyes on you. I wanted sex the first time I saw you."

"It's okay. I know it's not easy to have feelings for people. Like with Joel, if I could love him, I would. Everyone tells me I should. But I can't and I don't."

He kneaded her shoulder. "When you knew me back then, when we were together, there was still a gap in my life that I thought I might fill with someone. Since then, I took certain terms out of my dictionary. Like 'love' and 'caring.' They're gone."

"That's not true. You care about people. You're just not admitting it."

"Hey. I like you. I admit that. I'm nuts about Amy. And I like your friends. But 'love and forever' doesn't play on in my life like an expensive TV commercial. For me, love and forever are more like snapshots."

She held her chin up. "That's okay. I mean, I've told you long relationships don't work for me, either."

"But the difference is, *you* believe in happy endings. I know you do. I saw the look on your face when Cile told us Eula's story."

"But I said I don't believe in it for me."

"You want to, though."

Finally, in frustration, she said, "Do you see a contract in my hand?" She reached for his hand, and stepped backward toward the front door. "I'm going to my room. Are you coming with me?"

He may as well have been a block of steel, for all she could budge him. His gaze seemed to absorb her as he stared up at her. A muscle flickered in his jaw.

Then, slowly, he lifted himself from the swing.

She swallowed past the lump of longing in her throat as heat radiated off his body. Dropping his hand, she turned and went inside.

The sound of his footsteps behind her as she walked through the kitchen made every inch of her body shudder with anticipation and desire. She moved down the hall to her bedroom, with him following her. She knew what she was doing. She wanted Daniel. He wanted sex. He made it sound as if any chance they'd had for a real, lasting thing had ended in the past, while she recalled it as a light, no strings attached affair. Now they'd gotten to know each other better, for their child's sake. This could be dangerous. She must remember one thing: she'd been without him for five years. She could be without him again. This was just sex to satisfy the craving. She'd been alone for so long, and so had he. Therapeutic sex. That was all it was.

Darkness blanketed her bedroom. In her hurry to get to the hospital to see Eula, she hadn't opened the blinds this morning.

They stepped around Amy's toys on the carpet, and she sank down on the side of the bed.

Daniel came and stood beside her.

Looking up at him, she pulled her sweater over her head.

His gaze followed her actions. When he looked into her eyes again, he said, "Are you sure about this?"

She couldn't speak, but nodded.

He sat beside her, and after she tossed the sweater on an old trunk, he reached out and touched her shoulder. With his rough fingers pressing against her bare skin, he pulled her close for a lingering kiss.

Her eyes half closed as he lay across the bed, pulling her down with him. His movements as he scooted them around to rest their heads on the pillows released the delicious spice of his aftershave, of his unique, warm scent.

Up on one elbow facing her, with his free hand, he slowly combed his fingers through her hair. Her scalp tingled at his touch.

"You're beautiful," he murmured.

When he withdrew his fingers slightly to caress her cheek, she turned her mouth into his hand and kissed his warm, rough palm. "So are you."

She closed her eyes as he brushed his lips against hers. And then he was gone. She opened her eyes, to find him staring at her. "Are you sure you know what you're doing?"

"It's been a while, but I think I remember. And I think you should kiss me better than that. Kiss me like you did in the cave."

His gaze darkened. This time when he leaned in to her, he put his hand behind her back and pulled her up close to him, holding her there, immobile, as his mouth pressed against hers. He parted her lips and plunged his tongue inside, probing.

She moaned and pressed closer, seeking to brush her breasts against his chest and press her hips into the hard ridge of his erection beneath his jeans zipper. Lust pulsed through her as his tongue danced with hers. But as he continued kissing her, he pulled his body a few inches away from hers.

She moaned in protest over the space between them. But when his hand covered her over the lacy cup of her bra, her complaint turned to a groan of satisfaction. She barely knew when he lowered the flimsy straps off her shoulder. He pushed the fabric aside and cupped both breasts. Biting her lower lip, she basked in the exquisite sensation.

His fingers played at her nipples until she wanted to ask him for more, until her crotch was so hot, she needed release. She kissed him back fiercely, desperate to destroy his patience the way he'd overcome hers, so that she could find release with him.

He broke the kiss and stared at her, panting. "My god, Gretchen," he said, before lifting up enough to unbutton his shirt and toss it to the floor.

She reached back, unhooked her bra and threw it in the direction his clothing had gone.

He leaned in, pressing her against the pillow again with his kiss. His tongue played and taunted, before he pulled his mouth from hers and trailed kisses down her neck. He licked and sucked gently against her collarbone, until she squirmed impatiently on the bedcovers. His thumbs flicked over her nipples again, making her wet her lips with anticipation. Suddenly his mouth replaced his hand at one breast. He lapped and tongued, and then there was only his breath making her nipple so hard. Her blood surged with need, deeper than she had ever experienced.

She became aware of his erection again, pushing against her leg. She'd been so focused on her bursting desire that she'd forgotten him. Now she remembered how to get what she wanted.

She wriggled, so that he released her breast and looked up at her, his eyes glassy. Leaning toward him, she kissed him again. He tasted of her body, and him, and it was a heady mix. While they kissed, she reached for his jeans, jerked them open at the button and yanked the zipper down.

As she released him from the opening in his boxers, he groaned deep in his throat.

She cupped her hand around him and stroked him up and down. He was so hard, so ready.

She pulled away from him.

He drew back, panting, and she could almost feel the smoldering heat of his gaze as she tugged off first her jeans, and then her panties. When she glanced at him, she caught the appreciative gleam in his eyes.

His chest, lightly covered with soft brown hair, expanded as he drew in a breath. In one swift move, he hopped off the bed and peeled his pants down, followed by his shorts. Kicking them aside, he climbed back onto the bed.

His body was beautiful, hard, muscular.

As he bent and placed a kiss on her belly, he murmured against her skin, "How'd we wait this long?"

Through the haze of desire, she briefly wondered if he meant during this visit, or if he was wondering why it'd been five years. In the next instant, all she could think of was what his hand was doing, and how his fingers felt between her legs. She gripped the covers as he entered her wetness, and bit her lip, longing for all of him inside her.

"Damn," he whispered in her ear. "Hold on."

He leaned over the edge of the bed, rummaged around in his pants, and returned with a condom packet in his hand.

She took it, and he rolled onto his back.

When she had it in place, he groaned and threw his arm over his eyes.

"Are you okay?" Her voice wobbled with desire.

"Hell, no!" he ground out. "I can't do this."

"I think you *can*. I don't think there's any doubt."

His hand shot down and grabbed her wrist to stop her massaging.

"We can't do this." He pulled her toward him until he held her in his arms. Pressing her cheek against his pounding heart, he said, "Though God knows I want to."

"Me, too."

He sighed and rubbed up and down her back with his palm. "This is a first." He laughed, a low, guttural sound. "I've never said no to a willing woman."

Hurt shot through her. "Then why now?"

"I just don't want you to read this the wrong way."

Oh. Well, if that was all that was bothering him, they could carry on. "I know what it means." She pressed her hand against his hardness. "Lust."

He turned his head and looked at her. "You're driving me mad and I'm having a hell of a time convincing you not to."

Her eyes held his. "Then go mad."

With a growl, he rolled over onto her and spread her legs with his knees. He pressed against her, and she reached down and guided him inside.

They moved together slowly, with Daniel's breath at her neck, and her hands on his buttocks. A rush of delight spread between her legs, and he moved in her with more urgency.

She relaxed into their rhythm as her body grew hotter and hotter. Digging at Daniel's shoulders with her nails and pressing her face into his neck, she let go and her body contracted around him again and again.

He held her face between his hands, and kissed her, and murmured her name, softly, roughly. He was still inside her when she returned to Earth and became aware of his rocking. After a few moments, he thrust harder, and his body convulsed.

He stayed very still atop her a while, breathing hard. Then he bent and kissed her nose, and rolled off of her. He didn't release her, but pulled her along with him until she rested beside him.

They lay that way for a while, steadying their breathing.

She could lie there with him forever, safe and sated. Just for now, she had Daniel again.

Daniel stared up at the ceiling. They'd made

love again. He'd tried to stop himself. He'd told himself as soon as Joel admitted his love for Gretchen that he should be a gentleman and get the hell out of Dodge. He liked her too much. He honored her commitment to Amy, and the way she didn't want guys waltzing in and out of their lives. He was a waltzer now, the way people had always been with him. The way Gretchen had been with him.

He wasn't ready to be thrown back out of her life yet, but he knew he would be, because he couldn't measure up to Prince Charming for her. Yet what had he done instead of leaving? He'd wandered onto her porch and sat there waiting for her, like a wolf. Like the worst type of guy, the ones he did not want Amy to ever meet. From Gretchen's first step toward the porch, he'd wanted to taste her, to feel her, to explore the hollows and hills of her body.

He turned and looked at her. Her head was tilted back a little and she watched him with eyes still heavy-lidded from her release. He could see the rosy flush of passion across the top of her breasts, and the fullness that lingered on her lips where he'd kissed her.

"That was amazing," he murmured.

Her sultry blue gaze held his. "Yes, it was."

He swallowed hard. Damn. They were in bed together again. Maybe it was fate. Whatever the reason, he had to deal with this gnawing guilt now. Why? They'd used birth control. There wouldn't be a child this time. They'd both wanted sex and were clear on what it meant. Then why did he have this feeling that he should stay and cuddle and protect her?

He looked at her again. And he knew. It wasn't just the guilt. It wasn't just that he *should* hold her or that he *should* stay. He wanted to do those things. Suddenly he felt as if he was trying to hold on to a rope and climb up, but someone had greased the thing and he kept sliding down. Confused, he said gruffly, "This doesn't change things."

She looked down, and he noticed the curve of her lashes and wanted to touch them, too, and feel their softness. She looked up again, "I know," she said in a quiet tone.

He thrust himself out of bed and reached for his jeans. He couldn't look at her anymore. Didn't she know how she tore his insides out? She was beautiful, vulnerable. She could almost make him believe she would love him forever.

"Will you be around for dinner?" she asked, in a small voice. "Amy wants macaroni and cheese again, and I—I thought I'd try to make some from scratch this time."

He glanced at her while he buttoned his shirt. "Sorry, I can't. I'm taking Wally into Cincinnati."

"Okay."

He didn't even know if Wally could go, since he'd just come up with the plan. But any plan would do. He had to get out of here and go somewhere, anywhere, to try and get Gretchen out of his blood. There. He'd begun the downward shift, the drive toward separating himself from these damned feelings she'd started. And yet, the disappointment in her "Okay" dug at him like a knife.

After snatching his keys off the floor where they'd flown from his jeans when he tossed them, he breezed out of the room.

As soon as he'd escaped the house, he grabbed the porch support and gulped in chilly air.

Cold bastard. That's what you are. Are you happy? What was the point of making love with her? To prove you could walk away afterward? To hurt her, because you want her and you know she won't keep you?

He thought of Joel's threat that he'd hurt him if he hurt Gretchen. He pushed back from the porch post, and then slammed his palm against it, before taking the steps on a run. Let Joel have her. Let her figure out the baker was the right man. They had a much better chance at forever, since they'd already been in this cloying town together their whole lives.

It was sex, he told himself as he floored it down the road.

Forget it. Forget her.

But how could he, when even as he considered it, he turned his face into his shoulder to inhale deeply of her soft scent on his clothing?

****

Gretchen turned her face into her pillow and let it absorb a tear that trickled down. Daniel couldn't get out of there fast enough. And now, with her body still swollen and tingly from their lovemaking, her heart felt bruised and sore.

What had he done to her? He'd raised her body to amazing heights before sending her crashing to the ground. How could she be so receptive to him? How could it mean so much to her and just be sex to him?

Because you're a woman, and a stupid one at that!

He'd offered her multiple chances to get out of it, every step of the way. And she'd thrown herself at him. Remembering how she'd practically begged him for sex made heat rise in her face. She hadn't felt this dumb since she'd come back here with Amy.

She tried to make herself think of it as just sex in the afternoon. But there was that empty feeling inside one minute, and in the next, such a longing that she thought she might be ill. She knew that feeling. It'd been her downfall before. It was love. This time, though, it seemed to knock her down with its power. Had she felt it this strongly before, even with Daniel?

What could she do about it? He'd be leaving in a

matter of days. She didn't want him to. So she'd done the one thing she thought might keep him there. That *was* why she'd done it. To try and keep him.

It hadn't worked. It'd only served to prove what he'd made her see about herself the first time around with him—that she was the type who threw herself at men and never had one stick around.

And even now, as she scooted over in the bed and rested her head on the pillow where he'd rested his, she wanted him so much it hurt.

Chapter Eleven

Daniel stalked back and forth in the foyer of Marydale Casket Company's administrative offices, checking his watch every few minutes.

On his fourth sweep past her desk, Wally's receptionist glanced up. "He really should be finished soon." Fluttering papers, she sent him a wary look before returning to her work.

He drew up short near Wally's office door, and listened to the low drone of his friend's voice. Wally would probably yammer on forever, and he needed him now.

He had to get out of here, away from all that reminded him of Gretchen. He kept trying not to think of her. But how, when everything about her seemed stamped on his brain? He knew her now, from the delicate curve of her chin to the precise turn of her bottom. His fingers tingled from touching her in both places and everywhere in between. His mouth longed to taste those sweet lips, to savor the unique flavor of her skin. What had she said to him on the porch? What words had seemed to caress him then? Hell if he remembered, he'd been so consumed with need for her at the time. Still, it was something about want, and need, spoken softly and meant only for his ears.

Or so he hoped, like the damned fool he was.

Heaving a sigh of exasperation, he tuned in to Wally's phone conversation.

"So you'll go with the high grade satin lining, in champagne. Five from our Sherbourne Collection."

He leaned in and saw Wally jot something on a slip of paper. "Got it. We can get them into production on—" He reached for his calendar, glanced in Daniel's direction and froze. His red brows shot up. "Merle, there's something I need to attend to right away. Call you later and firm this up? Right-o."

Tossing the portable phone on a pile of papers, he stared at Daniel. "What the hell happened to *you*?"

"What do you mean?"

"You look like you lost your last friend."

"I'm fine." Daniel shifted his weight from foot to foot.

"Listen, I need a favor."

"What is it?"

"I need to go into the city tonight."

"To Cincy?" Wally eyed him. "What for?"

He tapped distractedly at the doorframe. "I feel like a trapped rat."

"Hm. I would too, with a photographer trailing me from town to town."

"It's not that. It's this place." He glanced around Wally's cluttered office, and out the window, before returning to him. "This town's getting to me."

Wally tightened his thin lips and seemed to contemplate Daniel a moment, before shoving his chair back from the desk. "What're we waiting for, then? Let's go." He snapped his fingers. "I know what we're waiting for." A car engine roared to a stop outside, and he craned his neck toward the window. "That looks like him right now."

Seconds later, Daniel pivoted at the sound of the front door opening. "*Sam?*"

Wally came to stand beside Daniel in the doorway. "He stopped by a little while ago, looking for you."

Sam motored down the hall with such haste that the flaps of his suit jacket billowed, and his red-print tie swayed like a ticking pendulum. Coming to an abrupt halt a few paces from Daniel, he set his hands on his hips and eyeballed him. "What happened? You look like hell."

"I'm beginning to get that impression," Daniel deadpanned.

Offering Sam a handshake, Wally said, "I think he had a fight with Gretchen."

"I didn't fight with her." If only it'd been that easy. Then maybe he wouldn't feel this way.

Sam clapped him on the shoulder. His serious gaze drilled into Daniel's. "I don't know what the woman is holding over you here, but I've come to your rescue. We're booked on the first flight out in the morning. I've scheduled meetings with Toyco's lead brass for tomorrow at four. With you there, we stand a chance at salvaging the account." He glanced at Wally. "This account is huge, international. It'll make Daniel a key player in advertising."

Why do you have to be so intense all the time? Daniel wanted to chastise. But then another idea struck him, and made him feel light and happy again as his gaze drifted back to Sam. Now that his brother was here, he could see Amy. He could meet his niece. They could leave now, go by her school and—

No, better not. Best to go to Cincinnati, party Gretchen and Amy out of his system, and then be ready to return to his old lifestyle.

Sam dropped his hand off Daniel's shoulder. "I'm not getting through to you, am I? Well, I've covered for you so far. The minute that rag paper ran the photo of you and the councilman's daughter, I contacted Toyco's reps and explained it was a setup, an invasion of privacy that we were pursuing with litigation. Then I convinced them we're the ones to go with. Their other choice, Chroma, is old-guard and safer, but I told them not as likely to score big with the younger parents of the world, while Nicholson Agency is young and edgy. I deflected the attention off you and your 'edgy' nightlife of late."

"That's what I hired you for, Sammy. You're great at running interference for me."

Sam held his gaze. "But you have to get back there and get some face time with these guys. I may have convinced them for now, but if Chroma commissioned that photo from Eddie Artis in the first place—and I'm convinced they did—you can bet they're still waving it under the leading Toyco officers' noses."

The weight of Daniel's job slipped onto his shoulders again, and sank straight into his bones. Sam was right. He should go and defend himself. And he would. But right now, at this moment, it just wasn't his overriding concern.

He glanced at Wally, an unspoken SOS.

"I'm ready when you are, boss." Wally turned to Sam. "We're headed to Cincinnati. You tagging along?"

"Good idea! We'll go straight to the airport and see if—"

Wally shook his head. "Daniel is covering PR for me for the festival this weekend. He's helping pull people in to check out my casket factory."

Sam's ears reddened. "Daniel is *not* some carnival hawker. He owns a multi-million-dollar agency. He doesn't have time for this nonsense."

"That's enough, Sam," Daniel shot out. "I *am* helping my friend, here, on my own time and out of my own pocket. But at the moment the roles are reversed and he's gonna help me find some TLC by way of a pitcher of B-U-D. And women. Lots of women."

Wally smiled smugly. "Told ya he and Gretchen had a fight."

Sam threw Wally a withering look before turning back to Daniel. "At least two women are anxiously awaiting your return. One even sent flowers to the office. Twice." He glared at Daniel. "You can't make it to Chicago without a fix?"

He shook his head. "Can't wait that long."

Sam's eyes glazed over, but he said, "Let's go, then. Sooner you get this out of your system, the sooner I can get you home."

As Daniel herded them to his car, he heard Wally say to Sam, "Loosen your tie a little, Big Bro. Let some oxygen get to that uptight head."

Forty-five minutes later, Daniel drove across the interstate bridge over the Ohio River and entered downtown Cincinnati. Twenty minutes after that, they stood drinking beer at the bar in a slick city establishment. Women made eye contact with Daniel, then wound their way through the crowd to meet him. Soon he'd attracted four female friends who studied his eyes when he spoke, tossing their long, shiny hair over their shoulders, and leaned in to him. When one particular blonde injected herself into the group, the other women slanted looks at her and took a few steps back, as if in deference to her exotic perfume, wide green eyes and beauty queen smile. As she slipped in sideways to order a drink, her rounded breasts, tightly bound up in a black number with straps as thin as tinsel, brushed Wally's chest. The flesh above the casket salesman's collar and all the way up to his scalp turned red. Sam and Daniel exchanged amused looks. But once the blonde had her martini in hand, she turned on the charm for Daniel. By the time she'd finished her drink, she'd whispered into his ear that her car was parked outside. They could be at her Mt. Adams apartment in ten minutes—if they wanted to wait that long.

Daniel smiled back at her. She was exactly what

he needed. Couldn't be less like fresh-faced Gretchen, with her gentle scent, drown-in-my-ocean blue eyes and genuine smile.

Swigging the last of his beer, he tossed his keys to Wally. "If I don't return, go on home without me. I'll take a taxi back to town." He didn't bother to look Sam's way. He knew "irresponsible" would be written all over his brother's face.

Wally didn't exactly give him a thumbs up, either, and as he started to walk away, he heard Sam's smug, "*That's* the Daniel I know."

While they weaved their way through the crowd, Daniel's new friend clung to his arm as if she were afraid he'd suddenly try to slip away. Her long nails dug like claws. Her smile seemed to suck him into this swirling vortex that made his head throb.

He frowned. But when she tipped her head back to look up at him, he recovered with a quick grin.

They cleared the doorway and stepped out into the cool night air. "Where's your car, sweetheart?"

"I love it when you call me that!" she purred, squeezing up against him and flashing the creamy curves of her breasts.

He looked down into her chardonnay-sleepy eyes. "The car?"

She pointed at a white four-door Jag in the parking lot across the street.

His face must have registered surprise, because she gurgled with laughter. "Got it in the divorce. Sorry bastard was cheating on me. Lucky for me, I had proof."

Christ. Didn't anybody stay together anymore?

They walked to the car, but she stopped when he started to open the front passenger door. Flinging her arms around his neck, she pulled him close and pressed her hip into his groin. "Let's just get in the back seat, hottie."

He held her loosely with his arms around her

waist and considered the offer. She was a pretty little tease, in a thin dress that left just enough to the imagination to be intriguing. And best of all, she seemed to be a good-time girl. She knew the bartender, and hung with a group of partiers. Yes, she was exactly the type of woman he was used to being around.

And there were no photographers here. Part of him wished there were, and Gretchen would see a picture of this and hate him. The other part of him kept an eye peeled for Eddie Artis and prepared to duck and run for cover out of guilt.

"What's wrong?" She gazed up into his face. Her lips looked full and kissable. "Don't you like me?"

"Sure." He dropped his hands away. "Maybe we should go back to the club."

"What'd I say?" She pressed her cheek against his chest.

He reached up, pried her hands off his nape, and took a step back. "You've had a lot to drink. Give me your keys and I'll drive you home."

Her smile spreading, she pushed the set of keys deep down in her dress's halter top.

Gritting his teeth, he ventured in just enough to pluck them out with his middle finger and forefinger.

"Aww, no fun!" she pouted.

With his palm on her back, he turned her around and guided her into the passenger seat of the Jag before sliding in behind the steering wheel. She gave him her address, and soon they were climbing the city's surrounding hills to the old, treed overlook known as Mt. Adams. He knew the area, with its tall, narrow apartments and retail establishments built in a time when most people lived close to town. He'd often partied in its string of bars on business trips.

The blonde rested her head lightly against his

shoulder, but it felt like a lead weight.

He hadn't even asked her name.

She tilted her head back, gave him another tempting smile, and at a stop sign, he relented and kissed her. She pressed herself to him, and her hand found his crotch, where she massaged him into awareness. But her hand wasn't Gretchen's hand. Her mouth wasn't Gretchen's sweet warmth.

Behind them, a car honked.

He pulled his mouth from hers, lifted her hand and set it on his leg. "Wait."

"More to come, then." She chuckled wickedly as he drove on.

When he stopped the car in front of her loft apartment building, he exited and helped her step up onto the curb. She leaned against him to the foyer entrance and showed him which key unlocked the door. He opened it for her, and she went inside. Then she spun on a spiked heel and flashed him a smile. "Well? Come on."

He stood there, thinking she was too thin, too rich and too young. "It was nice meeting you. I should go now."

"What? You can't go. This doesn't happen to me. I never get refused."

He turned back to the doorway.

"Hey! Don't go away!" Her words, shrilled by alcohol, lifted in the air. "I want you to stay."

Pivoting, he saw the guy at the security desk staring, brow raised.

Daniel reached out and gently grasped the girl's forearms. "I appreciate the offer, beautiful. But I'm tired. Another time, maybe."

"You were ready in the car," she whispered in his ear. She threw her arms around his neck. "I can wake you up."

He stared into her cat-shaped eyes. They were attractive. Gretchen's were wicked-sexy. He clenched his jaw. "Do you want me to see you to your room?"

She nodded, and swayed to the right. "Elevator's this way."

He guided her there with a hand against the bare skin of her back. Yeah, it was definitely a sexy dress.

When the elevator stopped on her floor, he stepped out with her. He still had her keys. He stuck them in her door, held it open for her.

She started in, then whirled and grabbed fistfuls of his shirt, and pressed her mouth against his.

He would do this. He could do this.

He pressed her lips with his, and she eagerly opened her mouth. He plunged his tongue inside, stirring her up, starting him up. Yeah. He could do it. Lose himself. Exorcise Gretchen from his blood.

His pickup date moaned around the kiss, and tugged on him, pulling him into her room.

He stepped back from her.

When she opened her eyes, her mouth tightened. "What is it with you? Don't you like women?"

"Yeah, I do." He swallowed, and raked a hand through his hair. "I—I don't know what's wrong."

"Well, when you figure it out, you know where I live." She shoved him backward and slammed the door.

Cursing, Daniel stalked into the elevator.

He hit the "Lobby" button with his fist, and when the door opened, entered and slammed his shoulder up against the side of the cage. Caged. That was it. He was caged in Marydale, trapped in Gretchen's domain.

He'd escaped tonight and it'd done no good. What was happening to him?

Once he was out of the building, he walked for a while, trying to clear his head. Then he flagged a cab and returned to the bar where he'd left Sam and Wally. On his way to them, he stopped by the table of girls the blonde had been partying with before joining their group. They seemed surprised to see him back, and when he told her friends that he'd just seen her safely home, one of them whispered a suggestive offer that involved the restroom. He politely declined.

He went to find Wally and located him in the adjoining room, playing himself in a game of pool.

Wally looked up as he approached. "Man, you scored faster than I could blink."

"I saw her home. That's all."

"Sure. Uh huh." Wally smirked. "All I can say is, I'm glad I knew you. When Gretchen hears about it—"

"There's nothing to tell. Nothing happened."

Wally tilted his head and studied him. "You want me to believe you took the hottest woman in here back to her place and just tucked her in for the night with a kiss on her forehead?"

Daniel ignored him, and rubbed his palm over his weary eyes. "Where's Sam?"

Wally pointed his cue stick toward the corner of the room.

He found Sam sitting alone at a table, his gaze cast upward. He had a beer bottle in front of him. But knowing Sam, it was either the same one from earlier, or his second and therefore his last.

He glanced back over his shoulder to see what he was so wrapped up in, and noticed a basketball game on a wall-mounted TV.

"Come on, party animal," he said, walking up to the table. "Time to call it a night."

"I was about to give up on you," Sam groused, but rose and followed him.

When they reached Wally, Daniel said, "Let's go home."

Let's go home. An odd sense of security dropped over him. For the first time that night, he was eager for something—eager to get out of the city and away from the club, the noise and the dating foreplay.

After they got onto the interstate, Wally glanced at Daniel, who was driving again. "I'd have paid you to teach me the ropes with women before I realized Crystal was the one for me. If only you'd come to town sooner. Now I've seen you in action, man, it's powerful!"

"Cut it out, Wally."

They listened to Sam snoring in the back seat. Poor Sam. He wasn't used to nights out. A beer or two had done him in.

"You aren't fooling me," Wally suddenly boomed, causing an abrupt stall in Sam's rhythmic breathing. "This night is proof you didn't drop that big account just to come visit your 'friend' Gretchen, like you told me."

"Why are you so interested in Gretchen and me?" Daniel demanded. Again the weird, threatening tone. He couldn't seem to keep it out of his voice tonight.

Wally was silent for a few seconds. Then he chuckled. "You've got it bad, pal."

****

Gretchen woke Amy and dressed her for school. The minute she had her fuchsia T-shirt on with her jeans and new pink clogs, she wanted to go next door and see if Daniel was up. But Gretchen told her not to, so she pouted as they walked down the driveway to the school bus stop.

They saw him standing at his SUV. Gretchen's breath caught in her throat as if it were a frigid January day instead of the unseasonably warm October one they were enjoying. Daniel looked a little rough this morning. He hadn't shaved, and lines of weariness showed about his eyes. His clothes were slightly rumpled. All those things just made him look sexier. He'd been to the diner, because he held one of their Styrofoam coffee cups in one hand, and her *Tribune* in the other. When he saw them walking up, he smiled and waved.

Amy ran to him. "Daniel!"

"Amy!" he yelled back, grinning. "What's up?" He caught Gretchen's eye. "My brother's in town. A personal escort back to Chicago to cinch that big deal I told you about. It's the final hour for negotiations."

Gretchen's chest felt like the house had just fallen on it. How, how could she have let him crush her like this so quickly? He hadn't. She'd done it to herself. From the minute he'd shown up, he'd planned on leaving again. She was the one who'd naïvely hoped he'd stay.

"But you just moved in." Amy's mouth turned down, and her eyes took on an ominous shine.

Gretchen bent to her and brushed a few curls out of her eyes. "I told you Daniel wasn't going to stay long. Remember?"

"I want Daniel to stay here now."

"People will come and go in our lives, sweetie." Gretchen sent Daniel a look of frustration. "It can't always be the way we want."

"Hey, Amy," he said quickly, "did you know I promised I'd stay until after the festival?"

She shook her head.

"When I'm there, I'll need some help passing out fliers, and I'm willing to pay whoever volunteers." He ducked his chin, in that boyish way that always gave Gretchen gooseflesh. "Do you think you're big enough to do it?"

She stretched up on her toes, and Gretchen bit her lip to keep from smiling. "I'm almost five!"

"Hm," Daniel said, frowning. Then he broke into a smile. "Okay, then. You're hired. High-five on it?" He raised his hand.

With a vivacious grin, she threw her hand back and whacked him one hard.

He laughed low. "That's some swing you've got on you. Maybe you'll play softball when you grow up."

Off in the distance a motor grew louder. Gretchen turned to check the road. "Here comes the bus."

Daniel reached down and lifted Amy up in his arms. She laughed, and clung to his shoulders as he strode toward the road. Gretchen followed, a lump in her throat at the sight of them, and at the thought of their final parting.

When the bus pulled up, Daniel said, "I'll just toss you on there. Ready?"

The bus doors swung open.

With devilment in his eyes, Daniel playfully swung Amy out toward the steps, and she giggled and squealed with delight.

Chuckling, he pulled her back to him and held her.

While the bus driver and Gretchen looked on, smiling, Amy took Daniel's face between her hands and kissed his nose.

He stood there, holding her tightly and staring at her pink cheeks and bright eyes.

"Put me down!"

He set her gently on her feet, and she flounced away and climbed into the bus.

The doors closed and off they went.

Daniel watched them go down the road. After a moment, he turned around, and the look on his face told Gretchen everything.

Daniel Nicholson was a man in love.

It was what she'd hoped for, dreamed about, and wished for on the candles of each of her daughter's five birthdays and her own past five birthdays.

For Amy to have a father.

And now it had come true. Not only did she have *a* father, she had her real father's love.

Hugging her sides, she turned away from Daniel. She knew she should be happy. But he'd reminded her that he wasn't staying. Whether he loved Amy or not, how could he really be part of their lives once the festival ended? She put her hand over her breastbone, where she felt the pain, and pressed.

"Gretchen."

She turned.

His eyes, his mouth, showed lines of stress at their edges again. "What's wrong?"

She shook her head.

He didn't come to her, the way he usually did. He was a touchy-feely guy, and she loved that about him. Now he kept his distance. Since they'd made love, he'd stayed away, making her keenly aware that she'd been the pursuer and he'd only acted on instinct. He was making sure it didn't happen again.

"It's just that Amy's so smitten with you. She likes you and you're leaving after this weekend. It'll hurt, seeing her sad."

"I know." He walked to her, and stood there a moment, looking down at the ground. Then he reached out and, after hesitating a few seconds, took her cold fingers into the comfort of his warm grip. Looking into her eyes, he said, "I thought we understood this was how things would go."

She nodded. "But I don't have to like it."

Lifting his other hand, he brushed a stray strand of hair back from her eyes. "I don't like it, either. As far as Amy's concerned, I'm jealous of you."

"Me? Why?"

"You've gotten to be here for the whole home movie."

"Hey, I *have* some videos." She leaned in to him, and inhaled his scent. Wishing she could memorize it. "We can watch them. And we haven't even gotten

191

into her four baby albums." She smiled. "If you have time before you have to go—" Again the weight threatening to suffocate her, flattening her smile. "Maybe I could put together a set of photos for you."

"I don't want them. When I want to see Amy, I want to see *Amy*."

No, Daniel wouldn't want one-dimensional statements of what Amy was like. He wanted to feel her, to hear her, to see her.

She knew the feeling. She wanted him now, the real thing, instead of black-and-white pixel images from the newspaper.

He cupped her neck with his palm, and bent his head and pressed a kiss to her lips. "Ah, Gretchen," he murmured, "You're so good to Amy. You've been good for me, too." He kissed her again.

She didn't mind that this gentler mood had come out of the blue. Savoring his kisses, she whispered back, "Then stay. Stay with us. Tell her at the festival that you're her father and you're not leaving."

He growled low in his throat as he trailed his mouth to her neck, and pressed a kiss below her ear, on her collarbone. "What would you give me to stay?" he said playfully.

"Anything." She sighed. "Everything."

"But for how long?" He lifted his face away from hers, out from the veil of her hair, to search her gaze. "Forever?"

Her nipples throbbed. Her lower region vibrated. "Yes, forever," she breathed.

His gaze dulled. He stopped caressing her arms, and slowly, she came back to reality and saw the dark shadow in his eyes.

"What? What did I say?"

"You said 'forever.'"

"Oh." She went cold inside, seeing the dead look on his face. "I'm sorry. It just came out."

He dropped his hands from her arms, and stared across the road. "I knew yesterday was a bad idea."

"Don't say that. Please."

He looked back at her. "You're right. It happened. We got together before, so it's not surprising it happened again."

"You make it sound so, typical," she said, with a humorless smile.

"You know I don't believe in attachments."

"I know. It just 'happens' with other women, too."

His jaw tightened.

She wanted to take the words back. But she'd dwelled on these thoughts half the night, tossing and turning as she pictured him with other women, kissing them and touching them the way he had her. She'd driven herself nearly insane with those scenes in her mind. And it hurt. Oh, how it hurt.

"Gretchen. We had a rule. The rule was 'no strings.' You said you didn't have a problem with it." He heaved out a harsh breath. "I thought, in light of your past, you were cool with it."

"I thought so, too." She swallowed, and tried to breathe over the pressure in her chest. "I was wrong."

"Well, I'm not. I want no repeats of my past."

Somehow, she found some remaining dignity and lifted her chin. "Then why did you ask me about forever? You're the one who wanted me to say it. Why?"

He shifted, hands on his hips, looking at the ground.

"Daniel?"

His head came up, and his gaze met hers. "I have a ticket home for Sunday, after the festival. Until then, I'd like to see you and Amy." His expression was hooded. "But let's keep things, light."

Her heart sank. So there it was, a definite end

date for them.

She'd known it would come, yet she'd pushed for something that frightened her so much, for so long. But apparently a lasting relationship no longer scared her as much as the thought of his leaving.

If she had to agree to chastity around him, her body would burn and have no relief. But she would have him, for three more days.

"Okay."

He smiled slowly, his mouth curving. "One kiss. To seal the deal."

One kiss. The devil on her shoulder whispered, "He hurt you. Now's your chance to make him burn, too."

"One chaste kiss," she promised sweetly. "Over there. Behind the apple tree."

She went around the tree to the side that faced the house, so they had privacy from the road. He came to her, and pulled her into his arms. He pressed his mouth to hers, and she pushed her body against him. He became hard almost immediately.

Good. *Suffer, Daniel.*

She moved her hips, and his erection shifted.

He groaned, and parted her teeth to grind his tongue into her willing mouth.

She tilted her head to allow him complete access, and thrust her tongue into his mouth, to play with him. To rouse him to the point where she was, that hot, sexual pivotal point.

With his hand, he molded her sweater to her breast, pushing its rough wool back and forth over her sensitive nipple. Damn. She'd thrown the sweater on without her bra to go to the bus stop. This was heavenly torture.

She'd had some game in mind. What was it? Fog had slipped into her brain, this incredible blindness that intensified her sense of smell, so that her nostrils filled with Daniel's warm, soapy scent.

Daniel pressed her against the tree, his strong, hard body pinning her there, but the rough bark only heightened her pleasure.

She reached between them and cupped her palm over his crotch, and as he groaned and pushed himself against her fingers, she had no idea what it was she'd started out to do to him.

Sex. All she wanted right now was him inside her. To stop this pounding, throbbing swirl of—

Wait a minute. Air. Nothing but air there.

He'd stepped away.

Slowly, she came back to awareness of the world, and opened her eyes to see him standing back a step, gaping at her with the strangest expression.

"I—I'm sorry." He stared at her mouth. "I don't know what got into me. I've never—"

"It's okay." Struggling against the dizzying thrill distorting her vision and her thinking, she managed, "It's me. I was trying to get back at you."

He just kept looking at her. Frowning. Finally, he murmured, "Yeah. It's you, all right. Definitely you." Holding out his hand, he pulled her off the tree so she stood in front of him. "Come on. Let's go in the house and try to act civilized."

He walked so fast toward the house, she stumbled to keep up with him. But he wouldn't let go of her hand.

Behind his back, she smiled. *Nice work, Devil.*

Chapter Twelve

Inside the house, Daniel wandered over and stood by the kitchen table. Gretchen grabbed the sponge at the sink and began diligently wiping the counter, trying not to appear knocked off her feet by his continued presence. That danged seductive move had sure backfired in her face.

Out of her peripheral vision, she watched him rap his knuckles on the table a few times, shift his feet, and stare at her.

What he was thinking? Was he bored with her? Frustrated, like she was? Sad at all, because he'd be leaving?

He flicked the cereal box around and examined the puzzle game on back for all of two seconds. Catching Gretchen's sideways glance, he growled, "Tell me again why you kissed me like that?"

Good. Verbal proof that he was frustrated, too. That or angry. "It was stupid. Forget it."

"I wouldn't call it stupid." Picking up Amy's bowl and spoon, he carried them over to the sink. When he turned to Gretchen, his gaze searched hers. Raw emotion seemed to flash there for an instant, before he closed his expression. "I should be going."

Clunk. Clunk.

They glanced toward the hallway where Scooby sprawled and was gnawing the huge bone she'd given him earlier. It banged against the floor as he repositioned it between his paws.

Daniel caught her gaze. His eyes twinkled.

She chuckled, silently thanking the dog for the

comic relief.

Daniel's pupils darkened. "I want to stay here today." His husky tone reminded her of their kiss. "Stay with you."

Her heart beat like a warning drum as she stared at his mouth, desire for him bubbling to the surface again. "I—I have to get to the shop."

"I know. I know your schedule now."

A nervous laugh escaped her. "You should. It doesn't change much from day to day." Yesterday's sex in the afternoon being the obvious exception. Remembering it left her a little breathless as she said, "By the way, how was Cincinnati?"

His gaze drifted downward, to linger on her mouth again. "Boring."

"Really?"

"Really." He touched her arm, and smoothed his fingers down from her shoulder to her wrist. He slid it back up again, stirring the warm embers of sexual energy inside her. "I've got to get to Wally's to wrap up his marketing plans. And you've got to get to the shop." He squeezed her shoulder, and regret seemed to shimmer in his gaze before he released her. Turning to the steps, he said, "Meet you and Amy at the park when school's out?"

"Okay." She remembered something. "Oh, I can't!"

He turned back to her, a question in his eyes.

"I told Cile I'd help her take in peoples' baked goods for the sale table at the festival. It's usually Eula's job, but since she's not well, a bunch of us volunteered to pull it together."

His mouth tightened, and he looked down.

"Why don't you join us there for dinner?" she said, sensing he felt left out. "We're doing a barbeque on the property, our kickoff party for the locals. It starts at six-thirty."

"I'll be there." He flashed her a grin, and left.

Gretchen sat at the table a while after he'd gone, thinking about that grin. Watching him smile was like watching Amy smile, and brought her that same sense that things were right with the world.

It was weird how at first she couldn't believe he'd come to Marydale and found them. Now she couldn't believe he'd be leaving in a few days. She wasn't sure how things had changed so quickly. But when she and Daniel were together, things always happened fast.

She wished she could throw away the clocks and calendars, close down the airport and hide all other forms of transportation.

Maybe then, Daniel would stay.

****

"Think the banner and fliers'll be enough of a lure?" Wally asked Sam. "Whadda ya think people will say about the caves museum? Will they like my collection of antique coffins and urns? And how about my replica of the catacombs? Think it looked real?"

Sam glanced over his shoulder at the casket warehouse they'd just exited, and croaked, "Not sure I'm the one to ask at the moment. My breakfast isn't sitting too well."

Wally clapped him on the back. "Not scared of death, are ya?"

"Uh...no?"

"Come on, now. It's part of the circle of life. Anyway, you'll get over it. You'll live."

"Coming from you that means a lot," Sam cracked, and turned and stalked to Wally's car. He climbed into the passenger seat, and as Wally opened the driver's door, said, "Make it snappy. I have to talk to my brother. I need to find out what happened to him in Cincinnati last night. That was not the Daniel I know."

"*I* know what happened." Wally pulled a pair of

aviator sunglasses out from under the window visor and shoved them into place on his nose. "And it happened before last night."

"Fill me in, then," Sam said as they headed away from the warehouse and back toward town. "Tell me what I need to know to get the boy back to Chicago. Don't keep me in the dark."

"It's my job to keep people in the dark," Wally drawled.

"Oh, brother." Sam expelled the words like a sigh. "How can Daniel work with someone with your sense of humor?"

"Work with me?" Wally glanced at him. "What about the way you try to micromanage him? Just the other day, Daniel said to me, 'It's different here. Nobody's breathing down my neck, expecting me to jump through hoops to make them happy.'"

"That doesn't sound like something Daniel would say. He's not the type to expound on his feelings."

"So maybe he didn't exactly say all that," Wally conceded. "All *I'm* saying is, maybe he's been concentrating on what makes him happy."

"Daniel thrives on his work. The tougher the deals, the better, as far as he's concerned."

Wally snorted but didn't say anything else.

Sam stared out his window. He wanted Daniel to be happy, and he was convinced he'd be happiest if he bagged Toyco. They needed it. They deserved it. No small-time guy in a small-town place would make him question his business savvy.

When they reached town, they parked near the square and strolled toward the diner where they were to hook up with Daniel.

As they approached their rendezvous spot, Sam saw his brother sauntering toward them with a slight, attractive woman and a little girl by his side. That had to be Gretchen Parks, and the child, Amy.

Daniel held the little girl's hand. Every so often, he'd stop their procession to twirl her around under his arm. Each time, her smile widened and she laughed, a jiggling, happy sound.

"Check it out," Wally murmured. "They look like a family."

"Yeah," Sam grated.

A kid in the park square let out a shrill whoop, distracting him, and he watched two boys chase each other around the bushes.

Wait a minute. What was that guy doing standing there with his camera pointed straight at Daniel?

Eddie Artis. Daniel had said he was stalking him.

But why?

He left Wally and started toward the park. Artis didn't notice, he was so busy snapping shots of Daniel, Gretchen and Amy. He almost reached the photographer before the leech looked up and happened to catch sight of him.

"What the hell are you doing?" Sam ground out between clenched teeth.

A woman sitting on a nearby bench glared at him.

He shrugged apologetically, and muttered to Artis, "Get out of here before I call the cops."

"What cops?" Eddie took his time looking around. "I've only met one around here. They call him Junior, and this time of day, he ventures into the bakery for an apple fritter."

Furious, Sam glanced back toward the sidewalk, where Wally had met up with Daniel. They were busy talking, and weren't looking his way.

"Who sent you here, Artis?" he hissed, kicking at his oversized camera bag. "Who's signing your paycheck?"

"Take a guess."

"Chroma Agency."

Eddie grinned. "You win the prize."

"Why?" Sam ground out between his teeth, while nodding to a mother who passed by with her toddler in a stroller. "Didn't they get their money's worth out of the councilman's daughter? What could they possibly find of interest here? What exactly are you setting up this time for that irreverent rag of a paper you sell to?"

Eddie shrugged. "Y'ask me, it's child abandonment."

So that was John Chroma's new plan of attack. He was using everything in his bag of tricks to garner negative press for Daniel. A smooth move, since they were in talks for a toy company's business, as in good moral values for children and families. The councilman's daughter issue had been swept under the carpet. But how could they run interference on child abandonment? He began to feel sick again as he visualized the photos and captions beneath them. Something like that could even hit the *Tribune's* more respectable pages. And that would spell disaster for Daniel's reputation.

With a last, threatening glare in Eddie's direction, he turned and marched back across the street.

"Sam!" As he reached his group, Daniel greeted him with a grin that quickly turned into a frown of concern. "You look a little green about the gills. You should've stuck to your one beer policy last night."

"It's the unusual flora and fauna around here." Sam glanced meaningfully in Eddie's direction. "I think I'm allergic."

Daniel followed his glance, but immediately flipped his attention back to Sam, his eyes communicating, "Ignore him."

"Gretchen and Amy have been excited about meeting you," he said, as if no cues had passed between them.

Sam met Gretchen's blue-black gaze. Very pretty. Nice smile she flashed at Daniel when he looked her way, too. Huh. He sure seemed different with this one. Because of her, though, Daniel had put the brakes on the Toyco deal, and that stung. "Nice to meet you," he murmured solemnly.

He looked down at the little girl.

When she tilted her heart-shaped face toward him, dark brows swooped down in a familiar, assessing move.

He flashed back to when he'd first held each of his boys. Even then, he'd noticed the definition of brows on their tiny new faces.

Did Daniel and Gretchen realize she had exactly half of each of them in her? No wonder his brother had nixed the need for a paternity test.

"Hi," he said softly.

She didn't say anything. She simply swung her hand in Daniel's and with those big eyes seemed to gauge Sam's value to the planet.

Gretchen took up Amy's other hand. Nodding at Wally and Sam, she said, "Sorry, but we have to run. Amy has a play date at her friend's, and I'm off to meet Cile for some marathon shopping for bake sale ingredients." To Sam, she added, "Nice meeting you."

He nodded.

Daniel sent her a tender look. "See you later."

She beamed back at him.

He watched them walk away.

Sam looked at Wally, whose expression clearly read, "See? I told you so."

Sam's gaze narrowed on Daniel. "You did it, didn't you? You slept with her again."

"Is that any business of yours?"

Sam smacked a fist into his palm. "I knew this would happen. I knew I should've come here earlier."

"You *slept* with Gretchen?" Wally sent Daniel a

look of exaggerated shock. "How dare you not allow your brother to orchestrate it? You've really ticked him off now." The chuckle lines at the outer corners of his eyes proved he was teasing.

Sam shot him a stony look, and turned back to Daniel. "I hope you understand you've put a severe kink in your custody case."

"Custody of what?" Now Wally's shock seemed genuine as he stared from Sam to Daniel.

"Sam, don't—"

"Custody of Amy."

"Dammit, Sam!" Daniel glared. Gretchen would eventually get wind of this and have his head. But right now, *Wally's* darkening expression meant he required an explanation. "She's my daughter, Wally."

"No way."

"Of course she is," Sam snapped. "Can't you tell? You said yourself they looked like a family."

Wally scratched his head, before spearing Daniel with an accusing look. "Then why'd you let Gretchen get away, back in Chicago? I told you, we all said whoever did that was a bastard."

"I didn't *let* Gretchen get away. She ran away from me. I didn't know she was pregnant."

"What was so bad about you that she didn't want to stay? She doesn't have a problem with you now."

"Yes, she does. She's afraid I'll run out on her."

Arms crossed, Sam leaned toward Wally. "I told you he was a player. Anyway, I'd like to believe in the two of them, too. But I'm afraid what's happening here isn't reality. Daniel's overwhelmed, so he's falling into something Gretchen wants from him. It's happened before, and it never works out for Daniel. He needs to get back to the city and into his routines."

Ignoring him, Daniel turned to Wally. "Can you

keep this to yourself?"

"Why?"

"It's just between Gretchen and me. Amy doesn't even know. She thinks I'm a friend of her mother's."

"That's ridiculous. Why can't you tell her you're—" Wally stopped short. "Oh, I get it. Gretch doesn't want you to tell her you're gonna leave."

Daniel's mouth tightened. "Can you keep the secret or not?"

"Yeah. Sure."

Daniel let out a breath and clapped Wally on the shoulder. "Thanks."

Wally nodded. "But if you hurt her..."

Daniel snorted. "Get in line behind Joel. I believe he mentioned something about ripping my arm off."

"*I'll* rip your arm off, if it'll work some sense into you." Sam checked his watch. "We've got a plane to catch. Are you coming or not?"

He shook his head. "I'm staying put until after the festival. I'll leave first thing Sunday morning."

"Kiss Toyco goodbye, then. Eddie's on Chroma's payroll. They're planning something to bring you down, and you're playing right into their trap."

"Eddie's followed me for years," Daniel shot back. "If he helped make me known, it's only fair that he could knock me down a notch or two as well."

"And that doesn't bother you?"

"Sure it does. But I never planned for that aspect of fame. I never thought reporters would come along and keep me in the papers as the agency gained success. It just happened, and for a while it was fun. But maybe its un-happening now is the natural course of things."

"Well, as your attorney, I say—"

Daniel held up a hand. "Tell me what you say as my brother and as a father. Should I spend a few more days with my daughter or not?"

Sam sighed, and with a last disapproving look, turned and walked away.

In the car on the way to the airport, he decided he'd try his best to save the deal, for Daniel and for him. His brother had been generous toward him with a percentage in the company, so he was heavily invested in The Nicholson Agency, planning for the boys' colleges and Beth's and his retirement. Daniel would be taking all of them down with him, though, if he continued on this crazy quest to lose major deals. Why wasn't he just getting out of Ohio while he could? He should leave Gretchen and Amy to their own lives.

He pictured the three of them again, strolling down the sidewalk toward Wally and him, with that happy aura surrounding them.

What was he thinking, saying Daniel should leave them? When had he gotten so jaded? He rubbed his knuckles against his sternum, trying to soothe burning indigestion, and murmured, "Beth." In a way, saying his wife's name was cleansing. Reminded him of what was good in him.

Maybe Gretchen was doing that for Daniel.

He'd hoped it was possible, back when his brother had insisted on coming here to see Gretchen and his daughter. Then he'd convinced himself it was a pipedream. Daniel had sworn he'd never do something so rash and so likely to turn ugly as to fall in love again.

But he *was* in love, wasn't he? Nothing else could explain this.

And his little brother didn't know it. He had no clue.

Sam grinned. Oh, to be a fly on the wall when he figured it out.

All he had to do now was try and keep the brass at Toyco from making up their minds too quickly. Give it a few more days and Daniel would figure out it wasn't just the lack of smog in Marydale that was making him act differently.

He'd come running home the minute he figured it out.

****

"Daniel's brother seemed like a nice guy," Crystal remarked, watching Gretchen inject helium into the balloons they had picked out for the pre-festival party.

"I barely met him, really," Gretchen replied, raising her voice to be heard over the hiss of canned gas inflating the balloons.

"I waited on the two of them in the cafe this morning." Crystal leaned against the gift shop's counter. "Do you wonder why he came here?"

One look at her friend's expression and Gretchen knew the other woman was dying to tell her something she'd overheard. So as she began to tie the dozen balloons together by their strands of curling ribbon, she said, "I do wonder."

After a quick glance around the shop, Crystal leaned in. "He wanted Daniel to go back to Chicago with him today. He kept talking about how some big deal was about to fall through and bring them down or something."

Gretchen didn't even focus on her friend's last words. She hadn't gotten past Sam's wanting Daniel to go back today. That thought instantly dragged her mood down. After she tugged on some of the ribbons to un-bunch the balloons, she took up her scissors again and curled their ends. "Sure you don't mind taking these over to Eula's on your lunch break? I'd do it, but—"

"But you're already taking food, a carload of kids, and toys to keep them occupied." Crystal sighed. "I don't know how you manage."

"What? I like picnics."

"*Saint Gretchen*," she mused, leaning against

the counter. "You sure Daniel Nicholson is one of the good guys?"

"What do you mean?"

"Gee, I don't know. Maybe I'm thinking there's more to the story." Crystal gazed dramatically into her eyes. "Remember when we were twelve and we swore we could read each other's minds?"

"Mm hm." She tried to act interested. But really, she wasn't much in the mood for whatever Crystal was cooking up. She just wanted to get the day's jobs done and see Daniel again. She turned to go back to her business, but her friend grabbed her hands, stopping her.

Crystal closed her eyes and emitted an "Ohmmmm." Her eyes flew open. "I got something!"

"Oh, brother," Gretchen muttered, and yanked her hands away, to start ringing up the balloons—a formality, since she was secretly paying the expense out of pocket. Crystal didn't need to know that, though.

"I see that you and Daniel were close before, in Chicago. Really close. And I see that he's Amy's father."

Gretchen's fingers froze on the register keys. "Ssh! I told you not to mention that. People will hear."

Crystal dropped her spooky psychic drawl and reverted to her usual light tone. "They should've figured it out by now, anyway. It's obvious the way you two stare at each other that you aren't strangers. Plus, all they have to do is look at Amy. Her hair may be lighter than Daniel's, but it sure curls the same way."

"Lots of people have wavy hair."

"Yeah, but when Amy's being flirty and dips her chin? She's Daniel's spitting image."

Gretchen closed her eyes. When she opened them again, she said, "We haven't told Amy yet. I'm

207

so scared about it. She'll probably be cool with it, but, I don't know. I guess what I'm saying is, Daniel isn't Big Bobby." She stuck a handful of furry pens into a cup holder and carefully fanned them out. "He hasn't exactly been around each week of her life like Bobby's been there for you and BJ. It didn't start out that way and it's not gonna end like that."

"But you wish it would." Crystal checked her teeth in a little rhinestone-encrusted mirror she'd pulled from her purse. "And girl, who can blame you? He looks like a toe curler!"

Her face heated.

With a knowing lift of her brows, Crystal turned the mirror around, to show Gretchen her reddened reflection.

She stuck her tongue out at her tormenter.

Crystal only laughed low and said, "I am so jealous."

Crystal? Jealous of *her*? She was a much freer being, and way more secure in her sexuality. Gretchen had always admired her for that, and for the way she turned the head of every man she met.

Daniel saw Crystal every day at the diner, and yet he spoke of her in the same tone as when he spoke of Wally or Eula...

Wow. She hadn't thought of that until now.

She smiled.

Crystal fiddled with the furry pens, and plucked out a purple one. Trying its ink out on one of the free pocket calendars that the card company sent, she said, "Is Daniel mad because you haven't told Amy?"

"It's a bone of contention. Every time he mentioned it before, I put him off. We have to tell her tonight or tomorrow, though. It has to be done before he goes."

Nodding slowly, Crystal studied her. After depositing the pen back in its holder, she took up the balloons that had been patiently floating overhead, anchored to the counter by the plastic bear-shaped weight. "You'll work it out, though. See ya tonight."

"See you." Gretchen watched her sashay out of the shop, juggling the balloons as easily as she juggled men. She wished she had half of Crystal's sex appeal. Maybe then she could keep a man. But then, for all her charm and looks, Crystal hadn't been able to keep Big Bobby.

She sank her chin into her hands. What exactly was she doing with Daniel? Why had she gone to bed with him again? He must think she was so easy.

What made her sad to think of his leaving? Was it his powerful body that had loved her, his arms that gently encircled her and provided a safe place to rest? Or maybe it was his throaty laughter as he bonded with Amy, or joked with Wally, or simply tried to lighten her mood.

A customer walked up, and she went back to work, glad for the distraction and determined to stop dwelling on Daniel's leaving for the time being. They'd cross that bridge when they came to it, and unfortunately that would be very, very soon.

Chapter Thirteen

Gretchen clapped for the children's silly dance routine when it ended. "You'll get a standing ovation when you show them this," she told them earnestly. She swung her legs off Eula's porch lounger. "Now I need to see what Amy's up to."

"She went to the barn with BJ," someone said.

Gretchen started to rise, but the Gerding twins leaned on her arms to keep her in the chair. "Stay! We have another dance."

"Well…" She glanced out at the yard full of pre-festival partiers milling around under two huge tents. "I should be helping Cile get more food out."

"I've got lots of help," Cile called out through the doorway. "Besides, you're keeping the munchkins out of the cookies until after burgers and hot dogs."

"Cookies!" they shouted in unison. Before Gretchen could breathe, they'd shucked their props and deserted her in their rush to beg food off their favorite baker.

Chuckling, she relaxed back in her seat.

"Hi," someone called, from outside in the yard.

She flinched, and glanced in that direction. *Daniel.* "You scared me." By now she welcomed the thrilling warmth that shot through her whenever they were together. "When did you get here?"

"In time to catch the last act." His eyes met hers. "You're very patient. That's why they pick you for their audience, you know."

She laughed. "They pick me because I'm a sucker."

He came to the screen door and let himself onto the porch.

He stood there, and just looked at her, his smile grooving his cheeks. Once again, his direct manner sent chills through her.

Tearing her gaze away, she noticed his jeans, open-collar shirt and shoes without socks. "Look at you. You've morphed into a country boy."

"That'll be the day." His smile accentuated those rich brown eyes as he stepped behind her and moved her hair with a brush of fingers against her neck.

Happy chills ricocheted through her. It was such a small thing, the slightest feel of his skin against hers, yet it seemed so intimate. So much for trying to keep her distance. Anyway, it was pre-festival night. Everyone had to be in good spirits, and that meant being friendly.

"Let's go somewhere quiet," he murmured in her ear.

His fingers moved away, leaving her with a sense of loss.

She got up, and he put his hand on her back and they strolled around the side of the house.

"Where's Amy?"

"The kids said she went to the barn with BJ. One of the cats had kittens."

They reached the front porch. Eula kept lawn chairs down at one end, and they opened them and sat, hidden from view of the road by the spreading maple tree in front of the house.

Once they'd settled in, Daniel said, "Sam saw Eddie again. Eddie says he's going to print photos of you, me and Amy and announce to the world that she's my daughter. He's going to present her as my love child I abandoned, and say I'm abandoning her again on Sunday."

Gretchen stared at him. "Why?"

"It's just how it works. Business politics are

dirty. Chroma Agency hired him to dig up dirt, and I guess I fell into the trap." He swallowed. "Sorry I led them here."

"Sorry doesn't stop Eddie, though, does it?" She sighed. "I could trust Crystal and Eula to know and not say anything, but not your buddy. I don't like him."

"He's not my buddy." He scowled. "Right now, I'd like to smash his expensive camera and—"

She shook her head. "It's a moot point now. We have to tell Amy right away." She met his gaze. "Now I'm more scared of *not* telling her."

He covered her hands with his. "We'll tell her, and then we'll spend as much time as possible together during the festival. We'll make it okay."

She wanted to close her eyes, to shut out the world and bask in the two of them right then. To imagine them there in that place at next year's picnic, having been through a whole year together. She drew her hand out from under his. "I wish you'd never come to Marydale."

"I'm glad I did."

She looked away.

He rose. "You'll feel better once we talk with Amy."

As Gretchen rose and followed him off the porch, toward the barn, her heart wrenched with pain. She wasn't mad at him because he'd come to town. She was mad because he was leaving.

Now they must tell Amy about him, and under the worst circumstances.

A chill of foreboding ran up her spine. This was exactly what she'd hoped would never happen.

****

BJ peeked through the old maple tree's fading fall leaves. "That's your daddy?"

Poking her head through the branches, Amy frowned at her mommy as she walked away with

Daniel. "He's not my daddy. My daddy's dead."

"Oh." BJ slid his sneaker-clad foot lower on the maple's bending branch. "Come down. I'm hungry."

"No." Amy usually climbed and climbed, being brave, then grew bored and slipped back down. This time, she clung to the tree's trunk, squatting in its branches and wishing she could just be a squirrel.

BJ lowered himself to where he could land on his feet. Letting go of a branch, he landed sideways instead. Dusting himself off, he said, "I'll be back," and ran to the house.

Amy didn't care if he came back or not. Daniel had told that stranger man that he was her daddy.

He wasn't her daddy. He was Daniel.

Sliding a sneaker down the trunk, she lowered herself the same way BJ had, using the limbs for support. But she was a big girl, and she didn't fall.

She didn't run to the house, either. She wanted to go somewhere by herself. She was big enough.

She'd go to the caves and see what everyone else got to see.

****

Standing under their maple tree, BJ bellowed, "A—my! I got cookies." He held them up in the napkin Cile had wrapped them in. "Come down."

He waited.

Plodding closer to the tree, he tipped his head back to see where its branches started from the trunk. "Amy?"

She wasn't up there.

He looked around, then walked to the bushes and kicked them. With his free hand, he rustled across their scratchy tops. She wasn't there. He went to the woodpile. Whooping, he hopped around to the other side, to surprise her out of hiding, thinking she was playing that game.

But she wasn't there, either.

Where could she be?

He looked down at the napkin in his hand. He set it down on the woodpile in case she came back hungry. Then he picked up a stick and headed for the creek. He wanted to catch a crayfish. He'd told Amy he could and she hadn't believed him. If he caught a crayfish, she'd show up to tell him she could catch a bigger one.

****

Gretchen hurried up to Cile in the back yard."Have you seen Amy?"

"Did you check the barn?" She glanced up from adding rock salt to the ice cream maker. "She wanted to see the kittens."

"We were just there." Daniel moved closer to Gretchen's side.

Crystal sauntered over from the food tables. "She and BJ said they were going to climb trees."

Daniel rested a palm against Gretchen's back. "The trees by the driveway? A little while ago?"

She swung her gaze to his, and caught his frown.

Crystal nodded. "They have a 'fort' in the old maple tree. It's really just a board someone nailed up there, and a—"

Daniel took off around the side of the house, while Gretchen sprinted straight through it.

As soon as they reached the front yard, they called Amy's name, making a beeline for the tree.

She wasn't there.

"Do you think she heard our conversation?" Daniel asked Gretchen. But he already knew the answer. She must've been in the tree the whole time.

Several partygoers had followed Gretchen through the house and onto the front porch.

"We'll search the house again." Crystal promised.

"Check the creek," Cile added as Gretchen and Daniel headed off again, this time across the deep side yard.

They found BJ at the creek. But the boy said he'd been fishing "a while" since he'd returned to the tree and Amy was gone. He asked if they'd heard Gretchen's and his conversation on the porch, and he timidly answered, "Yep."

Gretchen gripped Daniel's arm.

He stared hard into her eyes. "Do you think she went to the caves?"

Fear flashed in her expression, before she turned and ran stumbling up the hill toward the caves, yelling for Amy.

"You take the Ants' Hills and I'll check Lion's Den," Daniel ordered, outrunning her again.

The cave's rugged edges scraped Daniel's fingers as he hurried inside and thrust his way through passageways. The rocks jutting up from the ground tripped him once, and he fell hard on one knee. He pulled himself up, and ignoring the pain in his leg, bellowed, "A—my!" Her name echoed through the tunnels and seemed to mock him.

As he rounded the last curve, he saw the awesome pool, shimmering and quiet, but chilling him to the bone, just looking at it and wondering if—

Amy. He closed his eyes, doubled over and sucked in huge breaths.

Thank God. She's not in it, she's beside it.

He slid across the wet rocks and fell down on his knees, to grab her up in his arms. "Amy," he blurted, burying his face in her hair.

His eyes stung. His throat felt raw. Reluctantly, he released her enough to look down into her little face. "Are you okay?"

"I want Mommy." She'd been crying. Dried, muddy tracks marred her cheeks.

As his heart rate began to normalize, he sat down on his rear and stretched his sore legs. "She's coming. She's worried about you."

She nodded, and kept her face down now.

"Amy?"

She lifted her lashes and looked at him.

"Why'd you come here?"

She just sat there.

He sucked in a breath of cool air, expanded his tight lungs and then let it back out. "Did you come here to hide?"

She shook her head.

So much for their good rapport. Dammit, he would not blow this with her. "Did you come just because you wanted to?"

She didn't say anything.

"Your mommy's worried about you."

She started to cry again.

"It's okay." He tried to pull her close.

"No!" She pushed him away.

He sat back, shocked by the powerful sense of loss that rushed him then.

She crossed her arms. "You're not my daddy."

Closing his eyes, he dropped his head toward his chest. When he looked up at her again, she was still sitting there, her dark brows lowered over angry eyes.

"I *am* your daddy." He'd grasped the full meaning of it the second he saw the pool again, when fear reached down in his soul and yanked hard to get his full attention.

She shook her head violently. "My daddy's dead."

"No. I'm here." He reached for her again, but she put her hands out and pushed him away. Through raw pain, he somehow said, "Your mommy didn't tell you because I haven't been here for you. I haven't been a good daddy." Looking at her innocent face, he struggled for words of closure. "I want to be one from now on, though. Will you let me?"

Her "No!" echoed off the sweating, white-brown

walls.

She jumped to her feet, started backing away, and stumbled on the rocks.

"Watch out!" Daniel shouted.

But she lost her footing, and splashed into the pool's dark water.

Chapter Fourteen

Amy's scream reverberated off the cave walls and ripped straight into Gretchen's heart. She stumbled over uneven rocks in a mad scramble for the inner sanctum and its pitch black water. Bursting from the narrow corridor, she saw someone splash into the pool.

Oh, God, no.

The spray settled on Daniel in the water, thrashing to turn himself around to Amy, who bobbed beside him, wide-eyed and gasping for air.

"Amy!" Gretchen launched herself across the rock floor as Amy flailed her arms and knocked herself out of Daniel's grip.

Gretchen kicked her shoes off and prepared to jump in.

But Daniel had grabbed Amy again, and pulled her up against his chest before she could struggle away. "Tip your head back."

Gretchen knelt at the edge of the pool, shaking, terrified at the frightened expression on Amy's face. She'd swallowed too much water. She couldn't stop coughing. She looked so scared.

"You're okay," Daniel soothed. "Breathe and relax now."

Amy whimpered, with her face still contorted with fear. But she didn't fight anymore as Daniel floated her safely to the water's edge.

Gretchen leaned out over the water, desperate to grab her and take over.

Daniel turned her around to face Gretchen.

Holding her under her arms, with a grunt of exertion, he thrust her up out of the water so Gretchen could pull her into an embrace.

Once she held Amy firmly against her chest, she scrambled back several yards from the water. She sat there, holding her daughter and swallowing hard against the emotion that overcame her as the reality of what could have happened sank in.

She was vaguely aware of more splashes. Daniel must be climbing back over the pool's steep bank.

He appeared beside her. "Is she okay?"

She nodded, resting her cheek against Amy's head.

He brushed his fingers over Amy's hair, and Gretchen lifted her head so he could see for himself.

"You okay?" His words shook slightly. Amy moved her head up and down beneath his palm as he stroked her curls.

When he squatted beside them, Gretchen glimpsed worry in his gaze before he quickly covered it.

"She knows how to swim," she told him, with a wobble in her own voice. "Miss Peggy taught her last summer."

"She just panicked. But it's okay. We were here and it worked out. Right, Amy?"

Amy moved in Gretchen's arms, twisting to where she could see him.

Something spread through Daniel as he stood beside mother and child, something that left him with a sense of peace. Just as quickly, he shivered. He could have lost Amy to the water. What if he hadn't gotten to her in time? He became aware of the gray, tomblike cave walls, and his gut ached. This was his fault, a sign that he sucked at parenting.

Amy eyed him.

Wanting to comfort her in some way, he winked.

She blinked.

He smiled as his gaze soaked up her little rounded chin, chubby cheeks and long, damp lashes.

Gretchen glanced up at him. Fear hovered in her eyes, that same fear that hadn't yet released his pulse to its normal rate. "Thanks," she said. "I don't know what I would've done if..." Her voice trailed off.

He nodded. He didn't want to say anything with Amy there, but he tried to show Gretchen with his eyes that he understood. She seemed to get it, because a smile tugged at the corners of her mouth.

Amy stirred, and pushed away from her mother's chest. "You're hurting me."

"Sorry. I guess I was squeezing too hard." Gretchen looked down at her clothes. "You got me all wet."

Not wanting to think about what they'd just been through any longer, Daniel seized the lightness of the moment and quipped, "What about my shoes? Huh?"

Amy checked out his Italian loafers, whose tassels now resembled sea anemones. For a second, she looked as if she might smile. But then she turned her face into her mother's neck.

Gretchen's gaze caught his. Concern still glimmered in her eyes. She didn't bounce back that easily from the scare, and now he understood. Things weren't going to be as carefree as they'd been before now. Before he knew being a father could mean getting slammed up against a brick wall, and then somehow being pulled back away from it, bruised but still alive.

When they got up and started walking out of the cave, they met a handful of men following the narrow passageway toward them. According to them, many more people had gathered near the boulders, cautiously awaiting word on Amy.

At the entrance, while the men took Amy to the

cheering, whooping crowd, Gretchen touched Daniel's arm, to hold him back.

"She'll tell them all about it," she said. "How she fell in the water and you saved her." Her gaze softened on his. "Did I thank you?"

"Yes, but quit." Looking at the cave's walls, he said, "I have to get out of here."

"Come on." She turned to go, but he stopped her.

"I meant I have to get out this town." He clenched his jaw. "Gretchen, I caused what just happened. She must've overheard us, and she doesn't want me to be her father. I could see it in her face. I tried to explain, but she kept getting more and more upset. She fell in the water because she was trying to get away from me."

"You scared her because she wasn't prepared." She waved him off. "It's not your fault. You were right. I should've told her sooner."

"No. You were right. We shouldn't have told her at all. She would've forgotten me as soon as I left. But now she knows something she'll hold on to."

She'd know his face and his voice but she wouldn't have him. Just like when he lost his parents. Even those pictures of him in her head would fade after a few years. All that'd remain was a steady longing for someone you kept trying to remember. Or if you harbored resentment, the way he had for so long with his foster family, you'd keep trying to forget.

Which would it be with Amy? Would she wish to remember him, or long to forget?

Gretchen didn't know what to say. Daniel had a point. They could have left things the way they were. Hadn't she wanted that from the start, just wanted him to leave and never return? But she didn't feel that way now, and she couldn't blame Amy for reacting the way she had. It was what she'd expected would happen. Amy liked Daniel, just like she did. She *wouldn't* want him to leave.

Shivering in her wet jeans and sweater, she stepped out of the cave entrance. Daniel *had* told Amy what they should have told her together. He'd plunged into *her* parenting territory and taken initiative he shouldn't take. And yet, she knew now how much he really cared for Amy. He would never have intentionally hurt her.

She'd forgiven him. Now he must forgive himself.

Friends broke from the crowd and ran to greet her, offering towels and chattering about how great it was that Amy was fine.

Townspeople had gathered in a buzzing circle of talk and movement. They looked up as Gretchen and Daniel approached, and moved aside so she could see Amy standing safely in their midst. Cile had already slung towels over Amy's shoulders, and Crystal fussed over her and petted her hair. But though Gretchen had thought Amy would talk about the cave, instead she was strangely quiet. She wouldn't look at Gretchen or Daniel.

Though the rejection hurt, Gretchen covered her feelings with silence. Grabbing the towels Cile handed her, she offered one to Daniel, who'd followed her into the middle of the crowd. He waved it off, his gaze riveted on Amy as he knelt to her level. "We need to talk."

The sudden decrease in the crowd noise was palpable. Gretchen felt them waiting.

Amy looked into Daniel's eyes, into their mirroring toasted brownness. "Okay," she answered in an almost-whisper.

He rose, lifted her in his arms and strode out of the ring of adults.

They all followed his lead and began heading back toward the house.

What's he doing now? Gretchen wondered. Amy

was wet. She didn't want her catching a cold. She set her hands on her hips, hoping Amy might turn and look to her to seek permission, and see her shake her head. When Amy didn't glance back, she followed more closely, hobbling now that the excitement had receded and she noticed her sore muscles and the toe she'd stubbed on a rock.

Daniel carried Amy inside the quiet house.

She found them in the kitchen. As she came through the doorway, he glanced up.

When their eyes met, Gretchen thought she read need in his gaze. Need for what? *Forgiveness from Amy, silly. It's eating at him. He told you so.*

"This should wait." She turned to Amy. "Let's go change clothes."

"Please," he said softly. "Give us a minute."

"A minute. But I'm staying here."

Amy had climbed onto the tall stool that Eula kept tucked into a corner by the window, just for her. Daniel went to stand next to her. He kept his hands at his sides. Gretchen knew that was tough for him, being a toucher. He'd want to hold Amy, or take her hand. But he was correctly reading Amy's sullen look as "Back off."

"I wasn't a good daddy," he began. "I wasn't here for you since you were born. I didn't know you. But now I am here, and I've gotten to know you. And guess what?"

She shook her head.

"I like you."

Her expression remained passive.

He had the knack for talking to kids. He said just enough so Amy would understand. Gretchen ached to reach out and pull them into a circle, to be the family they weren't. But the sure knowledge that this was only a moment in time stopped her. This moment couldn't repeat, because Daniel was going away.

She willed herself to memorize the tilt of her little one's nose and the curve of her cheek as she looked up at her father for one of the very last times before he left. Daniel's chin angled down as he gazed at Amy. Gretchen noted the outline of his nose, and the intentness in his eyes. She didn't mean to memorize him. She was angry with him, for being like this. For caring about them. Why couldn't he just be a jerk, and make this easy? But watching him, seeing how earnest he was, her anger slowly melted away.

"I have to know something." Daniel reached out then and took Amy's hands in his.

Amy stared at their hands.

He placed her fingers against his and examined their lengths. He put his palm against hers, and touched her nails with the pads of his fingers. "I have to know," he repeated. "Do you like me?"

"You're not my daddy," she said, in a small voice. Her chin trembled. She pulled her hands away from his, and crossed her arms.

"I am."

She eyed him. "I'm cold."

"But it's so warm in here." He looked around at the old oven. "It must be ninety degrees from all of Cile's baking."

He looked back at Amy, and wrapped her towel more tightly around her.

Amy slid a glance Gretchen's way.

Gretchen stepped closer.

"Just one more thing," Daniel said to the little girl. "I want you to know that I'll always be here for you."

She looked at him.

"Do you understand that?"

She nodded.

"Good." He kissed the top of her head.

Gretchen moved in quickly then. With a

threatening look at Daniel, she scooped up Amy and hurried to the bathroom with her. She didn't want her catching cold and she didn't want her buying into Daniel's promises.

Cile gave Gretchen towels and saw to it that they had shampoo and soap.

After Amy's bath, as Gretchen sat on the bedroom floor brushing and drying her yawning youngster's hair, she thought of what Daniel had said.

I want you to know I'll always be here for you.

How could he say that, when he knew darn well it wasn't true?

"Gretchen?"

She glanced around to find Crystal at the door, and turned off the blow dryer. "What?"

"Daniel left."

Her heart dropped.

Her friend plopped onto the bed on her belly and propped her chin in her hands. "Boy, did he ever look good all wet like that. Why do some people look even hotter when they're—"

"Crystal!" Gretchen turned the hot air on and blasted her for a few seconds. "Stick to the point. He left because I was mad at him?"

"Nope. He said he'd had this brainstorm about how to showcase MCC, and he went to find Wally."

"Oh. You mean he left the *farm*." Relief flooded her, followed by irritation. He could've told her he was leaving. "That's Daniel. When things get hairy in real life, there's always money to be made."

"I don't see why you're so mad at him. He got Amy out of that water."

"Yeah. After he told her he was her father and she ran from him and fell in."

"Oh."

Gretchen snapped the dryer on. When she turned off again, she said, "So now you see why I'm mad."

Crystal looked down at Amy. "Are you still mad at him, Amy?"

"No."

"Good."

Gretchen untangled Amy's hair with the brush, and sent her out the door.

"If she's forgiven him, why can't you?" Crystal said when they were alone again.

"Because he's leaving, that's why!"

Crystal's smile spread. "I see."

"You see what?" Her gaze narrowed.

"That you're not mad because he told Amy. You're really hacked off because he's leaving you."

"No," she insisted. "The sooner he goes, the better."

"Right." Crystal headed for the door. She stood there a moment, looking at Gretchen. "Daniel looked just as sad as you on his way out the door." Chuckling, she shook her head. "You two are perfect for each other."

****

Daniel needed to clear his head so he'd quit this obsessing over Amy and his failures toward her. He had to talk to Wally about tomorrow, too, so he phoned him and suggested a run. Wally didn't exactly sound overjoyed at the thought, but agreed to meet him in the park as soon as they changed clothes.

Before they'd gotten much further then fifty feet in their jog, Daniel stopped, and leaned over to hide his laughter.

Wally pulled up short behind him. "You okay?"

Daniel looked up then, his eyes watering. "You run like a woman."

"Can't help it, man. It's these damned tight calf muscles."

That was an understatement. Wally's scarecrow

legs seemed stiff as sticks.

"Better shoes would help. I'll have my assistant send you some from Chicago. Those thirteens?"

"Fifteen."

"Whoa! She'll have to mug a clown."

"Yeah, well, just make sure she doesn't send me any loafers with sissy tassels."

They ran on, poking fun at each other good-humoredly. Daniel divulged his plans for tomorrow's festival, then filled Wally in on what had happened at the pre-party. Wally didn't say too much. For once, he just listened. But Daniel wondered about that look he sent him. It was as if he knew an answer Daniel was searching for, but wouldn't put it to words.

Daniel drove on, pushing his lungs to work around the day's tightness, the stress on his body. The endorphins calmed him, brought him back to an even rhythm.

"Lighten up, Nicholson," Wally implored, after they'd run several miles down the road. "You're killin' me. This ain't the Chicago Marathon." He stopped, shoved his hands on his hips and heaved in breaths. "You've run it, though, haven't you?"

"Twice. To qualify for the Boston." Daniel sucked in the air, too, filling his lungs. He was ready to move on. It was hard for him to slow his pace, though he wanted to hang with his buddy.

"Dude! I want to be you when I grow up."

"Nah. Be yourself. Crystal likes you that way." That reminded him of Gretchen, and his chest pulled. "Come on. Let's go back."

A short time later, he arrived at home.

Home at Gretchen's. He unlocked the door on his side of the house, wondering when he'd gotten so comfortable here.

He slumped in the chair and ran his hands down his face. Something gnawed away at him, something that came and went in odd bursts of pain worse than the tension headaches he'd grown used to over the years. It wasn't his guilt over leaving and not being here for Amy. He already recognized that ache. It wasn't the fact he'd miss Wally's friendship down the road, or the general sense of camaraderie in this town that had spread its arms and embraced him.

It was his longing to be with Gretchen.

He got this sense when they were together that they were this team, that they could handle things. Like Eula's stroke. Like their desperate hunt for Amy, though he hoped to God nothing like that ever happened again.

But they weren't handling their upcoming separation very well.

He rose and went to the door, put his hand on the knob and turned it.

Swearing, he thrust away from the door and stalked back to the table. He scraped the chair across the floor and sat in it again. She probably didn't want to see him anymore. She was tired of the whole thing, and thought Amy was better off cutting the ties now instead of tomorrow.

He stared at his keys lying on the counter. He could leave.

No, he couldn't. He had to stay for the festival. He wanted to stay, if she'd allow it. He wanted to spend as much time as possible with both of them tomorrow.

He went to bed and thrashed around in the sheets. *Gretchen.* His body hardened as he considered making love with her, kissing her and holding her and lying in bed with her for a lifetime.

She could live without him.

But could he live without her?

****

Gretchen lay in bed with Amy asleep beside her. She'd wandered in asking for water, and afterward refused to go back to her room. She hadn't done that in a long time.

This is your fault, Daniel. This is her way of acting out, of showing her confusion over your revelation today.

There. She'd said it, in her thoughts. But it didn't do a bit of good. She couldn't get around wanting him long enough to be angry with him.

She inched out of bed so she wouldn't wake Amy, and went to the bathroom to get an elastic band, to pull her hair back. She glanced into the mirror, frowned and stared.

How could she look that tired and still be wide awake?

And sheesh, she hadn't realized how unsexy she looked in her old, faded Marydale Elementary Fun Run T-shirt and men's-style undershorts.

Not like he's gonna see them. You're not going over there.

She slid her cold feet into her furry slippers, and padded to the kitchen. Maybe a cup of hot tea would soothe her.

In the kitchen, she quickly checked outside, to see if Daniel's SUV was still in the yard. It was.

He's in this house, just a door away from you.

Desire swept through her. Her nipples hardened against her T-shirt as other parts tingled with need.

She moved into the living room, paced around, and then sat and stewed again. She was angry with him for caring about them, for opening himself to them, and then leaving. Yet all along, she'd known he'd go. Because of that, she'd kept a tiny part of her heart safe from him. Until now. Now she knew in her heart that he loved Amy. Now she also acknowledged how, for a long time, she'd wanted to say, "See, Amy? Your father is smart and he's handsome and he's a hard worker." Now that she really knew him well, she could add that he was kind-hearted.

She wanted to ask him if he would stay. But what good would it do? She couldn't stop him from going. And that was what she couldn't stand. Anything was better. Lust. Friendship. Love. She needed to be left with *something* from Daniel, now that her feelings had run the gamut.

Her stupid wayward heart drove her to the door and made her pad in her slippers to Daniel's side, and forced her to knock on his door. She tapped. He probably wouldn't hear. She could turn and go, before she embarrassed herself and threw all caution to the wind for another night of bliss.

The door flew open and he stood there, in jeans, barefoot and bare-chested, his sculpted jaw softened by a scruff of evening beard. He stared at her, his dark-eyed gaze so intent on her that desire raced through her, pricking her skin with its force.

She glanced again at his tanned chest, at the path of dark hair spread across his upper body and then descending down his flat abdominal muscles.

Her already tightened throat went dry.

He didn't say anything. He just moved away from the doorway, and she stepped inside.

He didn't look at her slippers, her old shirt or her shorts. His eyes never left hers.

It was so quiet, she could hear her heart pounding, thumping hard inside her.

"I-," she began. "I wanted—"

But he cut her words off, reaching and taking her in his arms. "It's okay," he murmured against her hair.

She closed her eyes. She let him hold her, let herself melt into his hard, muscular body, enjoying the gentle way he stroked her back, loving the rough scrub of his jeans against her bare legs. She inhaled the scent of soap on his bare skin, and his chest hair tickled her nose. Then she pushed away, and fisted her hands and pummeled him lightly. "Why?" she groaned. "Why'd you have to come here?"

He pulled her to his chest again, and held her. "Don't be this way. Not now. Our time is too short."

His heart beat strong and fast where her cheek rested against his chest. She raised her head, tilting her chin up. Eyes closed, she said, "Kiss me, then. Say goodbye."

He didn't kiss her right away. She grew uncomfortable, and opened her eyes, to find his dark gaze on her. Searching hers. What was he looking for? He knew her feelings.

And then his mouth lowered to hers. It was a gentle, slow torture. Nibbles at first. Tastes that tantalized her and made her sigh and press against him.

He took his time, placing a hand along the column of her neck, rubbing his thumb back and forth against her nape and into her hair as his lips played against hers.

She opened her mouth, to let him know she wanted more. But he moved away from her lips, and placed his hands on both sides of her face, and kissed first one cheek, and then her nose, and her other cheek.

"I want this to last," he said, staring at her mouth. "I want you to know I'll remember every detail of this time forever."

And before she could think on his words, he pressed his lips to hers again. This time, he parted her teeth with his tongue and drove it into her mouth. He pulled it out slowly, and then entered again.

Oh, Daniel. Can you feel what you do to me?

She moved her tongue beside his, parrying with him. Showing him that she was with him. And when his hand touched her breast under her T-shirt, she moaned and pulled him closer, enjoying the rough feel of his fingers against her sensitive skin.

He lingered there a while, kissing her, before his hand roamed down her spine and dipped below the elastic waistbands of her shorts and panties. He squeezed her bottom, and pressed her closer against the hard column of his erection waiting beneath his jeans.

And then he pulled back.

She awoke as if from a crazy dream, worried, only to find such raw desire in his expression that she knew things were okay.

He bent and picked her up, and carried her down the hall to the bedroom. It was dark there, without even a nightlight. But that was okay. He was about to make love with her. She knew his kiss, his touch, his scent and his muscles. Daniel. Her Daniel, for now. For this one last time, she could delude herself into believing that he was all hers.

He leaned over her, kissing her as she sat on the low bed. Then he reached down at her sides, and she lifted her arms while he pulled her T-shirt over her head. He bent and went down on his knees between her legs, his hands on her breasts. She closed her eyes, tipped her head back and gave in to the rhythm of her heart beating hard inside, and his hands, kneading. She fully lived the pleasure, moaning when he leaned down and his tongue played over and then suckled at first one hardened nipple and then the other.

"Lie back, sweetheart," he murmured, turning his gaze, filled with devilish male intention, on hers.

When she obeyed and lay against the sheets, he placed chaste kisses on her belly, on her hipbones, tickling her and making her squirm in enjoyment.

"You're so beautiful, he drawled. "You taste good, too."

She drifted in a swirl of words, in the warm man-smell of freshly-showered Daniel, of his strong hands shoving her pants down, and then peeling her panties off. Then his shoulders were at her knees, pressing her legs apart as he stroked the soft flesh of her inner thighs, and pressed his lips there.

When his fingers found that wet, hard place between her legs, she turned her head from side to side and pressed her palms against his shoulders in a weak protest as he massaged. "Come here," she said, in a voice drunk with sex.

"I will."

But he didn't. For that moment, she could only focus on his massaging her clitoris, slowly, torturously, until she almost cried out for him. He slipped fingers inside her, and withdrew, in and withdrew, driving her mad, to where she clawed the sheets.

And then his mouth was there, his tongue replacing his finger, and oh god if he didn't stop now—

She groaned and leaned back on the bed, prepared for orgasm.

But he'd gone.

She opened her eyes and slowly realized he was stripping out of his clothes.

He stood there a moment, naked and gorgeous, and just looked at her. Then he climbed onto her, and pushed inside her, working in slowly as she groaned and thrust her hips to welcome him.

He brushed his lips against hers, and their tongues joined the rhythm, until he leaned back a little, to tuck his hand between their bodies and bring her to the brink with more massaging.

Her body clamped to his, begging for him to be driven as mad as he drove her.

His body tensed. He was holding back for her. She wanted him to—

And then she was on another plane, biting her lip, thrusting her hips against his as a well of wonderment washed over her in increasing circles of ecstasy.

He pumped harder, and came with her, every muscle tensed, his penis hard, spasming, thrusting.

He stayed in her a while, catching his breath between kissing her neck. Then he rolled off of her, but kept her close in his arms as they lay on their sides facing each other, breathing in rhythm.

He kissed the tip of her nose. "Wow."

She smiled against his damp chest. *Mm. Wow. This is love, Daniel. Can't you feel it? Can't you for once say you feel it?*

He took a strand of hair off her shoulder and rubbed it between his fingers. "That was incredible."

She moved a little, turned in his arms to face the ceiling. His gratitude made it all so formal, and seemed to distance them. "So, are you saying you'll remember this?"

He chuckled into the lock of hair he held, and inhaled, and kissed. "I'd say so."

Good answer. It wasn't "I love you." But this was Daniel. It was enough to make her sigh and remain in his arms a moment before she remembered Amy and began to move away.

"Stay," he said.

"I can't. I can't leave Amy alone." She scooted to the other side of the bed, stood and went around gathering her clothes.

He rose from the bed, too, and pulled on his jeans. "I'll come with you. I'll carry her over here and tuck her in on the sofa, and you can stay with me." She padded to him, barefoot, and hugged him. Against the tickly hairs of his chest, she said softly, "No." This was her life, hers and Amy's. This was how it would be, his leaving and her staying with their daughter. She couldn't think how much it would hurt on Sunday. She couldn't go there right now. She tipped her chin up, to look at him. "Think

234

about in the morning, when Amy wakes up. If she's here, and we're together, what will she think?"

He thought a moment. "That we're all together?"

She shook her head. "She'll think it's always going to be this way."

He looked down at her, and she saw something in his eyes then. It wasn't lust. It was something that came more slowly. A softening, an opening up to her that hadn't been there before. "What if it is?" His arms, encircling her, tightened. His lips turned up in a slow smile. "Would you have me?"

She arched her brows as feminine power unfurled inside her. "That depends on what you're asking. Do you mean would I have you as a long-term renter? Or did you have something else in mind?"

Chapter Fifteen

Daniel gave Gretchen a peck on the nose. "All I know is, I don't want to leave you and Amy."

"I don't want you to leave." She pressed her cheek against his chest. She'd stay just like this forever, except she'd rather be lying beside him in bed than standing here.

He brushed her hair out of her eyes, and tucked it behind her ear. "I don't know how to play house. I haven't tried since I was married. Not only am I out of practice, but I wasn't even good at it."

"Maybe you weren't married to the right person."

"True." He massaged the muscles in her neck.

She smiled up at him. "I thought you were walking me to my door."

He sighed against her hair. "If I must."

When she opened her door moments later, she went immediately to check on Amy. Returning, she informed him, "Our daughter is sleeping like an angel."

"She had a long day." His lashes lowered and he gazed at her mouth. "Well, if I can't persuade you to come back with me..." His words trailed off as he leaned in and his mouth met hers in a long, lingering kiss.

Reluctantly, he pulled away and backed off the porch.

Gretchen stood in the doorway and watched him go. He looked so good just in jeans, feet shoved into his shoes, forget the socks. His hair was mussed, his beard a bristly shadow that had tickled her skin and made her bite her lip with pleasure. How could she not go with him?

She shut the door, walked slowly to her own bed, and crawled under the covers in her clothes. They smelled of Daniel. She wanted that closeness, at least.

Her eyes closed, opened, and closed again. What if he stayed? He'd sort of offered that, hadn't he? Could it work, having him here? Having his arms around her every day, and his voice, murmuring in her ear? His mouth to kiss, his gazes to interpret? His little amusements, and his friendships, which were already her own? They had these things in common now.

They certainly had lovemaking in common. Fitting together so well in that area couldn't hurt.

Who was she kidding? It could destroy her. But to put it aside for the moment and hope against everything wrong in the past that they could have a future, that was bliss. Unreasonable, maybe, but bliss nonetheless.

She pulled the covers up to her ear and closed her eyes. It was late and she needed sleep in order to function fully at the festival. And yet, her mind was filled with Daniel. Each time she'd start to drift off, something would pop into her head. She'd see again the dark, deep wanting in his gaze. She'd hear his low, rumbling laugh and feel a quick surge of desire just by remembering their passion.

She sighed, flung the covers away, and stared up at the ceiling. She wasn't going to fall asleep anytime soon.

She was in love—full, deep, terrifying love—with Daniel.

****

Daniel whistled as he made his coffee. He'd been brewing his own since Gretchen had showed him how.

When the coffeemaker beeped, he poured himself a mug. Carrying it with him, he opened the front door.

Ahh. Excellent day for a festival.

As he drove to town to meet up with Wally, he recalled his first day there, when he'd wandered the sidewalks, wondering what people did in such an old-fashioned place. Now he knew. They lived here, same as people did in every other place. Somehow Marydale's days seemed longer, though. Maybe it was because he wasn't working, but he swore he'd experienced more in his short time here than he had in years in the city.

At the corner of the park square, he saw Wally unloading his truck and pulled up behind him.

"Daniel!" someone called as he climbed from the SUV.

He glanced around and saw Amy across the street, standing in front of the gift shop. She smiled and started running toward him.

"Look both ways!" he yelled, his heart in his throat.

She skidded to a halt at the curb as cars advanced down the road toward them on both sides.

He blew out a harsh breath. "It's okay now. Come on."

She scampered over.

When she reached him, he bent to her level. "Always stop, look, and listen at roads. Understand?"

She nodded soberly.

He smiled, satisfied. He swung her up in the air, and she giggled. "Did your mommy fix you pancakes today or what? You weigh a ton."

"No, silly. Waffles."

He winked at Wally, and set Amy down again. "Where *is* Mommy, anyway?"

"In the shop."

His gaze settled on the doorway across the street. He wanted to go over there. He wanted to see Gretchen, just see her. Then he could get on with his day's work.

"She said to tell you something."

"What?"

"We're going to the carnival rides at twelve."

"Oh." He waited, but she didn't say anything else. "Can I come, too?"

She nodded, and he smiled. She seemed to have forgotten all about yesterday's troubles.

He looked around at the truck. "Wally needs my help. Let me get him set up and I'll take you across the street."

"Can I pass out fliers?"

"Sure. Come on."

They set up the booth, cutout and ghost tour quickly. When they'd finished, Wally said, "Crystal's coming in ten minutes. You two go on. I'm okay here."

Daniel held Amy's hand and crossed the street.

Crystal came bouncing out of the diner, saw them and waved. "Hi, cuties. You gonna try the musical chairs to win cakes? We decided to make it a little different this year, so we're doing a cake 'sit' instead of a 'walk.' I donated coconut, chocolate with chocolate icing, and carrot to the cause."

"Then we're definitely doing musical chairs." Daniel smiled down at Amy. "Right?"

"Right."

They went into the gift shop and found it mobbed by kids and adults.

Amy found her friends and they played with stuffed animal puppets from a bin. Daniel roamed the card aisle, waiting to speak to Gretchen, who rang up sales at the counter.

Maybe he'd get her a card. Pulling a few, he

read the verses and replaced them, scowling. They didn't capture what he wanted to say. He wanted to leave her with just the right words and the perfect sentiments behind them. He wanted to tell her how he really felt about her. He'd decided last night that he would take that chance and open up. But if he did, how could he get beyond those feelings once he left town tomorrow morning?

He wandered to the doorway to check on Wally. Crystal stood by his side, posed in her black Victorian dress, hat and parasol. Wally had propped the cutout board sign next to her. The painted sign depicted a full-size person lying in a coffin with a hole where the face should be. Tourists could stick their faces in the hole, and Crystal would take a photo of them. This setup had already drawn a crowd of onlookers, who'd hopefully read the advertising printed across the coffin: "Ghost Tours of Marydale, presented by Marydale Casket Company. We're dying for your business."

"How's Wally doing?"

Daniel turned, and smiled. Gretchen had slipped up beside him. He glanced over at the register.

"I got Cile to cover for me."

His smile stretched, and he put a hand on her back and rubbed the very place where he'd kissed her last night during lovemaking. Well, one of the places.

She gazed up at him. Her eyes seemed to reflect openness to him now. Good. The closeness they'd shared last night didn't scare him, and he didn't want it to scare her.

"Is Cile cool with you being gone for the whole day?"

"If you want. I'm the boss, you know."

"I know." He looked into her eyes. "And I want."

She blushed then, and he started to pull her into his arms. But she moved away. "Amy's with BJ and their friend Kirsten. Let me just tell Kirsten's mom where I'll be." She went over to the stuffed toys.

While Daniel waited, he saw Eula's friend, Martha, leaving the drugstore. "Martha!" He waved.

She spotted him and tottered over. "Hello, young man. How are you?"

"Fine. Ready for this beautiful day?"

Gretchen came out, and stood by his side, and greeted the woman, too.

"When I was your age," she said, her head turning from one to the other, "I was being courted by three boys. I had to decide which one would get to take me on the festival hayride."

Daniel chuckled. "I'll bet you did." He turned to Gretchen. "Is there still a hayride?"

She nodded. "On the farm, before the fireworks."

He gazed into her eyes. "Will you ride with me?"

"Sure."

When he turned back to Martha, she was eying them keenly. "I'll be on my way. I'll see you at Eula's."

"Okay." Daniel turned his attention to Gretchen, taking up her hand and brushing his lips across her knuckles.

Her eyes half closed. "Don't do that." Her husky tone contradicted her words. "People will talk."

"Let them," he said, his voice strained. "Let them know I want you."

She pulled her hand away.

He chuckled low. "You're so proper. Except when we're in bed."

"Hush!" Her eyes shone with merriment as she kicked the side of his shoe.

He took her hand again, and they walked across the street. "Just wait 'til I get you in the hay."

"It'll be filled with people!"

"We'll be in the dark. They'll never know." His body hummed with need at the thought of riding beside her, bumping against her, holding her close and breathing in the scent of her under the cover of night.

She looked up at him then, and something in her expression should have made him drop her hand and ignore her. He'd seen it before in the eyes of women he'd never dated again. He knew what it meant. It meant if he didn't get out right then, he'd be hooked into settling down. It was a look he'd run from for years.

Instead of running, he bent and brushed a kiss across her lips.

She pulled back. "Daniel."

He followed her gaze, saw a group of festival-goers passing by, and shrugged. "I can't help it."

She moved away, and approached Wally and Crystal from the left side of the booth while he walked up to the front.

"Hi, guys." Wally tipped a goofy top hat. "Just sold out the first tour."

"Great!" Snagging the list of names and addresses from the booth's desk, Daniel skimmed them. "Nice assortment of future customers."

Gretchen admired Crystal's costume, and helped her straighten out the parasol's frets. "Are you going to take them through the museum first, and then the caves?"

"That's the idea. He'll do the museum, and then we'll ride them out to the caves and I'll be their guide for that part."

"I'm tending the booth during the tours." Daniel sent Gretchen a disappointed look. "I guess you and Amy will have to do the rides before I get finished. But I'll catch up with you later. Save me the cake deal."

She smiled. "We will."

By four o'clock, Daniel, Wally and Crystal had sold out six tours and had shown hundreds of folks the casket museum and caves. Gushing reviews from returning tour parties encouraged them. Word spread, and everyone clamored to see their peculiar sites. Daniel handed out several fifty-count packets of brochures on the tour, which included an insert on the casket company with a fifty-dollar off coupon.

"This should bring you business," he said to a weary-eyed, limping Wally when he showed up after the last tour.

He brightened. "If it works, I might hire you again."

"Wally was great!" Crystal gushed. "He came up to the caves after a while, and ran around and scared the beejeebers out of a few people."

"Wow, Wally." Gretchen laughed as she strolled up to the booth with Amy. "I had no idea you had the acting gene in you."

"Yeah, well, he was trying to impress Crystal." Daniel rubbed Gretchen's back in greeting. "How's the festival?"

"Lonely without you there. Ready to go?"

Wally invited them to go in the bus since the tour was over. So they piled in. As they pulled onto the highway, Daniel glanced toward Gretchen's shop as a crowd of people came out onto the sidewalk. He thought he saw a couple of the women he'd met in Cincinnati the other night, but decided they probably just looked like them. He doubted he'd even be able to recognize them since he'd known them such a short time.

The farm, when they got there, bulged near to overflowing with people. Cars were parked everywhere, but Officer Junior Nantz kept creating more spaces and flailing his arms to guide vehicles into them.

They parked and walked to the field, where they found pony rides, a moonwalk, the carnival rides and games, a dance band near the gazebo, and the musical chairs cakewalk.

Amy jumped up and down when she saw the sign for the cakewalk. "There it is! Ready?"

He smiled at Gretchen. "I think I've got a tough competitor. How about you, Mommy? Are you going to do it?"

"No. But I want to preserve the moment." She pulled a disposable camera out of her purse.

"C'mon, Daniel!" Amy urged.

In her excitement to get there, she stumbled, but he managed to tug gently enough on her arm to keep her on her feet and avoiding scraped knees. She was so light, so little. And his. His little girl.

He caught Gretchen looking at them and smiling. She seemed so happy. He wanted it to always be this way for them. He wished he could tell her with a glance what this time meant to him.

They arrived at the cake "sit," turned in their tickets and stood in line. When they were allowed to find a chair to stand by, he let Amy choose. "There! You stand there," she ordered, which was right beside her chair.

Gretchen called, "Daniel! Amy!" and when they looked her way, snapped a few photos. Then she smiled and waved.

Daniel stared at her. He took his own photo in his mind, snapping a mental shot of her, hair shimmering against her shoulders, eyes filled with childlike merriment, small, rounded breasts, slim hips, flat abdomen. When his gaze returned to her face after that leisurely assessment, she'd pursed her lips. "Concentrate!" she mouthed.

He grinned. "You want a cake, do you?"

With her free hand, she playfully indicated she'd like one to shove in his face.

The music began. Amy started for his chair, so he had to move to the next one. He kept looking around to make sure Amy made it to a chair. She would sometimes stop and look a little unsure. When the music ended, she was between chairs, so he reached out and tugged her into the one behind him.

They were safe, and she clapped her hands together.

"Good job!" he said.

They started up again. This time, several people including Amy were called out. The bully from her class grabbed her chair out from under her and shoved her out of the way, making a face at her as she was eliminated. Daniel glared at him, and the kid looked down at his shoes. Daniel was satisfied he'd let him know he was looking out for Amy.

It came down to Daniel and the bully. They went around the last chair a few times, the music stopped, and Daniel plopped into the chair.

The kid cursed.

Daniel shook his hand, anyway. "Good job. And if you say that word again before you're in high school, I'll tell your parents."

The boy glowered at him before he ran away.

Amy ran to Daniel and hugged his knees. "You won!" That was all he needed to feel like the winner. He didn't even need the cake.

Amy pointed at a two-layer one at the goody table. "Pick that one."

"What kind is it?"

"Pink." She looked at him as if he were king of all sillies.

Gretchen laughed. "Daniel, you're so slow."

He squeezed her arm. "Some people like that about me."

She blushed.

He pulled her to his side and wrapped his arm around her waist. She felt so good. She smelled good. He kissed her hair and smoothed it back from her face.

She leaned her head against his shoulder. He

caught people watching them, and a lump formed in his throat. They wouldn't see him with her tomorrow. By this time tomorrow, he'd be in Chicago.

They ate barbeque dinners sold by the Jaycees, sitting on the lawn atop a quilt Gretchen had brought over earlier. Amy didn't eat much. She was too eager to hurry off with BJ and jump around on the moonwalk. Crystal and Wally followed them, holding hands.

"Look at them," Gretchen said, smiling. "I can't believe it took them so long to find each other." Her gaze met Daniel's. "Crystal gives you all the credit."

"I just encouraged Wally to overcome his shyness and talk to her." He watched as they entered a large group of locals. Wally pointed at the caves and waved his hands as he talked. "Huh. Now I can't shut him up. I think I've created a monster."

"No. You've brought out the best in some of us. You haven't just helped Wally with his business. You're his friend. And you've been so great with Amy." She looked down at her plate, then back up at him. "And me."

He leaned in and kissed her full on the mouth. She pulled back. He knew she would, because she had this private side that shied away from public displays of affection. That was okay with him, since he knew she was anything but inhibited in private. Remembering her passion excited him and made him want to kiss her in public, so they were at an impasse. He settled for leaning on his elbow beside her while she sat up against the big old maple, wrapped in a plaid wool throw.

"Do you think Amy's cold?" she asked, watching the children thread their way in and out of the crowd as they went from game to game.

"I doubt it. She's moving around a lot."

She looked at him. "She's going to miss you."

He frowned. "I didn't want that. That's not why I came here."

"I know." She looked down, plucked at the fringe on the throw. "It's okay. We're used to consoling each other."

It was hard enough thinking about leaving Amy. Leaving them both...he couldn't even consider it right now.

He glanced up in the tree, where kids looked down on them and giggled.

He liked these trees. They grew in the ground here, instead of out of concrete in the sidewalk, like in Chicago.

He looked at Gretchen. She had her eyes closed. Her lashes brushed dark strokes onto her pale skin. Her lips were dark and full and in need of kissing. Her breasts rose as she breathed.

"Quit." Her lips moved, but nothing else.

"What?"

"Watching me."

He tickled her with a blade of grass, running it along her collarbone and the line of her chin. "Sorry. I can't help myself."

Her lashes came up, and he stared into her eyes. Their color was a promise of deep, wicked nights, their sparkle something to look forward to in the chilling months of winter to come.

He found himself saying, again, "What if I stayed?"

"We'd be together," she said, simply. "We'd make love again."

Her honesty was so sweet, he wanted to crush her to him and make a very public display, right there. The kids had climbed down from the tree and missed kicking him in the head by a hair's breadth. They'd scampered off. Now maybe no one would see Gretchen and him.

"We'd make love," Gretchen repeated, "and then

you'd grow tired of me."

That cut him deeply. He worked the muscle in his jaw. "I didn't do that last time. It's just what you chose to believe because you weren't sure of us."

She looked hard at him. "I really want to believe in us now."

"Then do."

She touched his arm, stroking the hairs there, running her fingers down to his and tracing them. He let her. He wanted to do so many other things, but he sat there, his body like a set trap, ready to pounce but controlled by the crowds around them.

"You don't know me, really," she said. "We have things in common, yes, but do you know what I want?"

He turned to see her. "Tell me."

She breathed in, and sighed.

He waited, watching her, seeing the concern lining her forehead.

She looked down at the blade of grass she'd taken from him. "It's stupid. Amy and I can take care of ourselves. But sometimes it gets lonely."

He squeezed her fingers. "I hear you."

She looked at him sharply. "*You* never get lonely! You're always with people."

"I'm with strangers. It's not like here. Here, you don't know a stranger."

"That's true, in a way." She looked around at the crowds. "Other than now, at festival time, everyone knows everyone. But that doesn't mean we're always happy about it. It's not all perfect here, the way you may think it is. We have crime and death and divorce and bankruptcy."

What was she saying? That he'd simply been vacationing? He thought about his busy days in Chicago, and his endless nights. He remembered Sam warning him to consider the time here as vacation time, a nice visit with his daughter, but nothing permanent. But he sensed that even Sam, who doubted he'd never lose his fear of attachment, and who wanted him back at the helm of the agency and their deals, had hoped he'd find more here.

Had he found a vacation spot and a fling? Or home and a family?

"If you stayed," she said. "What would you do? How long before you'd go nuts with boredom?" She pointed into the crowd. "How many of these people do you think need advertising?"

"I know one who does. Your landlord. He needs a better way to market the other side of your duplex."

"That's right," she said, her eyes dancing. "He needs to find a man for me who can move right in on that side. Then we could buy the place and tear out the separating walls and have one big house."

Daniel scowled at the thought of another man being there for Gretchen. Another man pushing Amy's swing or helping her with her garden.

Another man sharing Gretchen's bed.

He'd had enough of the conversation. They weren't getting anywhere. He wanted to stay, but he couldn't. It was pretty clear she wanted a man around. But she wouldn't come out and say she wanted him.

His insides ached. He rose, stretched his arms over his head and looked at the sun setting over the hills. Turning back, he held out a hand to help her up. "They're starting the tractor up for the hayride. Want to make our way over there?"

"Sure." She took his hand. "Give it another half-hour and it'll be dark."

When they'd thrown away their paper plates and folded up the blanket, they went to find Amy. A smiley face had been painted on her cheek, and she toted a bag full of plastic toys and candies she'd won at the kiddy booths. She begged to stay with BJ, and Crystal said she'd take them to the dance pavilion for kid "Hokey Pokey" and "Bunny Hop" time once they finished the potato sack race.

Gretchen and Daniel headed on to the pavilion because he owed Eula a dance. When she'd suffered her stroke, he'd promised her a dance and he intended to make good on that vow.

Afterward, Gretchen and Daniel headed for the hayrides. He helped her climb up on one of the first flatbeds, whose tractor was driven by Elmer Martin, the man who owned the farm across from Gretchen's house. He tipped his wool cap at Gretchen and they talked about his winter squash and root vegetables while the trailer loaded up with tourists and townspeople. Then Elmer started across the front yard and up toward the caves.

The tourist sitting on the bale of hay across form Gretchen and Daniel bubbled over about her tour of the caves. She had an MCC brochure sticking out of her purse, and when Daniel mentioned it, she said she was taking it home to a friend whose father was the funeral director of one of the bigger funeral homes in town. She wanted to tell him that Marydale made fine caskets out of local wood.

Daniel and Gretchen exchanged looks. Here was proof that Daniel's plan hadn't just provided more of the day's entertainment. Wally had garnered publicity that could lead to increased sales.

Daniel put his arm around Gretchen, and she snuggled in to him as the tractor chugged along. "Know anyone on here?" he said, low.

She shook her head.

"Good." He squeezed her. "We can be as naughty as we want and they'll never see us again." He moved his hand up her side, roaming close to her breast.

She squirmed, trying to get away, which only brought her closer.

His chuckle rumbled in his throat. "Now that's

more like it."

It was dark now. Stars twinkled in the sky above them. The other people on the ride were shadows, mostly, bumping along over ruts in the field, moving in rhythm with them.

Gretchen closed her eyes and let herself sway into Daniel, let his body take the shock from hers when they landed in a deep tractor groove. He didn't complain. In fact, each chance he got, he would push her hair out of her face, curve her body more closely to his, or kiss her head.

For a time, she'd forget he was the city playboy, going back to his life tomorrow. She was the country girl rooted in this town, invested in raising their daughter here.

She remembered their lovemaking. She longed to be with him again, and yet, she knew last night had been goodbye. So she clung to him this final time, burying her face in his neck and inhaling his warm scent. She rocked against him, loving his hard chest, and the muscles in his arms as he held her.

Memories would have to be enough.

He bent then and brushed his lips across hers. But she didn't want him to leave her. Her soul cried out to him. Her lips parted beneath his. But he drew back this time. "Later, sweetheart."

And the hayride went on and on and on. A lovely ride. A hateful trip. Deliriously contented one moment and in excruciating pain the next, she waited. Waited for it to stop.

Waited for Daniel to leave tomorrow.

All these years, she'd waited for him.

He had come.

And he was leaving.

Chapter Sixteen

They got home at ten o'clock. Daniel carried Amy inside. Draped over his broad shoulder that way, Gretchen thought she looked like a limp doll. He laid her on the bed and pulled the covers up while Gretchen watched, yawning.

Hands on his hips, Daniel stood at the side of the canopied bed that had once been Gretchen's. A tender look softened his face as he studied his sleeping daughter. He reached down, brushed her hair off her face. "Good night, angel," he murmured.

Amy turned, as if to curl her little body more surely into the covers and breathed an exhausted sigh. "Good night, Daddy," she said, her eyes barely open.

Gretchen watched as Daniel's hand that had been stroking her forehead paused. Standing in the doorway, she couldn't see his face. Still, she thought his fingers trembled slightly before he finally straightened from his bent position.

He moved quietly to Gretchen's side and glanced toward the bed, then back at her. "Did you hear that?" he said, his voice filled with wonder as he followed her out of the room.

She placed a finger to her lips. "I heard."

They walked hand in hand into the kitchen.

He shook his head slowly. "I can't believe she called me that."

"Well, you are her daddy."

He stared down the hall. When his attention returned to Gretchen, his eyes had grown serious.

"I'm going to send you money."

"I won't take it."

"I want you to take it. I wish you'd had it all along." He told her about the college fund he'd set up. Then he paced to where the living room carpeting started, and turned back to her. "I should've found you sooner."

"I wish you had. But not so you could give me money." The topic made it sound as if she couldn't handle things on her own. "Your time. *This* time. It's meant more than you'll ever know."

He walked back to her, and frowned down at the tabletop. When he looked up, there was resolution in his expression. "I want to stay."

"I don't think you should stay here tonight. I think it would—"

"Not tonight. I mean I'm not going to leave tomorrow."

"But if not tomorrow, then another day." Any day that Daniel left would be hell. She skirted the table and went into the kitchen, to busy herself with putting away clean dishtowels. "It's better to go now. Better to get it over with."

"I don't want to go back to Chicago," he drew out, moving toward her with purpose in his step. Reaching her, he took a towel out of her hand and tossed it on the counter. He lifted her palm and kissed it, then brushed his lips across her fingertips. His penetrating gaze seemed intent on piercing her inner being. "That kiss on the hayride. Did you mean it?"

She couldn't feel. She couldn't speak. She couldn't look at him, and couldn't look away, either. Everything stopped. Everything but the warm wetness of his mouth as he sucked first on her index finger, then her middle finger. She gasped for air. She had to close her eyes. She couldn't think. She couldn't breathe, except to breathe in Daniel. She wanted him so badly. Was she in love? "Yes," she said, on a sigh. "Yes, I'm in love with you."

He moved his mouth close to her neck, his breath warming and tickling her skin. "Then let me stay." He nipped her earlobe, teasing it with his tongue. "Trust me. I want to stay with you."

And she let him. She let him pull her to him, and hold her, and she let herself cry softly against his shoulder, diffusing the emotions she'd held in. He wiped her tears and kissed the salty taste from her mouth, making her know with his lips, his hands, his hushed words, that she was safe.

At last, she was safe with Daniel.

He walked her into her bedroom and tucked her into bed instead of making love to her.

"Good night, sweetheart," he crooned in her ear. "See you in the morning." Then he kissed her again, sending mind-tingling chills through her, making her want him more than anything she'd ever wanted. "Sweet dreams."

"Don't leave," she moaned. "Stay here with me."

"What about Amy?"

"I'll set the alarm and wake up early. You have to go to the airport before she'd normally be up, anyway."

"I *said* I was staying," he corrected.

Then he climbed into bed and they slept.

****

Gretchen awakened in the morning to the aroma of burning toast. She leapt from the bed and grimaced because she still had on her jeans and T-shirt from the day before, only now they were wrinkled.

Padding down the hallway, she heard Amy chattering away about her favorite cartoon. Daniel answered her in his rich baritone. When Gretchen got to where she could see them, she stopped and stared in amazement. Daniel had on one of the baker's aprons Joel had given her, and was pitching black toast into the trashcan. He stuck his thumb into his mouth at the same moment he turned and saw her. "Stupid stuff burned itself and me."

She whipped her hand over her mouth to hide her smile, and pretended a yawn. "Good morning."

Looking her up and down, he grinned. "You're a little rumpled."

He, on the other hand, had showered and shaved! He must have gotten up much earlier and gone to his side of the duplex, honoring her concern over what Amy might think of his being there. She glanced at the stove clock. "Nine-fifteen! Oh, Daniel. You missed your flight."

"Guess I'll have to stay longer." Holding her gaze, he smiled slowly. If you'll have me, that is."

She caught her breath. Until the next flight? Dare she hope he meant longer, like forever, maybe? But he hadn't said he loved her. Would she be content without knowing? Could she sacrifice her pride, and just hope loving him was enough?

She glanced at Amy. *Forgive me, Amy, but I have to have him. I'll try my best to keep him this time. For me. For you.*

She smiled. "What's for breakfast?"

He cast a glance at the stove. "Burnt eggs. Burnt toast. And limp bacon."

"Mm." She checked the contents in the pans. "I guess we're going to the diner, then?"

Daniel whipped off the apron, balled it up and tossed it onto the counter. "I'll drive. It'll give me a chance to return those tables we borrowed from the church."

She went to him and kissed him. "Thanks for the breakfast attempt. It's the thought that counts."

He squeezed her to him before playfully slapping her bottom. "Hurry up and get ready. I'm hungry."

****

When they arrived at the diner, they found it crowded with out-of-towners who'd stayed over from the festival. Several people waited for the tables to turn, chatting, reading newspapers and drinking "serve yourself" coffee from Styrofoam cups Crystal had set out beside a large insulated carafe.

They stood at the door, accepting coffee refills when Crystal sent it around via a waitress trainee. Gretchen sat on a bench beside an elderly woman who, between sips of her own hot brew, rambled on about "lovely, lovely Marydale" and especially the ghost tour, about how she and her husband had enjoyed it immensely.

Amy waited by Daniel's knee. She kept pointing at things and asking him to rhyme with them. It was a silly little game, but he enjoyed every minute of it. She'd call out "plant," and he'd say, "ant." Then he'd try to get her to spell it, something Gretchen had mentioned that she needed to be drilled on for school. Amy'd give it a try and usually have trouble. He'd spell the word and ask her to repeat it. This went on for about ten minutes, before she got bored and asked if she could talk with a little girl waiting beside them with her parents. Under Daniel's watchful eye, she introduced herself, and soon her new friend shared her coloring book and crayons.

Daniel shifted, restless. Why couldn't the early rush hurry up and finish their meals? He was hungry.

Even after they got seated and he'd eaten, he couldn't focus. Couldn't settle. Who was he kidding? He was just drawing out the goodbyes, because he had to return to Chicago.

When Amy went back to coloring with her friend near the front of the café, Daniel grabbed Gretchen's hand across the table.

"Come to Chicago with me, you and Amy. The

schools are great. We have the art museum, the galleries, and all the culture you two could ever want."

She shook her head. "Maybe you want those things. What I need are my friends here. I thought you understood that by now."

He clenched his jaw. "I have to go back, Gretchen."

She dropped her gaze. "I know."

"You don't have to raise Amy here. Think of all the opportunities for her in the city."

She looked up at him again. "I tried the city. Remember? I didn't fit in there. And what about all the people here that you said you liked, and that you wanted to help? Why can't you stay here and do your work?"

He dropped her hands and looked away. He ran his fingers through his hair, before pivoting back to her. "Are you sure this isn't you not trusting me? It's not like before. I'm not going back to the social scene. I have to get back for business reasons. This is the only alternative so we can be together."

"You could stay here."

His gaze searched hers, hoping for that openness he'd seen in her eyes yesterday. It wasn't there. Glancing around at the tables full of people, he said, "You said you loved me," in a lowered tone. "If you do, come with me."

"If you care about me, stay."

"Dammit, we're getting nowhere." He flung his gaze away from her. Snapping it back, he said, "My things are packed."

She looked out the window. "Goodbye, then."

He rose, went to stand by her and reached out to touch her, but stopped inches from her shoulder. "Gretchen, please."

"Goodbye."

He headed for the door. Glancing at Amy, he

half-turned to her. But no, he wouldn't put her through that. How could he? Swallowing the lump in his throat, he stormed out the door.

****

Twelve days later, Crystal stretched out on her back across the bottom of Gretchen's bed, her low-rise jeans exposing her flat tummy with its bellybutton piercing. She stared up at the plastic lei that she swung above her on her index finger like a pendulum. "I really thought Daniel was the man of your dreams," she said. "I can't believe he turned out to be another Walk-Away Joe."

It was a good thing Gretchen had her arm over her eyes and Crystal couldn't see how she didn't appreciate her worn clichés. She just wanted to be alone. But that didn't matter. Joel had already brought her over three cakes, two sacks of cookies and four pies. He'd scooted out, saying he knew she'd just want to be alone.

Alone with all those goodies?

They only added pounds and stomachaches to her troubles.

"I don't blame you, though. I'd have slept with him, too."

She groaned. If she could just wring Crystal's neck, she might feel better. On the other hand, she was just displacing her anger onto her well-meaning friends. She was really angry with herself for being a vulnerable dolt and allowing this loss of Daniel to pierce her heart. Maybe he was right. Maybe she should've gone with him. But she just hadn't felt it at the time. She'd made all the sacrifices up until that moment. She'd given him every reason to stay, too. It'd been time for him to show he truly cared and he hadn't. Though it'd killed her, she'd stood up to him. She hadn't been a doormat for a guy this time. When Daniel had walked out her door, she'd remained strong until he was out of town. Only then had she cried into her pillow, hugged her sides and given in to aching remorse.

Crystal shifted on the bed. "I'll go get us a cookie."

Good. Maybe she could sneak out the window while her friend was off to the kitchen. Everybody irritated her these days. She wasn't sleeping well. How many days had it been now since Daniel left? Ten? Eleven? No, twelve. It was Friday again. Hence the people forever coming and going at her front door once they got off work.

Ring.!

Speaking of doors...

"I've got it." Crystal called out.

"Tell them I'm busy." Gretchen didn't move a muscle. Her muscles had all melted into the bed an hour ago, once she'd gotten home from the shop and let down her guard. She'd gone to work each day so she wouldn't mope around the house feeling sorry for herself, hearing over and over in her head Amy's, "When is Daddy coming back?" She kept lying and saying, "I'm sure he'll be back soon," because she couldn't admit the truth just yet.

But once she was safely ensconced behind the cash register and the account books and the phone and merchandise orders each day, the town had come to find her. They'd come one at a time, either to her shop or her house, all the way up to until Crystal, the current one, making these sly daily rounds that were so, so obvious. They must have discussed not overwhelming her. They came the same way they had for her mother and her when her father left them.

The same way they'd come when her fiancé left.

First Wally came by the shop, with a testimonial on his new best friend, Daniel. "You know him, Gretchen," he'd said in his scratchy voice. "He wouldn't hurt you. The minute he saw you and Amy, he didn't care so much about that big ad deal his brother wanted him back in the city for. What about that? Doesn't it show how much he wanted to be with you two?"

She narrowed her gaze. "So why didn't he stay?"

Wally scratched his head. "You told him to leave."

"If he'd really cared, that wouldn't have mattered."

"Huh?"

"Oh, never mind." She shoved the cookies she was setting out in a "to sample" dish toward him. "Daniel doesn't deserve such a good friend, Wally. A good friend he'll never see again." And she went back to her duties.

Next, someone sent Eula in to try and play on Gretchen's emotions. She had recovered from her stroke and was rarin' to go. She marched right up to Gretchen and wagged her gnarled finger in her face. "Listen up, girlie. I know a good man when I see one, and that Daniel was a good man. Why, the way he looked at you, it was sinful!" Plucking up one of the order forms Gretchen was straightening, she fanned herself.

"He's a man, Eula. Men do that."

"I don't mean lust. I mean, he was moony-eyed, that one. He was in love."

"He's probably in love again in Chicago." The thought made her feel heavy-hearted.

Eula shook her white hair, which was becomingly corralled in a ponytail today. "He wasn't lookin' at *any* other woman around here with love or even lust in his eyes. He was lookin' at you."

Gretchen had brushed off her remarks as those of an old woman with a romantic streak.

Now, lying there on her bed and hearing Crystal coming down the hall with someone else in tow, she wondered. Had Daniel been in love? Could it be true that he loved Amy and her?

****

Elbows propped on his desk, Daniel sank his chin into his hands. "This is killing me, Sam."

"I know. But we have to do it."

"Our billings are way down. I let some of the new hires go. I've lost you money."

"Yeah, and then you busted your butt for two weeks over an intensive cost analysis that'll save most of the rest of us our jobs. Once we implement those changes you suggested, it'll save us money and allow us to continue making payroll. And voting Lieberman into your position is good. But only if you stick by your vow to help with the transition."

"You know I will."

"Perfect." Sam snapped shut the notebooks on the desk in front of him and rose. "Now get back to what really matters. I can't stand seeing that hangdog look on you."

Daniel frowned. "I'm not sure I can close this deal."

"Considering what you said about how angry she was, it doesn't sound easy. But from what I saw of you two together, I'd say you stand a fighting chance."

Daniel rose and strode to the window, to stare at people the size of ants many stories below being blown around by the city's famous winds. "I wish the odds were more in my favor."

"You've only got yourself to blame if you blow it."

He turned back around to face his brother. "I can't afford to blow this one. There's too much at stake." His brow tightened again. "Are you sure everyone was satisfied with the changes?"

"You were very considerate." Sam picked the notebooks up off the desk and slid them into his briefcase. He stared hard at Daniel. "You're dragging your feet. Get where you're supposed to be."

Daniel went to his brother and put his hands on his shoulders. "Being at your house the other night, with you and Beth and the boys, and our wrestling match, that was—" Emotion closed his throat and he had to look away a minute. He dropped his hands to his sides as he looked back. "It was great," he said, gruffly.

Sam clapped him in a bear hug, and then thrust him out from him again. "Go," he growled, with a shine in his eyes.

Daniel grabbed his jacket and hurried from the office, the building and the city. As he climbed into a taxi and headed for the airport, he thought of the last time he'd made the trip to Marydale to see Gretchen. He'd been angry with her for hiding a pregnancy, and uptight about meeting his child. He didn't know how she would react when he showed up.

Now his head swirled and his gut ached even worse.

He'd never been so unsure of how someone would receive him, until now with Gretchen. He'd never wanted anything as badly as he wanted her.

****

"Look who's here!" Crystal announced.

Who could it be now? Hadn't she already seen everyone in Marydale? With a heavy sigh, Gretchen turned her head toward the doorway. Then she jerked a hand to her mouth and swiped away cookie crumbs.

Daniel.

Crystal shoved him into the room and shut the door behind him.

Gretchen almost gasped at the sight of him. Dark circles claimed the area under his eyes. He'd gotten a haircut, but it looked ruffled and uneven. His face seemed thinner, his cheeks a tad hollow. And all that in just a two weeks' time.

"Hi." He stayed right where Crystal had pushed him. His arms rested at his sides. He wore his old uniform of starched white shirt, subdued tie and charcoal suit. Oh, and a new expensive pair of loafers, since he'd ruined the others here in the caves.

Gretchen sucked her breath in, trying to hide the extra pounds of cookie fat.

He looked at her. He seemed wary, his brown eyes weary, his mouth tense at the edges. "Mind if I loosen my tie?"

She shrugged.

He not only loosened it, he pulled the whole thing off from around his neck and tossed it onto her dresser. "Damned nooses."

She watched him. Seeing him again made her heart contract in pain. She'd wanted him so badly. She'd known they were right, that they might have a future.

She'd known it so well that she said, "That Sunday was the best day of my life and the worst."

His head came up. "Mine, too."

"I didn't think I'd ever see you again." She didn't look at him. It'd hurt too much earlier just seeing him.

"I had to come." He reached into his pocket. Something rustled. "I would've come sooner, but I had a lot of things to clear up first."

She looked then.

He had a folded piece of newspaper in his hand. He held it out.

"This might explain what I've been doing."

She kept her eyes on the paper as she took it from him. She opened it. It was a photo of two men, and at first glance she thought one of them was him. But the caption read, "John Chroma Wins Toyco Account." She read the article beside it, where it told how Chroma Agency and The Nicholson Agency had been in the running for the worldwide account. Then it said that after careful evaluation, Toyco had eventually chosen Chroma. Both agencies were competent to handle their needs, the president of Toyco was quoted as saying. But in the end, The Nicholson Agency had bowed out of the competition and the account had gone to a jubilant John Chroma.

She read this last line of the article twice. "But, this is the account you wanted," she said, her gaze still searching the picture, as if Daniel's image might suddenly pop up there to refute the article's words.

"Yes. I wanted the Toyco account very much at one time."

Now her gaze searched his. "Then why'd you let it go?"

"Toyco wanted me to prove I was worthy. They called me in and asked me to explain what I'd been doing here, and if I'd really abandoned my daughter." His gaze darkened. "I lost interest in them then. I didn't feel I needed to justify my life to them or anyone else. Anyone but you, that is," he said almost in a whisper.

She stared at him. "How much potential business did you lose with that deal?"

"All of it, in a way, since I just sold my share of the company to my partner." His gaze dropped to her mouth for a moment, before returning to meet her shocked gaze. "There's no pull for me in Chicago anymore, though I've stayed on as a consultant. You're more important to me. You and Amy."

"But—"

He thrust his hands into the front pockets of his slacks. "I wouldn't blame you if you wanted me to leave right now. But I'm not going."

He reached for her, and pulled her off the bed, and held her hands in his. "I'm in love with you, Gretchen. Your trust matters more to me than anything. I won't ever leave you now. Don't leave me, either. Okay?"

She looked into his eyes, and yes, she saw it there. He loved her! It bounced around in her brain and made her heartbeat pound in her ears. She could barely concentrate on what he was saying now, stuck as she was on those three little words: *I'm in love.*

"Can you forgive me for coming here for selfish reasons at first?" He brushed her hair back, and curved his finger around her ear, sending delighted chills through her.

Again, she nodded.

He pulled her to him and wrapping her in his embrace, in his scent, his warmth. "I love you."

She sighed and melted against him.

But he straightened away once more. "What if I started a little retirement business here? Daniel's Bakery, maybe?" His eyes teased.

She smiled up at him. "I'd love you for richer or poorer." Then, with a grin, she added a mild, "But didn't you make a fortune selling your share of The Nicholson Agency? That should set you quite well here in a consulting business on how to grow ad agencies."

"Sly girl" he growled. "Marry me tomorrow, before God and all of Marydale."

Her lips parted in surprise. She laughed. "No way. You know this town. They love a big, festive occasion."

"Well, if we must. But I won't wait long."

She gave him a peck on the lips. "Let's go tell Amy."

"I sent her outside with Crystal. Wally's probably driving them around in my car. They can't have gone far. We can go find them. But first things first."

He pulled her close and kissed her until she

throbbed with desire. Then he kissed her again, leaving no doubt in her mind that he wanted them together forever.

Epilogue

Daniel beamed down at the tiny baby in his arms. "Your uncle and cousins will be here any minute, Samantha. Stop rolling those eyes back in your head."

"She can't help it." Gretchen slipped the bib out from under her chin, and placed it on Daniel's shoulder. "Better get a burp before she falls asleep on you."

Lifting his little girl, he patted her back, and soon got his result.

"Good job, Daddy." After rubbing her sister's chestnut peach fuzz, Amy hopped off the glider. "I'm gonna go find Wally Junior."

"Okay. Crystal wants you to help him with those puzzles you brought him."

She nodded. "Don't worry. I'll show him how."

Daniel chuckled. He moved the sleeping baby to his other shoulder so he could squeeze his wife to him. "Our fourth anniversary. Can you believe it?"

She laid her cheek against his shoulder, alongside their daughter's terrycloth sleeper. "I love you. We're so lucky to have each other and our girls."

Daniel's throat tightened with emotion. He looked at the small garden area behind their old house, which was still in the midst of being renovated. It seemed another lifetime ago that he'd been in Chicago. He didn't miss anything about it. "I used to think I had everything I needed," he said against Gretchen's hair. "And then I got you, and now I *know* I've got it all."

Gretchen leaned up and kissed his cheek. "Crystal's watching Wally Junior, and Wally just told me Sam and the boys are running late. Let's put Samantha in her crib and take advantage of a few moments to ourselves in the bedroom."

He chuckled. "Lead the way, Mrs. Nicholson."

About the author...

Melissa Beck loves writing contemporary romances because it satisfies her passion for exploring what makes people tick, but she's not so sure acquaintances enjoy her psychoanalyzing them! She grew up mainly in Ohio, and returned to her home state of Tennessee to earn a degree in business at Vanderbilt University. After a career in the banking industry, she retired to raise her son and daughter with her college sweetheart husband. Hard Shell Word Factory published her first novel, a romantic suspense. She has placed in romance writing contests, including the Maggie Award for Excellence, and freelanced nonfiction articles. She's also passionate about her pets, gardening and needlework.

Contact her at www.melissabeck.com
or send her an email to melissa@melissabeck.com

Thank you for purchasing
this Wild Rose Press publication.
For other wonderful stories of romance,
please visit our on-line bookstore at
www.thewildrosepress.com.

For questions or more information,
contact us at info@thewildrosepress.com.

The Wild Rose Press
www.TheWildRosePress.com

Other Champagne titles to enjoy:

HOW MUCH YOU WANT TO BET? by Melissa Blue. Neil never thought a game of pool could change the course of her life, but against Gib she may lose both the game and her heart.

CATASTROPHE by Sharon Buchbinder. Cats! Twenty-three! Being evicted! Their handsome neighbor doesn't want to lose their curly-haired, curvaceous owner. So what's the rescue plan?

HIBISCUS BAY by Debby Allen. Picture love on a sun-drenched white sand beach surrounded by hibiscus-covered cliffs, with your yacht anchored in a blue Mediterranean Sea.

TASMANIAN RAINBOW by Pinkie Paranya. A concert violinist grapples with remote ranch life, intrigue and the mystery of a missing diary, the peril of a flood in which all could be lost, and the undeniable attraction of the man who would do anything to protect his son.

THREE'S THE CHARM by Ellen Dye. Rachel vowed never to speak to her ex-husband again, but her beloved horse needs a vet and Heath is the only one within three counties of West Virginia mountains.

DAMN THE MAN by Michelle L. Witvliet. Maggie believes she did the right thing in giving Nick his freedom. He is patiently waiting for her to realize divorce was the only mistake they made. What's a woman to? Damn the man, of course.

SEE MEGAN RUN by Melissa Blue. City-successful Megan goes home to the boonies to save her childhood home but finds she must not only agree to stay for her mother's wedding but also deal with the man she left when she hitchhiked out 12 years ago.

A MOTHER'S HEART by Misty Simon. Carrie wants a simple life. Helping Gran with the animal shelter: complication. When the new neighbor with two kids comes in for a dog, life goes out of control.

www.ingramcontent.com/pod-product-compliance
Lightning Source LLC
Chambersburg PA
CBHW070846250626
47159CB00003B/961